to Hugh M...

KT-416-543

James Lesl... ... ...s Grassic Gibbon', (1901–35), was born a... ...ght up in the rich farming land of Scotland's no... ...-east coast. After a brief and unsuccessful journalistic career, he joined the Royal Army Service Corps in 1919 serving in Persia, India and Egypt. Thereafter he spent a further six years as a clerk in the RAF. He married Rebecca Middleton in 1925, and became a full-time writer in 1929. The young couple settled in Welwyn Garden City where they lived until the writer's death in 1935.

Mitchell published a number of short stories and articles and his first book, *Hanno, or the Future of Exploration* appeared in 1928. Seven novels followed under his own name: *Stained Radiance* (1930); *The Thirteenth Disciple* (1931); *Three Go Back* (1932); *The Lost Trumpet* (1932); *Image and Superscription* (1933); *Spartacus* (1933); and *Gay Hunter* (1934). In the same year Mitchell collaborated with Hugh MacDiarmid to make *Scottish Scene*, which contained three of Mitchell's best short stories, since collected in *A Scots Hairst* (1969).

He adopted his mother's name for his finest work, the trilogy *A Scots Quair*, which comprised *Sunset Song*, *Cloud Howe* and *Grey Granite*, written between 1932 and 1934. Dogged by ill health at the end, Mitchell died of a perforated ulcer at the age of only thirty-four. An unfinished novel, *The Speak of the Mearns*, was published in 1982.

Lewis Grassic Gibbon

GREY GRANITE

Introduced by Tom Crawford

CANONGATE
CLASSICS
34

First published in 1934 by Jarrolds, first published as a Canongate Classic in 1990 by Canongate Publishing Ltd, 16 Frederick Street, Edinburgh EH2 2HB. Introduction copyright Thomas Crawford 1990.

The publishers gratefully acknowledge general subsidy from the Scottish Arts Council towards the Canongate Classics series and a specific grant towards the publication of this title.

Set in 10pt Plantin by Hewer Text Composition Services, Edinburgh. Printed and bound in Denmark by Nørhaven Rotation.

Canongate Classics
Series Editor: Roderick Watson
Editorial Board: Tom Crawford, J. B. Pick

British Library Cataloguing in Publication Data is available on request.

ISBN 0-86241-312-5

Contents

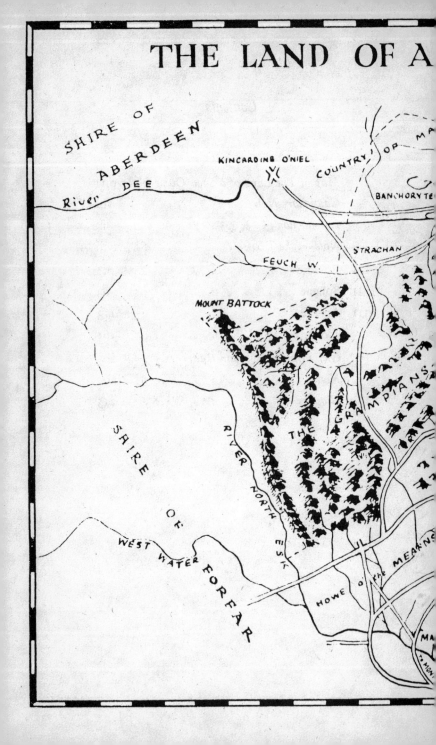

Cautionary Note

The 'Duncairn' of this novel was originally 'Dundon'. Unfortunately, several English journals in pre-publication notices of the book described my imaginary city as Dundee, two Scottish sheets identified it with Aberdeen, and at least one American newspaper went considerably astray and stated that it was Edinburgh—faintly disguised.

Instead, it is merely the city which the inhabitants of the Mearns (not foreseeing my requirements in completing my trilogy) have hitherto failed to build.

L. G. G.

Introduction

When *Grey Granite* was published at the end of 1934 it was advertised as the last volume of a trilogy. Yet many who had missed the first two novels were swept off their feet when they read it. This seems to have been the experience of Tom Wintringham, the influential editor of *Left Review*, who termed it 'the best novel written this side the Channel since Hardy stopped writing'.[1] And it was certainly that of the *Sheffield Daily Telegraph* reviewer, who was glad he had not come across the earlier volumes because, after the overpowering experience of *Grey Granite*, the 'pleasure of their first perusal' was still to come (31 January 1935). Page Cooper of Doubleday (Gibbon's American publisher), who did of course know the other books, could not keep it out of her mind and found it 'a bigger, more disturbing, and beautiful book than *Cloud Howe*. One hesitates to label anything with the word genius, but there isn't any other for the quality of his mind.'[2] Of those who went in for comparisons, the *New York Times* reviewer was almost as enthusiastic, calling it 'Gibbon's most swiftly moving book and most adventurous in ideas' (3 February 1935). More significantly, perhaps, Gibbon's greatest Scottish contemporaries, Hugh MacDiarmid and Edwin Muir, both liked it: MacDiarmid enthusiastically, Muir less so (though he preferred it to its predecessors).[3]

The majority of those who had read all three parts seem to have agreed with the *Glasgow Herald* in the judgment that is still, I think, standard among 'common readers': '*Sunset Song* stands by itself, a good novel; *Cloud Howe* and *Grey Granite* are two rather ramshackle outhouses which have been added to it.' This, however, is to forget that Gibbon had planned a

trilogy from the first,[4] and to ignore the fact that each of the
outhouses has its own effective structure, however different
from nineteenth-century and Edwardian norms. Like all
creative writers Gibbon had not worked out the total shape
right at the start; once begun, the novels flowed with their
own momentum and took on new features as he wrote. That
his original title for *Cloud Howe* was *The Morning Star*
indicates that he cannot at first have thought of organizing it
around contrasting cloud-formations passing over the vale of
the Mearns, but perhaps around heavenly bodies ironically
conceived. And when he came to grips with *Grey Granite* he
scrapped his original plan of a Prelude that would make the
beginning of *Grey Granite* formally parallel to those of the
earlier novels, with their milieux firmly set in place and time
(this is given in the Appendix). The result is that Duncairn
has depth, history, and background only for those in the
know; for them, Gibbon's city is more like Aberdeen than
Dundee, Glasgow or Edinburgh, and the glancing identifica-
tions and allusions provide, quietly and unobtrusively, many
of the in-jokes of which Gibbon was so fond.[5] For the wider
readership, Duncairn is an imaginary city, the crumbling
backdrop to the personal and political paradigms set within
it. The novel has thus a much freer form than *Sunset Song*,
framed by Prelude and Epilude; its frame consists of two
passages about Chris, where interior monologue deftly
incorporates third-person narration. With the first, we begin
in medias res with Chris—'old at thirty-eight?'—puffing and
panting as she lugs her groceries up the urban height of the
Windmill Steps, and end with her in the countryside, above
the croft she has 'retired to', enigmatically losing conscious-
ness on top of the Barmekin.

When Gibbon began *Sunset Song* he told his wife the whole
trilogy was to be written round 'a woman',[6] and the framing
just mentioned seems to show that this is as true of *Grey
Granite* as it is of the earlier novels. But Chris, though as
moving and convincing as ever, is in a sense peripheral to the
main action, the growth and development of her son Ewan,
which parallels and contrasts with her own rural adolescence

in *Sunset Song*. The book's four sections are called after different constituents of granite: Epidote (a greenish silicate of calcium, aluminium, and iron), Sphene (whose crystals are wedge-shaped and which contains the element titanium—strong, light, corrosion-resistant), Apatite (consisting of calcium phosphate and fluoride), and Zircon ('a tetragonal mineral, of which jacinth and jargoon are varieties'—jacinth is reddish orange, and jargoon brilliant and colourless). They mirror the stages in Ewan's transformation into the kind of person required by the stark, sure creed that will cut like a knife:

> Cold and controlled he had always been, some lirk in his nature and upbringing that Chris loved, who so hated folk in a fuss. But now that quality she'd likened to grey granite itself, that something she'd seen change in Duncairn from slaty grey to a glow of fire, was transmuting again before her eyes—into something darker and coarser, in essence the same, in tint antrin queer.

Gibbon's theme reflects one of the commonest spiritual sequences of the thirties—the process whereby a bourgeois intellectual came to join the Communist Party and decided to give over his life to it. Many have felt with Isobel Murray that 'the greatest weakness of the book is the character and role of Ewan';[7] others have seen in him its main strength. That was certainly Eric Linklater's view before he had even finished it. He has left a unique record of his immediate responses in a letter written towards the end of 1934:

> Chris, I think, has lost a little of the character—but she's lost it to Ewan, who's coming very robustly alive; & the curious angular growth of his mind is very true to type. So far I can sympathise with his nascent politics very comfortably, & if the police had behaved in that manner his bottle-throwing would have been not merely noble, but natural.[8]

The function of the granite symbolism is to highlight Ewan's willed transformation into the 'more than human': Ewan comes to be like granite just as Stalin means steel and

Molotov means hammerman. He inherits from Chris a still centre, a refusal to be anything other than himself, an aloofness that others find unsympathetic and haughty. He respects what Gibbon sees as the cool detachment of science and is utterly blind to the arts; his sense of humour is, to put it mildly, limited, and at one point Chris says, 'human beings were never of much interest to him.' Yet it would be wrong to say he is emotionless; it is merely that he can keep his ordinary feelings under control—his admiring affection for Chris, his detestation of what breeds nauseous slums and stunts the wretched of the earth, his contempt for the inchoate, the indecisive, and the second-rate. His most intense emotions are those of the communist mystic, which come on him towards the end of the novel, an essentially religious identification with the enslaved and the exploited throughout recorded history. They are only made possible by what Ewan learns in the factory, the working-class movement, and the police cell, but they are rooted in a character trait he displayed even in boyhood, in his friendship for Charlie Cronin the spinner's son and his strange bond with old Moultrie, survival from an age of pre-industrial knacks and skills, who on his deathbed shared with Ewan the precious essence of the old ways (*Cloud Howe*, Canongate Classics edition, p.192). They also link him to Chris and show that despite his crystalline hardness, his sensibility is akin to hers—to the Chris who in her girlhood saw visions of prehistoric hunters and farmers and identified with the tortured Covenanters in the Whigs' Vault at Dunnottar.

William K. Malcolm, in what is perhaps the best critical presentation of Ewan to date,[9] draws attention to his literary precursors in the Soviet Pantheon, and links him to the Russian and international debate over the nature of the Communist Hero and how to present him. He sees Gorki's *Mother* (1906) and Gladkov's *Cement* (1925) as the most important analogues, and Ewan's brusque rejection of Ellen as being in their tradition, where 'the protagonist demonstrates his heroic fortitude . . . by resisting the threat made to his greater political destiny by romantic involvement' (p.161). But it is not strictly correct to speak of a 'socialist realist' influence here: the dogma was not theoretically formulated until 1934, and therefore could have had no influence on either *Mother* or *Cement*. Orthodox communists have always criticized Gibbon's presentation of Ewan. They have felt that the ideal communist leader should be warm, sympathetic, many-sided, and richly human—all the things that socialist realism said he should be, and which Ewan is not. His coldly analytic mind drives him to extreme and 'super-revolutionary' conclusions, to 'an intellectualized and at times inhuman conception of the workers' struggle for Socialism', and his remarks on tactics do not in the least resemble the real communist tactics of the time; they are pure fantasy on Gibbon's part.[10] But the whole course of history since 1934 seems to show that they were not fantasy. The book is dedicated to Hugh MacDiarmid, and as early as 1926, in the *First Hymn to Lenin*, MacDiarmid had proclaimed that the horrors of the Cheka were not merely necessary but even insignificant when compared with the role of Death in the whole Cosmos, and had asked

> what maitters't wha we kill
> To lessen the foulest murder that deprives
> Maist men o' real lives?

Solzhenitsyn has shown how the Leninist Cheka was a precursor of the Yezhov terror, and it is only a step from MacDiarmid's lines to 'What maitters't what lies we tell, or how we deceive the poor lumpen proles?', since we, whatever our actual social origins, *are* the working class, and *our* will is the 'real will' of the proletariat, whether they know it or not. Jim Trease makes the point, at first grimly joking:

> *For it's me and you are the working-class, not the poor Bulgars gone back to Gowans.* And suddenly was serious an untwinkling minute: *A hell of a thing to be history, Ewan . . . A hell of a thing to be History!*—not a student, a historian, a tinkling reformer, but LIVING HISTORY ONESELF, being it, making it, eyes for the eyeless, hands for the maimed!—

Or again, when Ewan is with Trease and his wife:

[He] liked them well enough, knowing that if it suited
the Party purpose Trease would betray him to the police
tomorrow, use anything and everything that might
happen to him as propaganda and publicity, without
caring a fig for liking or aught else. So he'd deal with Mrs
Trease, if it came to that. . . . And Ewan nodded to that,
to Trease, to himself, commonsense, no other way to
hack out the road ahead. Neither friends nor scruples
nor honour nor hope for the folk who took the workers'
road . . .

In 1934 fascism seemed in the ascendant in Europe, and
possible even in Britain. Beyond the novel's open end there
lies for Ewan, as Gibbon saw it, a brief spell as a full-time
communist organizer and a long period when he would
'hunger, work illegally, and be anonymous', through 'a
generation of secret agitation and occasional terrorism'. As
things actually turned out in Britain and the world, Ewan
might well have fought in Spain with the International
Brigade, then spent several years as a industrial organizer in
Scotland and the English midlands before ending up as one of
the leaders of the British Communist Party. But in both the
Ewan-Trease vision of a fascist Britain and the 'real' future,
Ewan would have had to live through the Moscow trials and
the Stalin purges: he would have had to justify what he knew
to be false in the interest of what his theory told him was the
lesser evil. Many communists tricked themselves into believ-
ing that the accused were always guilty, that there were only a
very few labour camps, that socialist planning in the East was
economically successful. Ewan, as Gibbon presents him,
would have faced up to the truth in private and deliberately
suppressed it for the public. And if the communists had come
to power in Britain, a mature Ewan, given his attitude to ends
and means at the end of *Grey Granite*, might have been
capable of sending comrades and rivals to their deaths after a
show trial—or else of stoically signing his own confession if
the Party decided that he was the one to be sacrificed.

It is Ewan's final scene with Ellen that shows the New Man
most appallingly in action. Though Ellen is depicted criti-

cally—she is about to 'sell out' to ordinary values—yet she was after all the person who helped him through his psychological crisis after police torture, and she is consistently straight and above board in her dealings with others. Ewan rejects her in the most brutal way possible:

> *But what are you doing out here with me? I can get a prostitute anywhere* . . . He stood looking at her coolly, not angered, called her a filthy name, consideringly, the name a keelie gives to a leering whore; and turned and walked down the hill from her sight.

As Deirdre Burton has put it, 'It is that recourse to the irrelevant insults of sexuality that finally marks Ewan out as the person of limited vision, limited growth—both personal and political.'[11] Yet, horrified, we empathize with him in his rejection. Writing with hindsight in the years after communism's collapse from within, one is impressed by Gibbon's refusal to endorse Ewan's ethics in this scene, and by the deft impressionism with which he portrays his flawed hero.

Because ideas play such a large part in *A Scots Quair* there has been a tendency for critics to impose an abstract 'meaning' on the trilogy as a whole. What is certain is that, as Edwin Muir put it, Gibbon 'was firmly convinced that man once lived a life of innocence and happiness' in the Golden Age of the Gay Hunters; 'but all his impetuous energy was concentrated on drawing the vital conclusion from this, which was that by breaking the bonds imprisoning him man can live again.' He certainly believed that revolutionary communism was the sword to cut those bonds; but he had also, to continue with Muir's appreciation, 'a passionate devotion to such things as truth, justice and freedom, and a belief in their ultimate victory that nothing could shake'.[12] In the beginning he seems to have seen the *Quair* as propaganda for socialist action ('I am a revolutionary writer . . . all my books are explicit or implicit propaganda', Letter in *Left Review*, February 1935); but the fact surely is that in the white heat of composition it turned into a method of *thinking* about contemporary morals and politics in aesthetic terms—thinking by means of the images which we call characters. Gibbon's aesthetic thought points to conclusions somewhat different from the sort he was accustomed to formulate in articles or arguments with friends. As Ewan says:

> *There will always be you and I, I think, Mother. It's the old fight that maybe will never have a finish, whatever the names we give to it—the fight in the end between* FREEDOM *and* GOD.

It is Chris whose whole being is inseparable from the truth, justice and freedom which Muir claimed were such strong values for Gibbon, and Ewan whose communism is religious at bottom, as Ma Cleghorn notes quite early in the book:

> she wouldn't trust Ewan, a fine loon, but that daft-like glower in his eyes—*Och, this communism stuff's not canny, I tell you, it's just a religion though the Reds say it's not and make out that they don't believe in God. They're dafter about Him than the Salvationists are, and once it gets under a body's skin he'll claw at the itch till he's tirred himself.*

It would seem likely, then, that Chris's oblivion on the hilltop must have something to do with Freedom and God. In W. K. Malcolm's interpretation, it signalizes a union between the two categories attained by Chris on the very last page, 'for just before she finally becomes insensate to the feel of the rain and oblivious to the noise of the passing lapwings, she ultimately recognizes God in the constant working and reworking of her natural surroundings, identifying the power of Change which holds sway over life as the final truth.'[13] This is quite some distance from earlier allegorical interpretations which identified Chris with the Land or the Scottish nation, and saw her 'death' as symbolizing both the final destruction of the peasantry and the end of Scotland, and indeed of all other nations, in favour of the proletarian internationalism of the industrial working class. One mystical experience is balanced against another—Ewan's visionary identification with all the oppressed, and Chris's recognition of God in the ever-changing natural world—and each epiphany is, in the last resort, religious.

                                        Thomas Crawford

NOTES TO INTRODUCTION. MSS in the National Library of Scotland are quoted by kind permission of the NLS and of Gibbon's daughter, Mrs Rhea Martin.

1. Letter to Gibbon, 29 January 1935, NLS MS. Acc. 26065(8).

2. Doubleday Circular of 30 January 1935, NLS MS. Acc. 26065(15).

3. *Listener*, 5 December 1934.

4. Ian S. Munro, *Leslie Mitchell: Lewis Grassic Gibbon* (Edinburgh, 1966), p.71.

5. Ian Campbell, 'Lewis Grassic Gibbon and the Mearns', in *A Sense of Place*, ed. Graeme Cruickshank (Edinburgh, 1988), p.18.

6. Munro, p.71.

7. 'Action and Narrative Stance in *A Scots Quair*', in *Literature of the North*, ed. David Hewitt and Michael Spiller (Aberdeen, 1983), p.117.

8. NLS MS. Acc. 26109(61).

9. William K. Malcolm, *A Blasphemer and Reformer* (Aberdeen, 1984), pp. 157–70.

10. Ian Milner, 'An Estimation of *A Scots Quair*', in *Marxist Quarterly* I (4), 1954, p. 214. Similar points were made by Jessie Koçsmanova, 'Lewis Grassic Gibbon, Pioneer of Socialist Realism', in *Journal of Brno University* (1955), and by John Mitchell in his Epilogue to the East German translation of *Grey Granite* (1974).

11. Deirdre Burton, 'A Feminist Reading of *A Scots Quair*', in *The British Working-Class Novel in the Twentieth Century*, ed. J. Hawthorn (London, 1984), p.45.

12. Edwin Muir, 'Lewis Grassic Gibbon: An Appreciation', in *Scottish Standard* I (March 1935), pp.23–4.

13. Malcolm, p. 184.

Note on the Text

The present text follows that of the first edition as scrupulously as possible, except in such matters of typographical styling as the use of small capitals, not italic capitals, for words emphasized in direct speech. Misprints that were not picked up in later editions have been corrected, and the map of 'The Land of *A Scots Quair*' has been prepared from the one in the first edition.

A typescript of *Grey Granite* survives, all but the last page, in NLS MS Acc. 26042. It includes phrases and short passages which Gibbon altered for his final version. Thus at p.1, line 10, the typescript reads 'and paused, breathing deeply, she could hear her heart, afore tackling the chave of the climb', and at p.2, line 3, '*And at sixty, with sweirty and creash combined, they'll have carted you off to the creamery!*' Sometimes there is a weakening of the Scots, as at p.3, line 18, where the typescript has 'hap of the fog', the printed text 'peace'. The NLS also has a complete set of uncorrected galley proofs. These appear to embody all corrections made on first proof: a spot check revealed no differences from the published text.

ONE

Epidote

ALL AROUND her the street walls were dripping in fog
as Chris Colquohoun made her way up the Gallowgate,
yellow fog that hung tiny veils on her eyelashes, curled wet,
and had in her throat the acrid taste of an ancient smoke.
Here the slipper-slide of the pavement took a turn that she
knew, leading up to the heights of Windmill Place, and
shortly, out of the yellow swath, she saw come shambling the
lines of the Steps with their iron hand-rail like a famished
snake. She put out her hand on that rail, warm, slimy, and
paused afore tackling the chave of the climb, breathing
deeply, she could hear her heart. The netbagful of groceries
on her arm ached—she looked down through wet lashes at
the shape of the thing—as though it was the bag that ached,
not her arm. . . .

Standing still so breathing that little while she was
suddenly aware of the silence below—as though all the
shrouded town also stood still, deep-breathing a minute in
the curl of the fog—stilling the shamble and grind of the
trams, the purr of the buses in Royal Mile, the clang and
swing of the trains in Grand Central, the swish and roll and
oily call of the trawlers taking the Forthie's flood—all
pausing, folk wiping the fog from their eyes and squinting
about them an un-eident minute—

Daft, she said to herself, and began climbing the stairs.
Midway their forty steps a lamp came in sight, at last,
glistening, it flung a long dirty hand down to help her. Her
face came into its touch, it blinked surprised, not expecting
that face or head or the glistering bronze coils of hair that
crowned them—hair drawn in spiralled pads over each ear,
fog-veiled, but shining. Chris halted again here under the

lamp, thirty-eight, so she couldn't run up these steps, stiff's an old horse on a Mounth hill-road.

Old at thirty-eight? You'll need a bath-chair at fifty. And at sixty—why, as they'd say in Segget, they'll have carted you off to the creamery!

Panting, she smiled wry under the lamp at the foul tale told of Duncairn crematorium—the foul story that had struck her as funny enough even hearing it after the burning of Robert. . . . Oh, mixed and queer soss that living was, dying, dying slowly a bit of yourself every year, dying long ago with that dim lad, Ewan, dying in the kirk of Segget the time your hand came red from Robert's dead lips—and yet midmost the agonies of those little deaths thinking a foul tale flouting them funny!

Daft as well as decrepit, she told herself, but with a cool kindness, and looked over the Steps at the mirror hung where the stairs swung west, to show small loons the downward perils as they pelted blue hell on a morning to school. She saw a woman who was thirty-eight, looked less, she thought, thirty-five maybe in spite of those little ropes of grey that marred the loops of the coiled bronze hair, the crinkles about the sulky mouth and the eyes that were older than the face. Face thinner and straighter and stranger than once, as though it were shedding mask on mask down to one last reality—the skull, she supposed, that final reality. Funny she could stand here and face up to that, not feel sick, just faintly surprised! Once it had been dreadful and awful to think of—the horror of forgotten flesh taken from enduring bone, the masks and veils of life away, down to those grim essentials. Now it left her neither sick nor sorry, she found, watching a twinkle in sulky gold eyes above the smooth jut of the wide cheekbones. Not sad at all, just a silly bit joke of a middle-aged woman with idle thoughts in a pause on the Steps of Windmill Brae.

Below the quiet broke with the scrunch of a tram wheeling down from the lights of Royal Mile to the Saturday quietude of Gallowgate. Chris turned, looked, saw the shiver of sparks through the fog, syne the sailing brute swing topaz in sight, swaying and swearing, with aching feet as it ran for its depot in Alban Street. Its passage seemed to set fire to the fog, a little wind came and blew the mist-ash, and there was Grand Central smoking with trains. And now, through the thinning bouts of the fog, Chris could see the lighted clock of Thomson Tower shine sudden a mile or so away over the tumbled rigs of grey granite.

Nine o'clock.

She lowered the netbag and stretched her arms, saw herself wheel and stretch in the mirror, slim still, long curves, half-nice she half-thought. Her hands came down on the railing and held it, no need to hurry tonight for a change, Ma Cleghorn would have seen to supper for them all—the nine o'clock Gallop to the Guts as she called it. No need to hurry, if only this once in the peace of the ill-tasting fog off the Forthie, in the blessed desertion of the Windmill Steps so few folk used in Duncairn toun. Rest for a minute in the peace of the fog—or nearly at peace but for its foul smell.

Like the faint, ill odour of that silent place where they'd ta'en Robert's body six months before—

She'd thought hardly at all what she would do after Robert's funeral that so shocked Segget, she'd carried out all the instructions in the will and gone back with Ewan to the empty Manse, Ewan made her tea and looked after her, cool and efficient, only eighteen, though he acted more like twenty-eight—at odd minutes he acted eighty-two she told him as he brought her the tea in the afternoon stillness of the sitting-room.

He grinned the quick grin that was boy-like enough, and wandered the room a bit, tall and dark, unrestlessly, while she drank the tea. He hated tea himself, with a bairn-like liking for bairny things—milk and oatcakes would have contented Ewan from breakfast to dinner and some more for his supper. Ayont the windows in the waning of the afternoon Chris could see the frozen glister of night on the Grampians, swift and near-moving, Ewan's shoulder and sleekèd dark head against it. . . . Then he turned from the window. *Mother, I've got a job.*

She'd been sunk in a little drowse of sheer ache, tiredness from the funeral and the day in Duncairn, she woke stupid at his speak and only half-hearing: *A job?—who for?*

He said *Why, for little Ewan Tavendale all by his lone. But you'll have to sign the papers first.*

—But it's daft, Ewan, you haven't finished college yet, and then there's the university!

He shook the sleekèd head: *Not for me. I'm tired of college and I'm not going to live off you.* And thought for a minute and added with calm sense, *Especially as you haven't much to live off.*

So that was that and he fetched the papers, Chris sat and read the dreich things appalled, papers of apprenticeship for four years to the firm of Gowans and Gloag in Duncairn. Smelters and steel manufacturers—*But, Ewan, you'd go daft in a job like that.*

He said he'd try not to, awfully hard, especially as it was the best job he could come by—*and I can come out in weekends and see you quite often. Duncairn's only a twenty miles off.*

—And where do you think I *am going to bide?*

He looked at her curiously with cool, remote eyes, black didn't suit him, hair and skin over dark. *Eh? Oh, here in Segget, aren't you? You used to like it before Robert died.*

Sense the way he would speak of Robert, not heartlessly, just with indifference, as much as to say what did it matter, would a godly snuffling help Robert now? But a queer curiosity moved Chris to ask *Does anything ever matter to you at all, Ewan?*

—Oh, lots. Where you're going to stay, for one thing, when I've gone.

He'd slipped out of that well, Chris thought with a twinkle, sitting in the deep armchair on her heels, her head down bent, he ran his finger along the curve of her neck, coolly, with liking, as she looked up at last:

I'm coming to bide with you in Duncairn.

★

When they'd sold the furniture and paid off the debts there was barely a hundred and fifty pounds left, Segget took the matter through hand at the Arms, the news got about though both Chris and Ewan had been secret about it and never let on. But Segget would overhear what you said though you whispered the thing at the dead of night ten miles from a living soul in the hills. And it fair enjoyed itself at the news, God man! that was a right dight in the face for that sulky, stuck-up bitch at the Manse, her with her braw clothes and her proud-like ways, never greeting when her man died there in the pulpit, just as cool as though the childe were a load of swedes, not greeting even, or so 'twas said, when they burned the corp in there in Duncairn. And such a like funeral to give a minister, burning the man in a creamery!

And the Segget Provost, Hairy Hogg the sutor, said the thing was a judgment on the coarse brutes both, he never spoke ill of the dead, not him, but what had his forefather, the poet Burns, said?—

Ake Ogilvie the joiner was having a dram and he sneered real coarse: *You and your Burns! The gawpus blethered a lot of stite afore they shovelled him into the earth and sent all the worms for a mile around as drunk as tinks at Paldy Fair. But I'm damned if he'd ever a tongue like yours. What ill did Robert Colquohoun ever do you—or his mistress either, I'd like to know, except to treat you as a human being?—B'God, they showed themselves soft enough there!*

Alec the Provost's son was in having a nip, he wanted to fight Ake Ogilvie for that, the coarse Bulgar of a joiner to curse that way at a poor old sod like the Provost his father. But the wife of the hotel-keeper was back of the bar, folk called her the Blaster and Blasphemer for short, she was awful against a bit curse now and then: and she nipped Alec short as a new-libbed calf. *None of your cursings in here*, she cried, *I won't have the Lord's name taken in vain*. Alec habbered he'd nothing against the Lord, it wasn't Him he'd called a Bulgar, but the other one—and got in a soss, fairly upset at the Blaster's glower. Folk thought her an interfering old runt, ay God! she'd find her custom go.

So the most in the bar took a taik to the door with their drams in their hands and sat on the steps and looked at the sky, evening in Spring, bonny the hills, the seven o'clock dirling down Segget High Brig, peesies out on the long flat field that went mounting up to the bend of the hills. You minded Colquohoun, how he'd haunt those hills, the temples of God the creature would call them, him that died in the pulpit preaching a sermon—fair heathen it was, ay, a judgment of God. And now this slip of a wife of his had less than a two hundred pounds to her name, living up there in one room, folk said, all by her lone now that her loon, Ewan (ay, a son by her first bit man) had gone to work in Duncairn toun. It just showed you what happened to proud-like dirt, she'd intended the loon for an education and a braw-like life in a pulpit, maybe, nothing to do but habber and haver and glower over a collar on back to front: and instead he'd be just a common working chap.

Ake Ogilvie had new come out and heard that last speak of wee Peter Peat's. *Well, God,* YOU'RE *common enough,* he said, *though it's damn little work you ever manage.* And then he went swaggering across the Square, past the statue of the War Memorial Angel, a trig-like lassie with a pair of fine hips, and spat at it, coarse-like, fair a tink Ake, aye sticking up for the working men, you were maybe a working man yourself but were hardly such a fool as stick up for the brutes.

Syne Feet the Policeman came dandering along, he was due to leave for a job in Duncairn, folk cried out *Ay, Mr Leslie, fine night,* respectful-like, for he'd fair got on. And he stuck his thumbs in his belt and said *Ay,* majestic-like, like a steer with the staggers, and squashed out his great feet and looked up at the Angel as though to speir where she'd mislaid her stays. Syne folk saw that he'd gotten his sergeant's stripes, he'd come out to give the bit things an air; and he said he was off to Duncairn in a week, he'd been kind of put in charge of the toun, you learned, him and some other skilly childes, or at least in a bit that they called Footforthie where the factories were and a lot of tink workers, low brutes, for they hadn't a meck to their name and lived off the Broo and

Ramsay MacDonald, draining the country and Ramsay dry. But did that content them?—No, faith, it didn't, they were aye on the riot about something or other, stirred up by those ill-ta'en Bulgars, the Socialists. . . . Feet said that he'd use a firm hand, by God you thought if he used his feet there wouldn't be a Socialist left in Duncairn that didn't look like an accident with a rhubarb tart. God, how the meikle-houghed sod could blow!

Folk ganted a bit and began to taik off, but halted at the hint of a tasty bit news, and cried *No, man?* and came tearing back. *What's that? God be here!* and Feet swelled out his chest and started to tell his tale over again.

And the gist of the thing when you got to the bree was that Sergeant Sim Leslie had been in Duncairn, on business, like, that very forenoon—colloguing with the other heads of the Police and learning the work that he'd have to take on. Well, he'd finished the business and looked out for lodgings, awful expensive up in Duncairn and you needed a fine salary, same as he had. The second bit place that he keeked intil was a boarding-house on Windmill Brae, fell swell it looked, a braw bit house on the high hill that rises over Duncairn. But the terms were hardly as much as he'd feared, and he clinched for a room with the mistress o't, a meikle bit woman, Cleghorn the name.

Well, they had a bit crack when he'd ta'en the room and she told to Feet, fair newsy-like, she'd had the place all decorated of late at an awful expense she couldn't have afforded but that she had advertised for a partner with a bit of silver to lay down as deposit, and syne help as a maid attending the lodgers. Feet had said *Ay?* and *Well, that's right fine*, not caring a damn one way or the other till she mentioned the new bit partner's name.

But when he heard THAT Feet fairly sat up, as every soul did now in front of the Arms: *Mrs Colquohoun? Where might she come from?* And the Cleghorn body had said *From Segget. Her man was a minister-creature there, though I'm damned if she looks it, a fleet trig woman that could muck a byre more ready any day than snuffle a psalm.* At that poor Feet was took sore aback, he never could stick the proud bitch at the Manse; but he'd made a deposit for the lodgings already and couldn't well ask for the silver back. So off he'd come home and got ready to pack—and faith, did you ever hear the like of that?

Afore night was out all Segget had heard, and half of the Mearns afore the next day, postmen ran for miles over parks with the news, old Hogg hammered four soles on the same pair of boots he was in such a fash to give the tale out. And when Mrs Colquohoun went down to the station, straight and cool, with her trig-like back, her hair coiled over each lug, fair daft, some thought it bonny, you were damned if you did—the half of Segget was keeking from its windows, and wondering about her, how she'd get on, what was she thinking, what was she wearing, had she had a bath on the previous night, did she ever think of a man to sleep with, how much did she measure around the hips, could she greet if she liked, what was her temper, how much of the hundred and fifty was left, was that loon of hers, Ewan, as dour as he looked, would he land in jail or would he get on?

At half-past five the clock would go *birr!* in the narrow long room you had ta'en for yourself, you'd wake with a start and find yourself sprawled in weariness right across the great bed, dark the guff of the early Spring, no cheep of birds here on Windmill Brae, clatter of the clock as it started again with a hoast and a rasp; and you'd reach for the thing and switch it off and lie still a minute, hands under your neck in the pad of your hair, fingers rough-seamed and scraping your skin. And you'd stretch out under the bedclothes, long, till your muscles all creaked, legs, hips and ribs, blessedly, you'd still a passable figure. Syne you'd throw off the blankets and get from the bed, the floorcloth cold as a Christian's heart under the naked soles of your feet—off with your nightie and stretch again and look from the window at the coming of dawn, lacing its boots and grabbing its muffler and pelting across the roofs of Duncairn. In a hurry the same you'd wriggle in your vest, stockings and knickers, slip on your dress, getting warm already in spite of the floor and the

frozen gleam of grey granite outside. And you'd open the
door and go down the stairs, quick, and looping back your
hair, to the cold prison walls of the kitchen, smelly, fling
open the window, in rushed the air and a smell of cats you
could cut with a knife. At first that smell had made you near
sick, even Jock the house-cat, a clean beast enough, but
you'd no time for such luxuries as sickness now-a-days,
lighting the gas, the kitchen range, your hands swift on
kettles and frying-pan, eyes on the clock and ears wide open
for the first stir of life in the morning's morgue.

At six you were up at Ma Cleghorn's room with a cup of tea
and a knock at her door and go in and draw back the window-
curtains, let up the blinds, bang! She'd wake up and groan
Is't you, Chris lass? Losh, you spoil me, just, she meant the tea,
and you'd say *Oh, havers,* she spoke Duncairn and you'd got
the same gait. And Ma Cleghorn would give another bit
groan and drink up the tea and loup from the bed, swack as
you like, an old woman only a minute afore but filled now
with tea and a fury to work. *The Bulgars'll soon be on the howl
for their meat. Whatever made me take to the keeping of lodgings?*

You'd say A BOARDING-HOUSE, *please, Mrs Cleghorn,*
one of the jokes that the two of you shared, Ma'd give a great
snifter through her meikle nose: *Boarding? B'God, it's
leathering they want. And I haven't a pair of bloomers to my
name that's not darned so a body can hardly sit down. I've a fair
bit padding of my own to ease it, you haven't, get out of the damn
trade, lass, afore you're like me and take to bloomers instead of
them frilly things you wear—God be here, they'll kill you yet dead
with cold. Aren't your legs froze?*

You'd say *Not them; fine legs,* and Ma struggling into her
blouse would say *You're no blate. Who told you they're fine?*
And you'd say *Oh, men,* and she'd nod to that, great red face
topped with greying hair like the face of a war-horse out of
Isaiah (as you'd once thought, minding back through the
months to Robert's reading from the Bible in Segget).—*Ay,
no doubt they have, and enjoyed them fine. And would again if
you gave them the chance.*

Syne you'd to tear to the kitchen again, in time for the ring from Miss Murgatroyd's room, dying for her tea the poor old wretch, solemn you'd carry it up to her room, the best in the house, three guineas a week. She'd quaver out of a lace nightcap: *Is that you, Mrs Colquohoun? And you have my tea? Oh, that's Such Fine*, she was awful genteel, poor spinster body with her pensions and potterings, not a soul in the world hers and respectable down to her shrivelled toes, wabbling hands and meek quiet eyes, Episcopalian, serving tea for the whist drives up at the Unionist Club. . . . And Ma Cleghorn, watching her taik down the street, would ask who in God's name would be an old maid? She'd often used to think when her Jim was alive and would come back from the Fish Market stinking so bad that his shirts hung out on a washing day would bring the cats scraiching for miles around—she'd used often to think *I wish I were single, trig on my own, not handled, not kenned, with nobody's seed ever laid in me!* But losh, when he died she had minded him sore, night on night and would fain have had him again though he smelt like a kipper mislaid in a drain when he'd cuddle you, feuch! They were sosses, were men, but you'd only to look at the Murgatroyd creature to make you mad to go tearing out and grab the first soss that you met in breeks—*Half-past six, Chris; will you waken your Ewan?*

He slept in one of the two rooms of the upper floor, the other empty, his window looked down on the glare of Footforthie at night that changed to a sick yellow furnace-glow, unstill, staining the sky on the morning's edge. You'd wanted him to change to another room, and he'd asked you why and you'd told him he'd surely get sick of it—working down there all day and seeing it all night. But he'd shaken his shapely, sleekèd head, no fancies or flim-flams with Ewan at all: *It'll neither wake me nor send me to sleep. Only a light in the sky, you know, Chris.*—So you'd turn the handle of his door and go in and meet the sting of the sea-wind there, the window wide open, the curtains flowing, Ewan dim in the light of the early dawn, lying so still, so still he slept that near every morning you'd be startled the same, feared that he lay there dead, so quiet, you'd shake his shoulder and see as you bent the blankets he'd thrust away from himself, pyjamas open wide to the waist, curling dark down on a boy's breast. Strange to think that this was your Ewan, once yours and so close, so tiny, so small and weak, sexless, a baby, that had grown a body tall as your own, slimmer, stronger, secret and strange, blossom and fruit from that seed of yours. . . . In a queer pity you'd look and shake him awake: *Ewan, time you were up!*

He'd start awake quietly, at once, like a cat, and look at you with those deep, cool eyes, neither grey nor green, grey granite eyes. *All right. Thanks. No, I don't want tea. I'll get an apple for myself, mother.* MOTHER! *I said I'd get it for myself!* And he'd be out of bed and have reached the dish and caught an apple afore you got near. *You've enough to do without waiting on me.*

—*But I like waiting on you. Wouldn't you wait on me?*

—*I suppose so, if you were sick or insane. What's the time?* And lean out half-naked from the window ledge to peer over Duncairn to Thomson Tower. *Splendid. I've time for a dip in the Forthie.*

He'd be out of the house as you gained the kitchen, an uproar by then of banging pans, Ma Cleghorn cooking porridge and bacon and sausages and coffee and cocoa and tea, and swearing out loud at the young maid, Meg, who slept at her home away down in the Cowgate and was supposed to come up each morning at seven. *Call that seven?—Then you're blind as well's sweir. Stack up the range and be nippy about it. Mrs Colquohoun, will you lay the table?*

You were aye *Mrs Colquohoun* when Meg was about, Ma Cleghorn treating you distant, polite, for the sake of discipline, so she said. You'd gathered the way of setting the table in the big ben room so quick your eyes hardly followed your fingers, porridge plates for Sim Leslie (who'd come from Segget where they'd called him Feet) and Mr George Piddle, the *Runner* reporter, thin and *he-he'ing*, minus his hair so that he could go bald-headed for news. Bacon for Miss Murgatroyd and Mr Neil Quaritch: Mr Quaritch worked on the *Runner* as well, a sub-editor creature, aye reading books and sloshing them to death in the *Runner* next day. But you rather liked the wee ferret man, red eyes and red hair and a red nose as well, and a straggle of beard on an unhappy chin, Ewan said he'd gone sozzled with reading rot rather than with knocking back gills of Glenlivet. . . . Mixed grill for Miss Ena Lyon, the typist, powdered and lipsticked, and awful up-to-date, baggy a bittie below the eyes and a voice like a harried peahen, poor lass. Porridge for young Mr Clearmont, nice loon who went to the University and was awful keen on music and jokes, you could never make head nor tail of either as he always guffawed out, young and hearty, right at the point—if there was a point. Ma Cleghorn didn't think much of him, she said if ever he'd a thought in his head it'd be easy to tell it, you'd hear the damn thing rattling about like a stone in a tin. But she was jealous a bit, you thought, of the lad's university and books and book-learning. . . . Bacon for young John Cushnie, all red, the clerk in Raggie Robertson's Drapery Depot, half-sulky, half-shy and would spend half an hour roping up his neck in a speckled tie, he shared Archie Clearmont's room but nought else. . . . Eight o'clock and you hit the gong, breakfast all ready set on the table.

And down they'd all pour and sit in about, Miss Murga-troyd sitting neat as a pin, Such Fine, and eating her grape-fruit up like a sparrow pecking at a bit of dung (you laughed: but you sometimes wished that Ma wouldn't say those things about folk so often: the picture stuck, true or untrue, and you never saw them in real likeness again); Sergeant Sim Leslie supping his porridge and goggling at you over his collar; Ewan eating quick, clean and indifferent, lost in his thoughts or else in a book, all squiggly lines and figures and drawings; Miss Ena Lyon, complete with complexion, eating her bacon and talking to Clearmont, he'd been to a concert the night before and Miss Lyon was saying she liked music as well—just loved a talkie with a Catchy Choon. Poor Mr Piddle with his long thin neck and his long thin head, as bald as a neep and something the shape, would snap up his meat in a haste to be gone in search of news for the *Daily*

Runner, a fine big paper, the pride of Duncairn, and awful useful for lining your shelves; Cushnie, red-eared and trying to speak English, would call out above the folds of his tie *Will ye pass the cruet? I'm in a gey hurry. Me and Mr Robertson have the Spring Sale on;* and Mr Neil Quaritch would push down his cup, *May I have another, Mrs Colquohoun?* he'd left his breakfast untasted as usual.

And Ma Cleghorn would sit at the top of the table, her big red face set square on its neck, sonsy and sturdy, you'd liked her from the first, she you, you supposed you'd neither of you frills, you'd seen over much of this queer thing Life to try hide from its face by covering your own with a ready-made complexion out of a jar, or ready-made morals from the Unionist Club, or ready-made fear and excitement and thrill out of the pages of the *Daily Runner*. . . . And you'd sit and stare at your own porridge plate till Ma would call out: *Will you fill up the cups?*

By ten the lot would have clattered away, on trams and buses, on foot and a-run, tripping along like a sparrow, Miss Murgatroyd, Mr Piddle whirring away on his bike like a snake going pelting back to the Zoo, Miss Ena Lyon with her heels so high that her shoulders drooped and her bottom stuck out, quite up-to-date, Ewan in dungarees, no hat, books under his arm, black hair almost blue, shinning down the Steps of Windmill Brae two at a time, hands in his pouches. . . . And they left the real work of the house to begin.

You and Ma Cleghorn couldn't run to more help than Meg for the washing-up in the kitchen, Ma took the first floor with the dining-room and sitting-room and swept them and dusted them and tore up the rugs and went out to the back and hung them on the line and thrashed them to death in a shower of stour. You had the bedrooms, Ma'd asked if you'd mind—*Some of them stink like a polecat's den.* You'd said you didn't care, we all stank sometimes. And Ma had nodded, *Fegs, and that's true. But fancy you being willing to let on—you that was wed to a minister body!*

You'd mind that speak as you redded the rooms, gathered

the mats and pulled wide the curtains, opened the windows and made the beds, swept out and polished each of the rooms, emptied slops and carried down washing, and cleared the bathroom of razor blades and bits of paper stuck with shaving-soap hair, other things that Miss Murgatroyd would half-hide, so would Miss Lyon in a different way. . . . Wife to a minister—wife to Robert: it faded away in the stour of the days though only last Spring you had been in Segget, had slept beside him in those chill hours that had come trailing down a blanket of dark to cut you off one from the other, Robert sleeping sound while you woke and heard the wail of sleet from the Grampian haughs. All ended, put by, Robert himself no more than a name, you'd loved him so deep that the day he died something had broken in you, not in your heart, it didn't break there, something in your belly went numb, still, and stayed so . . . but the queerness of things! You could hardly mind now the shape of his face—his eyes, were they grey or blue?—Oh God! . . . And you'd sometimes stop and feel sick to think how quickly even your memories went, as though you stood naked in an endless storm shrilling about you, wisp by wisp your garments went till at last you'd stand to all uncovered—love, pity, desire, hope, hate put by under the sail of the endless clouds over Cloud Howe, the Howe of the World—

Then you'd shake yourself to sense, get down with pail of water and a scrubbing-brush, scrub and scrub till your finger-nails, so smooth and round-shaped in your years at Segget, come jagged again, hacks in your fingers that caught the blankets as you turned in unease of a night and sent a shrill stream of pain up your hands. Queer to work again in such fashion, use all your body till you ached dead tired, by the time you'd finished the upper floor your hips were filled with a stinging and shooting, like a bees' byke with bees, bad as having a baby, sweat in runnels either side your nose—you felt like a greasy dish-clout, just, ready to be wrung and hung out to dry. And when you got down to the kitchen at last Ma Cleghorn would skeugh at you over her specs, *Fegs, lass, you take well with a slammock of work. Like a cup of tea?—Here,*

gi'me the basses, I'll take them out while you sit down a minute.
You'd say *I'll shake them myself, I'm fine,* and she'd look at
you grim, *It's your funeral, then. But die where it's easy to
spread out the corp.*

A blessed minute that when you'd gotten back, though, sat
down to drink the strong tea Ma made, hot, steaming and
thick, Ma drinking another cup the other side of the table,
Meg pleitering still at the kitchen sink. You felt all revived,
throat, belly and—better not further. (Miss Murgatroyd you
were sure never went further, Ma Cleghorn on the contrary
seldom went higher.) You'd see yourself as you sat and
drank, your head and hair and face and breast in the kitchen
mirror over the range, flushed face, not pretty, it was never
that, sulky eyes and the mouth men had liked well enough in
your time—long ago, afore you grew old and took to
scrubbing! . . . And you'd finish your tea and loup to your
feet and be gone to finish the rest of the ploy, and be back in
the kitchen to lend Ma a hand to plan out the dinner for those
that came home—Mr Clearmont from the University, Ewan
seldom, Mr Piddle sometimes, Mr Quaritch and Miss Ena
Lyon never, John Cushnie when Raggie's rag Sales would
allow, Sergeant Sim Leslie sure as the clock.

Ma had a great cookery-book of her own, made up of
recipes cut out of the papers, daft ones and good ones and
plain damn silly ones, Ma'd say *What stomachs some folk must
have to eat the dirt that the papers say!* But she cooked well
enough, passable yourself, Jock the cat would sit and purr
under the red-hot glow of the range, half-roasted the brute
had been since his birth, and liked it: Ma said he'd enjoy hell.
And she'd lift him aside with a meikle great foot, impatient-
like, and he'd purr all the time, while the foot was under him,
while he sailed through the air, while he landed with a thump
out under the sink. And Meg would give a bit scraich of fear,
and maybe drop a plate, inviting death.

In the first few days you'd been sorry for the lass, Ma
Cleghorn treated her worse than dirt, bullying her, sneering
at her, upbraiding Almighty God for making such a trauchle
to pest decent folk. Syne you saw that Meg, thin, schlimpèd

and pert, wasn't feared a wee bit, sleekèd and sly with a sideways glint in her eyes at Ma, taking her in and her measure unfeared. And Ma that could skin a body alive with her tongue and hang out the hide in the sun to dry wouldn't send Meg out on a message if it rained, heaped her plate with great helpings at dinner, and when she saw the bit maid over-trauchled with a job would swear at her and go tearing to help. . . . So you didn't interfere but got on with your own work, plenty of that—how you'd ached at first afore dinner-time, hungry as you'd never been in a manse: genteel appetite going with all else, walking now with a quick and a hasting step not the long lope that had once been yours, face altering as well from the drowsy mask that had come on you under the yew-trees of Segget—waiting, half-asleep, sitting deep in a chair, for Maidie to bring tea out on the lawn, the peesies flying over Segget blue in smoke, smoke in sun smother, long ago, long ago; and Robert coming striding across the lawn, whistling—and you looked, and he hadn't a face—

And once Ma came on you as you stood and wept, tearless, sobbing dry-eyed, and stared and knew, shook you and hugged you tight, it hurt: *Don't greet, nothing's worth it, not a damn thing, no man that ever yet was, Chris!* You'd stopped from that daft carry-on at once, shamed of yourself, bothering Ma, weeping like a fool over something as common as kale, losh, weren't there thousands of widows in the world worse off than you and not snivelling like bairns? And you'd shaken Ma off, gentle as you could: *I know. I'm just giving myself a pet. My father would have said it was salts I needed.*

Dinner and the feeding of all the faces, funny to think a face was mainly for that; and then out shopping for the morn's meat. You went down Windmill Steps in the blue Spring air, the grey granite walls rising about you, if the day was clear you'd see below Duncairn spread as a map for show, far off, north-east, the sheen of the Beach beyond the rolling green of the Links, Footforthie a smother of smoke ayont the Docks, the Fish Market and the trawlers' rig, the Forthie gleaming grey under its brigs. Cleaving the jumble of warrens and wynds went Royal Mile like a south-driven sword, to the left the new biggings of Ecclesgriegs, Town Hall and courts and Thomson Tower, the Tangleha' trees that hid the University, the gentry's quarters, genteel Craigneuks—to the right in jumbles around Grand Central the Cowgate and Gallowgate, Paldy Parish, and far off in the west beyond Footforthie the fishers' wee toun, called Kirriebem.

You waited a tram by the Windmill Steps, it came showding and banging up from the Station, green like a garden slug, in you got, and sat down and closed your eyes and thought hard, the things you'd to order, where you'd best get them. Fish, beef, eggs, butter, go swear at the grocer, the laundry hadn't sent back those sheets, Ma Cleghorn wanted the chimney-sweep, you needed a new frock and must bear with the need. . . . Out into Royal Mile you stepped,—there on his stance, unmoving, King Edward, bald as a turkey and with much the same face, ready to gobble from a ton of grey granite. In the seats round the plinth the unemployed, aye plenty of them, yawning and wearied, with their flat-soled boots and their half-shaved faces, they'd cry their bit bars as they stared at the stir, or chirp a bit filth to a passing quean, sometimes though seldom they did it to you. You didn't much mind, were you wearied yourself and half-fed, you thought, with nothing to do, you'd do worse than chirp.

Only once had that worse ever happened to you, you'd run down the steps from the Mile to the lane that led to the Gallowgate's guff one evening, to a dairy there that sold good eggs. Day above, but already half-dark in that place, no body about as you hurried along, or so you thought till you sighted the man. He'd been leaning in the doorway of an empty warehouse, heard you coming and looked up and down: and as you came near he got in your way. *I'm starving, wifie. Gi'me a tanner*.

His face was thin and dirty and brown, he'd no shirt, his jacket pinned over his breast, smelt awful, great knuckled hands, should you scream? And then you'd known that that would be daft, you'd said *All right, though I haven't one to spare*. And you'd opened your bag, heart thumping as you did it, what if he grabbed and made off with the lot? But he didn't, stood waiting, face red with shame. You'd found him the sixpence, handed it over, he'd nodded, no thanks, and looked away. And you'd hurried on down the lane to the dairy, suddenly trembling and your lips grown wet.

You'd get back to tea with the netbag full, have a first cup ere the others came, Archie Clearmont first, banging up the stairs, he'd meet you and smile, *'Lo, Mrs Colquohoun. That's a nice frock*. You'd tease him and say *There's a nice woman in it*, and he'd blush, boy-clear, *I know that as well*. If only Ewan were as simple as he! . . . Mr Piddle tearing in from his office, all in a fash to be off to the Station and catch the 6.30 bound for Dunedin. Not that he'd catch the train himself, he'd send off the latest news of Duncairn and make a bit extra salary, *he-he!* from the linage the *Tory Pictman* would print. . . . Miss Ena Lyon trailing in half-dead from the work in her office, half the rouge gone, the other half sprinkled about like a rash, she'd drawl on the Awful Rush in the firm, and the Boss no more than a Vulgar Keelie. . . . Ewan at last, black-streaked, black-haired, as cool and composed from Gowans and Gloag's as he'd been when haunting the hills of the Howe seeking the flints of the ancient men.

More clearing away, more tidying-up, getting ready supper, eating it, clearing it—you might almost have hated the sight of food with the number of times you messed the stuff. But you didn't: instead, you were hungry all day, ate a large supper at nine o'clock, found work nearly done and yawned a bit, and sat listening to Ma's radio in the sitting-room, a deserted place most nights but for you. And you'd listen to talks on ethics and cocktails and how to go hiking on the Côte d'Azur, minding the baby, copulation in catkins, and the views of Jacob P. Hackenschmidt on Scotland and Her Ancient Nationhood; and you'd switch the thing off, losh, that was better, worth paying a licence to keep the thing quiet, drowse instead and think of the countryside, corn coming green in clay parks this night as often you'd

seen it when you were a quean, wedded to Ewan in Kinraddie
long syne—you that waited the feet of another Ewan now.

In Paldy Parish as the June came in there came a wave of heat
with the month, it lifted the guffs from the half-choked
drains and flung them in under the broken doors down
through the courts to simmer and stew, a body could hardly
bear the touch of his sark as he lay in bed by his wife of a
night, the weans would whimper and move and scratch on
the shake-down over under the window—stewing in the
front of a half-open furnace. And a man would get up in a
Paldy tenement and go along the passage to the WC, blasted
thing crowded, served a score of folk, not decent, by God
what a country to live in. On the Broo since the War and five
kids to keep, eating off your head—och, why did you
live?—never a minute of quiet to yourself, nothing but the
girnings of the wife for more silver, the kids half-barefoot,
half-fed, oh hell.

And the wife would turn as she heard him come back, lie
wakeful and think on the morn's morning—what to give the
weans, what to give the man, fed he must be ere he took the
streets to look for that weary job he'd not find—he'd never
find one you had come to ken. Hardly believe it was him you
had wed, that had been a gey bit spark in his time, hearty and
bonny, liked you well: and had hit you last night, the bloody
brute coming drunk from the pub—a woman couldn't go
and hide in booze, forget all the soss and pleiter, oh no, she'd
to go on till she dropped, weans scraiching, getting thin and
like tinks, and the awful words they picked up every place,
the eldest loon a street-corner keelie, the quean—oh God, it
made a body sick.

And the quean would turn by the side of her sisters, see the
faint glow of the dawn, smell the reek of the Paldy
heat—Christ, would she never get out of it, get a job, get
away, have clothes, some fun? If they couldn't afford to
bring up their weans decent why did father and mother have
them? and syne nag and nag at you day on day, on this and
that, the way that you walked, the way you behaved (*take care*

that the loons don't touch your legs), the way that you spoke—nothing pleased the old fools, and what you brought home they thought should be theirs, every meck that you made, nothing for yourself, stew in the reek of the Cowgate's drains till you died and were buried and stank to match. My God, if a lassie couldn't do anything else she could take a bit walk out to Doughty Park, fine there, though the place was littered with Reds, fair daft, the Communionists the worst of the lot, aye holding their meetings and scraiching and bawling that the workers all join up with their unions and fight for their rights and down with the gents.

But no decent lassies would listen to them, for they knew the Communionists were awful tinks who wanted to break up the home.

Every day as the Cowgate stirred Meg was up at the cheep of dawn, seeing to young Jessie and Geordie for school, getting ready breakfast, snapping back at Mother, Father the old devil lying snoozing in bed, he didn't go down to the Docks till ten. He swore he could hardly get a wink of sleep because of the old trawl-skipper next door, awful religious and fond of a nip, who thrashed his old wife near every night, singing out hymn-tunes like hell the while. If other folk could sleep through the old skipper's roar of *Rock of Ages, cleft for me* as he cleft his old woman under the bed, why couldn't Father sleep as well?

Alick, Meg's brother, would get into his clothes, grumbling as usual when he'd only porridge. He was barely Meg's age, an apprentice-lad down at Gowans and Gloag's in Footforthie. That might have been fine, the beginnings of a job, but when his apprenticeship was up—well, everybody kenned what happened to apprentices. They were sacked right off when they needed men's wages, and Alick like others would be chucked on the Broo.

Alick said this morning when Meg sneered that, *Ay, maybe to me the same as the others, but not to the dirty college sods*. And he said that Gowans took college pups now, with a special apprenticeship, easy as winking, they served the first six months at the Furnace, same as the others, but what happened to them then? They squatted their dowps in office jobs, and put on clean collars and gave out their orders, bloody toffs, though no better than you or me. There'd been two of them in the last two years, training as managers, *they* weren't sacked, when the last machinery came into the Works that would do all the doings without working-chaps: you'd still need somebody to oil it about, and they'd keep the mammie's pets to do that. Another had come a two months back—a black-haired, stuck-up gypsy Bulgar, over-fine to speak to a chap like Alick, he'd get a sock in the kisser sometime.

Meg said *Don't blether, you haven't the guts; you're jealous he's brains and you haven't, that's all.* Alick snorted *Brains? Him? He's only got swank. And me and the chaps in the Furnaces are planning a little bit of a surprise for Mr Bloody Ewan Tavendale.*

—WHO?

Alick said *Wash out your lugs. Ewan Tavendale's the name if you want to know. Here, get out of my way till I get on my boots, the hooter'll be howling in a minute or so.*

So that was where HER son worked, was it then? What had She to be stuck-up about? A lassie could bear with old Ma Cleghorn, an orra old bitch but not a bad heart. But the way that that Mrs Colquohoun took on, and looked at you cool, put a body off. And who was she to put on her airs that kept a lodging-house for a living and had her son only an apprentice like Alick?

Meg grabbed her hat and set out for Windmill, the Cowgate slowly unwreathing its fug, up in Royal Mile the lorries were lolloping over the calsays, Paldy Parish littering its doors with weans, snuffy and ragged, kids off to school, scrawling dirty things on the pavements, some throwing filth and cheeking a lassie. . . . She'd get out of this place, get a lodging somewhere in Tangleha' or the Ecclesgriegs.

But who should she meet where the Cowgate lane climbed up to the stour and whirr of the Mile than Big Jim Trease the Communionist, red-cheeked and sappy, everybody kenned him and called him *Jim* when bobbies weren't looking. But

Meg had no use for those coarse brutes the Reds that would
do away with the gents and her job, and when Big Jim smiled
all over his face twinkling his wee pig eyes at her she made to
go by with her nose in the air. He'd a creature with him she
didn't know, thin, brown, ragged, with an ill-shaved face;
and Jim cried *Meg, I've been looking for you. Has your Ma still
got that spare bed to let?*

Meg snapped *Supposing you gang and speir at her?* Big Jim
smiled at her sappy and kind, she felt half-shamed though the
beast was a Red: *Right, and we will. Many thanks, Meg.*

Would you credit that?—trying to land a Red in the
house, maybe rape you and gut you in the middle of the
night, as the coarse tinks did with hardly a break, night on
night, in that awful Russia. If Ma wasn't soft she would keep
the door snibbed. . . . *Oh to hell, there's the Windmill tram!*

She caught the thing by the skin of the teeth and got out
under the Windmill Brae, ran up the Steps and met face to
face young Ewan Tavendale coming down them—three at a
time, no hat, in overalls, hands in his pouches, two books
alow his oxter, his eyes went over her, why need he be proud?
The like of him made you think the Reds right, he needed to
be jammed by a wall and shot.

Morning, Meg, he said, *Didn't notice you*, and smiled as
sweet as a kid at you. Oh, losh, and the things you'd been
thinking about him!

And the things Alick said they were doing today—

Gowans and Gloag made metal containers, bolts and girders
and metal trestles, fine castings for sections of engine casings,
a thousand men working in great rattling sheds built to hold
the labour of three times the number in a rattle and roar of
prosperity. Ewan Tavendale would think of that now and
then, Gowans had flourished just after the War, high wages
and bonuses dished out to all, pap for the proletariats.
Wonder what they did with the high money then?—Spent it
on the usual keelie things, dogs and horse-racing and
sleeping with whores, poor devils—it had nothing to do with
him.

Hardly anything to do with the others at all, stoking his shot in the Furnaces, stripped to the waist, he stripped brown, mother's skin, and tightened his belt over shovel and barrow, cleared out the clinkers and wheeled up a load and flung it deep in the whoom of the flame, the Works kittling up as the morning woke, bells snarling hell if the heat now and then went low in one fire or another. In an hour or so Ewan'd be dripping with sweat, and drink and drink from the tap in the rear, water that gushed out again from him, a sponge-like life and tremendous fun. The other apprentices, keelies the lot, didn't seem anxious to chum up at all, thank goodness, it gave him time to tackle the books of the trade, metallurgy twice as exciting as flints. He stacked the books with his coat in the sheds, till dinner, and went up and scrubbed himself, put on his coat and went down to the Docks with books and a sandwich and swotted up Castings. But the other apprentices stayed behind and laughed and joked in the lavatories, insanitary devils, no business of his.

But this forenoon was the worst he'd faced in the Furnaces, hours clogged with heat, lungs going like bellows, once the foreman Dallas came swearing down, about fires, not Ewan's, it was drawing fine. He looked at Ewan and gave him a nod *Take it a bit easier, Mr Tavendale. Yours is fine. It's the fires of those other muckers.* He'd hardly gone up the steps to Machines when the pimply keelie Alick Watson called out to another of them, Ewan didn't know his name: *D'you know any poetry this morning, Norman?*

—*Oh, ay, a fine bit. You other lads heard it?*—

There once was a gent Tavendale
(Oh-Rahly-the-guff-makes me pale!)
    A pimp and a sucker,
    A dirty wee mucker—
And his name, as I've said, Tavendale.

. . . . Oh ay, the toff bastard heard it fine, but he didn't let on, just went on with his work, all the lads laughed, you'd known he'd no guts. Syne Norman Cruickshank sang out another bit, you laughed till you split, a funny sod Norman, about the toff mucker's mucking mother. He threw down the shovel as he said that, Norman, getting ready for the toff when he louped to bash him, as any body would do when he heard THAT about his mother. And he heard it all right and gave Norman a look, fair damn well maddening, as though Norman were dirt and not very interesting dirt at that: and went on with raking the clinkers, calm. But Alick you could see was warming up to him, you all warmed up, led him hell's delight, serve him right with his bloody show-off. Wee Geordie Bruce couped his barrow when he wasn't looking, and Norman nipped back for the urine pan and slung it right slap in the toff Bulgar's fire, it sent up a guff that near killed you all and the toff had to stoke it up afresh.

He'd only just finished when the hooter went, Alick Watson had nipped up a minute afore bent on some deviltry you could be bound. When the rest of you got up the stairs he was just coming out of the washing-sheds where all the lads left their jackets and pieces. He winked and you knew he'd been up to something, and grinned and waited for Tavendale.

Ewan went in and washed and took down his jacket, and put it on, and put his hand in his pocket. . . . For a minute, certain, he knew he'd be sick, damned sick, and then swallowed his throat and didn't think as he washed his hand and wrenched off his jacket. Nuisance—miss most of that section on phosphor bronze now.

The five keelies were waiting for him to come out, they held their noses and capered and laughed, Ewan thought *The pimply keelie, I suppose*, and walked quietly over to where the five stood. The keelie's eyes in his thin, dour face didn't change, scornful of gentry, hands in his pouches, *Damn shame, he's no chance*, said Ewan's mind as he hit him and felt his arm go numb.

Alick shot like a stone from a catapult half across the yard crash in a bowie of lime, Ewan knew he'd be back in less than a minute, the only other dangerous one in the gang the one called Norman, an unscrubbed little swine—*about three inches higher than yourself*—still, *little*. And he swung up his left, keelie on the point, he whirled about and went flump in the stour; and it seemed to Ewan suddenly all the day cleared, Duncairn clear, bright and sharp to his finger-tips' touch, he'd never felt so well or so keen for life, he laughed: and Alick Watson came at him head down.

The foreman and another man heard the fighting back by the sheds and came round to see. The childe with the foreman grunted *That's him: another of those gentry apprentice sods*, but the foreman Dallas of course had his favourite, he called out *Steady a bit, Tavendale!* Ewan dripped blood like a half-killed pig, but he didn't know that, infighting, they were both thick-streaked with blood and snot, holding and fighting, Alick tried to kick, Ewan felt a stab of pain like a knife, and loosened his hold and Alick broke away—looked, swung, and struck, it caught Ewan's neck, he gave a queer grunt and twist, the fight finished, queer that silence to Alick and the way the sheds shook.

When Chris woke next morning the first thought that came in her mind was of Ewan. She didn't lie in bed and stretch as usual, got out and dressed and went down to the kitchen. Outside the early dawn of Duncairn lay pallid on the rigs and rinds of grey granite stretching away to the feet of the morning, east wan-tinted, no birds crying, the toun turning to yawn awake below. Jock came and purred and circled her legs, sniffed and sneezed, but she hardly noticed, taking up Ma's tea, syne Miss Murgatroyd's, and so at last gained Ewan's room.

He lay fast sleep, head bandaged, neck bandaged, she thought *He's so young!* as she saw his arm, dimpled and smooth of skin, lying by his side. And then as she went nearer she saw his face, the bruises upon it, the broken skin, the swollen lips: and went soft inside in a blaze of rage. How could they—to Ewan, he was only a bairn!

She picked up one of the apples he'd want and sat down on the bed and shook him awake. He woke with the usual quick lack of blink, but half unguarded for a minute, Chris thought, as though she'd peeped down in his eyes for once to that queer boy-self that so puzzled her. Son of herself but sometimes so un-sib she felt more kin to Meg Watson the maid!

She told him that, idly, as though it were a joke, and he put his hands under his head and considered, and said something about hormones and egg-cells, whatever they had to do with it—*I'm not so different; but I want to* KNOW THINGS. *And I love you up to that phosphor-bronze hair—more than Meg Whatname'll ever do.*

Chris said it was Watson, not Whatname, and Ewan said that was a funny coincidence, wondered if she were any relation of the keelie that had bashed him so yesterday.— *Perfect hiding he was giving me, Chris; and I struck it unlucky, head bang on a girder. Fought like a rat and so did I.*

Chris said *What was it all about?*

He lay still a minute, still in that posture. *Oh, filth. Nothing you need worry about. They don't much like me, the keelies, Chris.*

She'd heard him use that word before but the queerest thing happened to her now. She said sharply: *What's a keelie, Ewan? Your father was a ploughman afore we were wed, and I was a quean in a crofter's kitchen.*

Bandaged, undisturbed, he lay looking at her. *A plough-man's not a keelie. And anyhow, Chris—*

Her heart tightened in a funny way. There was something else. She said *Yes?*

—Oh—just that though my father was a ploughman and you came from a kitchen—that's nothing to do with me, has it? I'm neither you nor my father: I'm myself.

All that day and the next Meg didn't turn up, Ma Cleghorn swore at the lazy limmer and did all the washing-up by herself, and broke two plates in the first half-hour—*all through that lazy bitch of a quean!* Jock hardly knew where he was after that, his feet more often in the air than not, as Ma kicked him from the range to the dresser and back, he purring like a red-hot engine the while, Chris saw the last act as she brought down a tray—Jock scart his claws in Ma's sonsy leg and give a loud scraich and shoot out of the window.

And the sight was so funny Chris heard herself giggle, like a bairn, Ma rubbing her leg and swearing:

Malagaroused by a cat and forsook by a jade. Will you go to the Cowgate and see what's come of her?

So down Chris went, not taking the tram, better acquainted with Duncairn by now, down Windmill Brae with its shelving steps, across the Meal Market where they didn't sell meal, sold nothing, old, a deserted patch, dogs and unemployed squatting in the sun, through Melvin Wynd into Little Mart where the ploughmen gathered in feeing-times in Paldy Fair in the days long syne. They didn't now, two or three shops littered here, shops everywhere that a body might look, how did they all live and manage a trade? The pavements were sweating a greasy slime as she made her way to the Cowgate's brink, steps leading down to Paldy Parish.

She'd never been so far into Paldy before, seeing the broken windows and the tattered doors and the weary faces of the women going by, basket-laden, all the place had a smell of hippens, unwashed, and old stale meat and God knew what, if even He knew, Chris thought He couldn't. And she passed a Free Kirk with a twist to her thought: if there was a God as Robert had believed couldn't He put it into the heads of those folk they'd be better served filling the wames of their weans than the stomach of some parson clown in a Manse? But then she'd never understood religion, thought it only a fairy-tale, not a good one, dark and evil rather, hurting life, hurting death, no concern of hers if others didn't force it on her, she herself had nothing to force in its stead.

Robert once had had with his Socialism. And looking around that evil place in the stew of the hottering rising June she minded that verse he'd once quoted in Segget, long ago in that other life:

Stone hearts we cannot waken
    Smite into living men:
Jehovah of the thunders
    Assert Thy power again!

And dimly she thought that maybe that was what the Covenanters had believed when they faced the gentry in the old-time wars. Only God never came and they died for Him and the old soss went on as it always would do, aye idiot folk to take dirty lives and squat in the dirt, not caring a lot were they letten a-be to rot as they liked. No concern of hers—she belonged to herself as Ewan had told her he belonged to himself, she'd have hated the Covenant giving her orders as much as she'd have hated its enemies, the gentry.

. . . And all far off from a middle-aged wife looking for a missing maidie, Meg. Where was it Ma said the creature bade?

She found it at last, a deep narrow court, used to the smells she went in and up the stone stairs, chapped at the door and waited and listened. In a tenement near a row was on, furniture crashing, Chris heard a woman scraich and grew white to the lips. Syne she heard a loud voice raised in a hymn:

> Count your blessings, name them one by one,
> Count your blessings, see what God has done,
> Count your blessings, name them one by one
> And it will surprise you what the Lord has done.

There followed a final thump on that, somebody cried *I'll ha'e the bobbies on you*, and then a door banged: and then a loud silence.

Chris chapped again, heard a noise inside, the door opened, she said: *Is Meg Watson in?*

The man who opened the door was the same who'd once stopped her in the Upper Cowgate and asked her for sixpence.

They both stared like gowks a minute, speechless, he'd shaved and wore a second-hand suit, over-big for him, bulging at paunch and bottom, the thin brown face didn't look so starved, cocky and confident till he met her eyes. Now he flushed dark and licked his lips:

Meg Watson's gone off to look for a job.

Chris nodded. *I see. Will you tell her I want to know why she left me? My name is Mrs Colquohoun and if she comes back the morn you can tell her that I'll say nothing about it.*

. . . So that was who the sulky bitch was, boorjoy and

stuck-up—he'd heard the tale, Alick had sloshed her son down at Gowans. A stuck-up toff, he'd said; like the mother, damn her and her glower and her ice-brick eyes.

Meg was feared to go back when she heard from her brother he'd bashed your son in a bit fight at the Works.

Chris said *I see. Well, she needn't be,* and turned and went down the stairs, stare on her back; turned again: *I think you owe me a sixpence.*

He dived in a pouch and brought one out, flushing again, but looking at her cocky: *There you are, mistress. Enjoy your money while you have it. There's a time coming when your class won't have it long.*

Chris's temper quite went with her a minute, silly fool, the heat she supposed, she didn't care:

My class? It was digging its living in sweat while yours lay down with a whine in the dirt. Good-bye.

Ewan was tired enough of the going next week, lying in bed, reading in books, feeling the throb under the bandages go. If only they'd leave him alone with the books. . . . And he thought *Most people—how they hate you to read!*

They were at him all hours: Chris in the morning, decent sort Chris, though you'd never got very close to each other since that winter in Segget, further off now since you'd made it plain her notions on begettings weren't necessarily yours. But once or twice when she put her arm under your head and unwound the bandage in the early morning, stuck on the lint, hands and arms so alive you felt queer—as though you were falling in love! You'd gathered the reactions were something like that, and possible enough for all that you knew, those psychoanalyst Jewboy chaps had had cases enough, record on record, Œdipus the first of the Unhanged Unhygienics— *Rot! Let's dig in the phosphor bronze!*

She'd hardly have gone than a thunderous chapp, and in would come waddling Mrs Cleghorn, very fat, very oozing, you rather liked her. Supposed it was her jollity, easily come by, it didn't mean much and couldn't mean much, but a bearable ingredient—so damn scarce. She'd plump on the bed and ask how you were, not stop for an answer, instead start in to tell of the time when her husband, Jim, was ill—with mumps, so he'd said, and looking like a tattie scone. And he'd been fair ashamed to have mumps at his age, the daft old tyke, Ma had wondered a bit, funny-like mumps for a body to have. So she'd hauled in the doctor, will he nill he, and then could you guess what his illness was? You couldn't, you were over innocent and young, but the cause turned out to be one of those trollops down in Fish Market, Jim had chased her and gotten her and got tally-ho. And he'd got more than that when the doctor left.

Ewan had said *Oh?* not caring a rap, and Ma had nodded, *Mind out for the women. You're over bonny a lad to be taken that way.* Ewan'd said, grave, he'd be sure to mind, and Ma had said *Fine*, and gone, thank God. Back to that chapter on phosphor-bronze smelting, house cleared with the others all off to their work. All?—No luck, a knock on the door.

Miss Murgatroyd this time, thin and peeking, tittering and shy like a wren gone erotic, *Eh me, in a Gentleman's Room, such a scandal! I thought you'd maybe like an orange or so*, she'd brought two of the things, great bulging brutes. You said you were sorry you never ate them, and she shrivelled in a way and you really felt sorry—why couldn't old people leave one alone?—always in need of pity, compassion, soft words to fend off the edge of things, cuddling in words, oh, damn them all!

So you'd put on a kind face and said you were sorry—*it was nice of you to think of me*. And at that she'd unshrivelled like a weed in the rain, peeking and chittering in your bedroom chair all about herself and her life and her likes; and Ewan'd sat and listened, half-wishing she'd go, half-wondering about her in an idle way. Queer to think she'd been born for that, been young once like oneself and wanted real things: food, wind on the sea, phosphor-bronze smelting . . . maybe not, but books and sleeping with men. Surely at least she had wanted THAT—her generation had seemed to want little else, blethered in their books about little else, Shaw and the little sham-scientist Wells running a fornication a folio before they could pitch an idea across: gluey devils, the Edwardians, chokers and chignons, worse than the padded Victorian rabbits. . . . And now at the end she had none of it, went to tea-fights, the Unionist Ladies, she liked Mr MacDonald and the National Government and read lots of faded verse in Scots, the new Scots letters the Edwardian survivals were trying to foist on the Scottish scene—*Have you read Dr Pittendrigh MacGillivray's pomes? Such lovely, I think, and Clean and Fine. And Miss Marion Angus, though they're awful Broad.* And Ewan said he hadn't, he didn't read poetry. Then she tweetered from the room and came back with a book of Mr Lewis Spence's for him to read, all about the ancient Scots, they'd been Awful Powerful in magic. And Ewan said that was nice; and he was sure they had.

Tired after that and a spot of sleep. Chris would waken him up at noon, with a tray and dinner, gleam of bronze hair, dolichocephalic heads scarce in Duncairn, his own one only a betwixt-and-between. And he'd eat, not much, and read some more, Duncairn outside in its afternoon haze, far off the foghorn on Crowie Point lowing like an aurochs with belly-ache—the cattle that Cæsar said couldn't lie down, no knee joints, they kipped up against a tree. . . . What the devil had that to do with a chapter on Castings?

Five o'clock, shoes on the stairs, a guffaw, a knock, young Archie Clearmont. Decent chap Archie, if a bit of a bore, baby face, a long story about a Prof: he'd turned round in the lecture-room and said to Archie, and Archie had turned and said to the Prof—, and Ewan nodded and wondered they hadn't grown dizzy. Rectorial elections coming off soon, Archie thought he'd support the Nationalist. Ewan asked why, and Archie said for a bit of a rag, the Nationalist candidate was Hugo MacDownall, the chap who wrote in Synthetic Scots. Ewan asked *Why synthetic? Can't he write the real stuff?* and Archie said *I'm damned if I know. Sounds more epileptic than synthetic to me—that's why I'm interested, I'm going in for Medicals!*

John Cushnie next, sure as fate, poor devil with his English and his earnestness, smart, in a new Raggie Robertson suit, he'd brought Ewan an Edgar Wallace to read—*you must feel weariet with lying there*. And he said 'twas a gey thing when decent chaps, just because they spoke well with a bit of class, were bashed by keelies down in Footforthie. They were never letten into Raggie Robertson's Depot, time the bobbies took they kind of wasters in hand. . . . Ewan said *What wasters?—Raggie or the keelies?* and Cushnie gawked above his tight collar oh ay, *ha-ha*, but Raggie was all right, he'd a good job there and a chance to get on. A chap didn't need a union to help if he put his back into a job of work—though Labour wasn't so bad, look at Bailie Brown. But the Communists—along in Doughty Park on Sunday he'd stopped and listened to that dirty Red, Trease, paid from Moscow as every body knew, splurging away about all workers uniting and yet pitching glaur as fast's he was able at decent folk like Bailie Brown. . . . And then, thank God, the tea-bell went, and Cushnie with it, tie, spots, and all.

Mr Quaritch came up in the evening to see him, with a pile of review-books from the *Daily Runner*, and his pipe, ferret-twinkle, and unhappy wee beard: *Want anything to read? What's that you've got?* Ewan showed him the text-book and he shook his head: *Dreich stuff. Would you care to review a novel?*

Ewan shook his head, couldn't be bothered with novels. Mr Quaritch said he might count himself lucky, *he'd* to bother enough with the lousy tripe, twenty or so of the damned things a week. Ewan asked who wrote them—and what on earth for? and Mr Quaritch said mostly wee chaps without chins—but what for God might know, He kept quiet about it, unless it was to provide the deserving reviewer with half a crown a copy when he sold them at Burnett's.—*Piddle makes a fortune flogging reviews. Have you heard what happened to my colleague last night?*

Ewan said he hadn't and Quaritch told him the tale, Mr Piddle was racing for the six-thirty train with his copy, Duncairn news for the *Tory Pictman*, gey late, in a hell of a sweat that he'd miss it. You knew the way the daft Bulgar would ride?—head down over the handlebars, neck out like

a gander seeking the water, all in a flush and a paddy for time.
Well, he wheeled out from the *Runner* offices in Wells Street,
into Royal Mile, and pedalled like hell up the Royal, tramcars
and buses and lorries about, dodging the lot and beating
them all. Dark was coming down and the street-lamps were
lighting and Piddle's feet were flying like the wind when,
keeking his head a bit to one side he noticed a lot of folk
yelling at him. Well, he took no notice, half Duncairn yells
whenever it sights our reporter Piddle, just thought that the
proletariat,—*he-he!*—was living up to its lowness, *yes?* And
then next minute his bike left the earth, his head went over
his heels and vanished, and when he'd finished wondering
with a sheer despair how he'd ever get copy about the end of
the world down to the *Tory Pictman* office when there
wouldn't be a *Pictman* left to print it—he looked up round
the curve of his haunches and saw two or three folk looking
down at him, one cried *Are you killed?* Piddle wasn't sure, but
he managed to stand up, and was dragged from the hole by
the crowd that had come, the rest of the survivors of the end
of the world. And then he found what had happened was he'd
fallen head-first into road-digging in the middle of the Mile,
he'd passed the red lights with never a glance, that's what the
shouts had been for as he passed. The bike looked like a bit of
string chewed by a cow, but Piddle had no time to attend to
it: the next things the gapers around the hole saw were
Piddle's legs scudding away up the Mile, bent on catching the
Pictman train. . . .

Ewan lay with his hands under his head, drowsing and
thinking of Quaritch and his tale when both had gone down
to their supper. Now the night was coming in by, lamps
lighted; through the window and up through the night the
ghost-radiance of Footforthie flecked the blind.—People
thought that kind of a story funny, everyone laughed,
Quaritch had expected him to laugh, and he hadn't, he'd seen
nothing funny about it. What was funny in a queer old wreck
like Piddle falling into a dirty hole in the Mile? He'd hurt
himself a bit, no doubt—that the fun? Enjoyment of seeing
another look ridiculous? And he thought of innumerable

stories he'd heard, overheard when a boy, been told in Duncairn with loud guffaws and glazed eyes of mirth—about women and their silly, unfortunate bodies, about babies and death and disease and dirt, and something he supposed was lacking in him, Robert had once told him he was born a prig, he'd no humour and couldn't be cheerful and lusty and scrabble in filth and call it fun. Fun? Real fun enough in the world—fun in the roar of the furnaces, in a sweeping door and a dripping trough of blazing metal a-pour on the castings, fun in the following of formulæ through trick on trick in the twists of maths, fun in the stars wheeling at night with long lights over the whoom of Footforthie, the breath-taking glister of the Galaxy. Fun in the deadness of Duncairn after midnight, you could stand by the edge of Royal Mile where it wheeled to the moving blackness of Paldy and think the end of the world had come—the shining dead streets of this land long hence, waving in grass, beasts lairing in culverts, the sea creeping up and up on Footforthie and a clamour of seals on the rocky points where once they launched the fisher-fleets, men long gone from the earth, not wiped out, not lost, vanished an invading host to the skies, to alien planets and the furthest stars, storming at last the rooftops of heaven, earth remote from their vision as the womb and its dreams remote from the memory of an adult man—

He woke late that evening to hear a commotion in the next-door bedroom, empty till then. Low talk and quick steps, Mrs Cleghorn, Chris, then a shivering bang, silence, a cough. Then Ma Cleghorn whispering *Will that have waked Ewan?*

His own door was opened a minute later and Chris came in, walking pussy-foot, she stood and listened till he called out soft, *'Lo, Chris. What's all the row next door?*

She said she was sorry they'd woken him up, a new lodger was coming in a hurry, late, and they were making her up a bit bed.

Ewan said he saw. What was she like?

Chris didn't know, a lass up from Dundee, the new

schoolteacher at the Ecclesgriegs Middle—English, she'd heard, though she hadn't yet seen her—

Then she saw with a smile that Ewan was asleep, human beings were never of much interest to him.

Taking up tea to Ma Cleghorn next morning Chris found the meikle creature already out of bed, getting into her stays like wool into a bottle. *God, Chris, just give a pull at they points, I'm getting a wee bittie stout, I'm half-feared*.

Chris put down the tray and pulled at the tapes, the house a drowse in the Saturday quiet, she asked why Ma'd got up so early, and Ma asked if she'd forgotten the new lodger-lassie, was Chris herself to do all the work? Chris said *Well, unless she's so awful big, she'll make no difference to me, I hope. What's she like?* and Ma gave a bit of a snort: *A stuck-up looking bitch from a school in Dundee. Schlimpèd and English and thin as a sparrow, I never could abide the stuck-up kind.* Chris said *Some folk say that I'm stuck up*, Ma said *So you are, and so's your bit Ewan. I'll maybe thole two of you about the house but I'll be danged to a cinder-ash afore I bear with another of the brew. . . . Och, lassie, go away, I'm in bad tune this morning. Take the teacher creature her cup of tea*.

So Chris did, and went up and knocked, a cool voice said *Come in*, in she went, the lassie lying in the double bed Chris and Ma Cleghorn had put up yestreen, window wide open, curtains flying, Chris lowered her eyes to the quean herself and saw her trig, neat, in a flowered nightie, slim like a boy, like Ewan almost, short black hair and blue deep eyes, great pools going down into darkness. She sat up and took the cup and nodded: *You Mrs Cleghorn's partner?*

Chris knew for certain then what was wrong, the English lass was shy as could be but carrying it off with a brassy front, the kind of cool courage Chris always had liked. And as Chris smiled the brassiness went, the quean flushed sweet as they looked at each other, was suddenly neat and demure and forlorn, no more; like a prize pussy-cat, Chris thought, with that faint line of down on her upper lip that one liked the look of, most folk didn't.—*I'm Mrs Colquohoun and you're Miss Johns*.

—I say, you're different from what I expected.

—You're a wee bittie different yourself, Chris said, and carried down the tray and went on with her work, nice to have had a nice quean like that for one's own sometime: as well as had Ewan. But that was just dreaming—she wouldn't have been one's own any more than was Ewan, the pussy-cat, wave of nice black hair by her smooth, soft cheek and that funny down and that youngness—oh, but they made one feel like an old trauchled wife, the young folk here in Duncairn!

And suddenly, washing the breakfast things, there came a waft of stray wind through the window, a lost wean of the wind that had tint itself in play in the heights of the summer Mounth, Chris nearly dropped the cup she was drying. Ma Cleghorn louped: *Steady on, lass! Mighty be here, have you seen a ghost?*

Chris said *Only smelt one*, and then, on an impulse, *Ma, I want the day off. Can you spare me?*

Ma said *If you like: you're hardly my slave*, Chris said she knew that, but would Ma manage herself? Ma said she'd managed a good fifty-five years, off and on, and as far as she kenned at the moment she was neither a cripple nor had brain-concussion. So Chris laughed and said *I'm off to the country*.

And she ran up and knocked at Ewan's door and went in and found him not in bed, up, naked, a long, nice naked leg and that narrow waist that you envied in men, lovely folk men, he was standing and stretching, stark, the bandage gone from his head. No shyness in Ewan, just a cool disinterest, he turned and grinned *I'm feeling my feet. Too hot to lie in bed. Chris: let's take a holiday out in the country!*

She said *I was off for one on my own*, his face fell a little, then he nodded *All right. Have a good time.—But aren't you coming?—Not if you want to be on your own.* And Chris said that was daft, she would always want him, and he said that was nice, and meant it, with a sudden glint of a grey granite smile nipped across to where she stood and cuddled her, funny to be cuddled by a naked man, she made out she was shocked, for fun, and he didn't see that, said *Oh, sorry*, and went back to his clothes. A minute Chris stood with the queerest feeling of lostness, staring at him, fun was beyond Ewan.

Then, because she knew that couldn't be helped, daft to expect him other than he was, she said *Be ready in half an hour*, and went down to her room and changed, looked at her clothes and found a light frock, took off all she wore and looked at herself, as of old, with cool scrutiny, seeing mirrored her face with the broad cheekbones, seeing the long white lines of thigh and waist and knee, not very much need to envy men. *The queer years that I've been with you!* she said to the earnest thing in the mirror, and the shadow-self smiled back with golden eyes, shadow and self no longer woe, light-hearted suddenly as she dressed in haste to be gone for a day from Duncairn and herself.

She went into the sitting-room for a book, the place half in darkness, half the blinds drawn against the sting of the sun without. And the place wasn't deserted as usually it was, Miss Johns was sitting in the biggest chair, on her heels, not reading, chin in hand looking out through the window, a little lost pussy-cat Chris thought, with her trim black hair and her lobeless ears. She smiled up at Chris with that fenceless smile that came when the brassy shyness went: and Chris was moved to an impulse again. *I'm going for a jaunt to the country today. Would you like to come—if you've nothing else to do?*

She hesitated a minute, flushed, demure: *I'd love to. Terribly. Only—I've no money.* And in a sudden rush of confidence was telling Chris she'd come dead broke from Dundee and wouldn't get an advance until Wednesday, she'd nothing till then and had settled herself to mope the weekend in Windmill Place. Chris said that didn't matter, she'd pay, and Miss Johns could pay her back some time; and the pussy-cat was shyer than ever, and Chris asked her name, and she said, *Oh, Ellen. Helen really, you know, but when Dad came down from London to work in Dundee I went to High School and they mis-spelt me Ellen.* . . . And Chris had almost expected that, she couldn't have been anything else but an Ellen!

She was dressed and down in the sitting-room a short minute before Ewan came down. Chris said *Ellen Johns— Ewan Tavendale. He's my son—sometimes. Ellen's coming out with us on our jaunt.* And Ewan, un-boylike, wasn't shy a bit, he said that would be nice, grey granite eyes on Ellen Johns as though she were a chapter on phosphor bronze, they were much of the same straight height and look, both dark and cool, Ellen cool as he was, no blush now, indifferently polite to each other. And a queer unease came on Chris that minute as she looked from one to the other: as though she were sitting in a theatre-stall and watching the opening of a dark, queer play.

But that fancy was lost in the hours that followed. The three went down to Mercat Cross and found an Aberdeen bus waiting there, ready to leave in a minute or so, crossing the Slug into Banchory, down by Deeside and Dunecht to Aberdeen, turning about and so back again. And they got in the bus, the two pussy-cats polite, not wanting either to sit by the other, manœuvring each to sit by Chris. Chris said *I think I'll sit by myself, right at the front*, and went and sat there, the other two on the opposite seat, Ellen by the window, hatless, hair braided, curling long lashes and secret face, Ewan hatless as well, cool and composed, staring about him as the bus moved off. Once he leaned over and asked where they were going, Chris didn't know, they'd get out at some place they liked.

In a minute, themselves near the only passengers, the bus was climbing Duncairn Rise up to the heights where the men of Montrose had marshalled three hundred years before, suddenly, on a Sunday, over-awing Duncairn and pouring down to a Sabbath of blood. Chris turned in her seat and looked down and saw the white sword gleam of Royal Mile, the haze that lay on the lums of Footforthie, shining boats dipping out to sea in the pelt and shine of the morning tide. And then the road wheeled up and around and paused: there below the Howe of the Mearns, crowned, shod, be-belted in green and gold, silver chains where the Mearns burns wound

and spun to the Forthie's flow, Stonehaven forward, Bervie
behind, far off the shimmer where the Grampians rode, the
farms gleaming below the bents, haugh on haugh, tumbling
green long corn-swaths under the wind. And syne the bus
stopped and took on a farmer, thin and mean-looking, he
starved his men and ate sowans to his meat, never cuddled his
wife except on Sundays and only then if he'd been to kirk.
And like a great squat beetle the bus crept on, oh, they were
cutting the hay in a park, the smell in the bus, drifting,
tingling—Blawearie's night and days, hush of the beeches in
a still July, pastures sleeping around Segget Manse with
Robert beside you as you drowsed on the lawn—Robert that
you looked at, and he hadn't a face—

And Chris shook that woe dreaming away from herself, let
nothing spoil the sun and the hay and the goodness of being
alone and alive, peering through lids at July unfold, birring,
up the blossoming Howe, deep-honeysuckled ran the
hedges, in parks outbye the gleg-vexed kye were tearing
about with tails a-switch, some eident body would have sour
milk the night. Ewan and Ellen at last were speaking to each
other. Ewan had turned his head and Chris saw the English
quean looking up at him, cool, like a virtuous panther-kitten
exchanging tail-switchings with a black-avised leopard.

The next thing she knew they were through Stonehyve,
windy, guarded by Dunnottar Woods, and were climbing up
the heath of the Slug, no hay-smell here but the guff of the
heather billowing up to the quivering heights. And there
came a sudden memory to Chris—a winter night twenty-
three years before when father and mother and Will and
herself and the loons long-lost and the twins that died had
flitted across these hills in a storm, with battered lanterns in
the on-ding of sleet . . . twenty-three years before. Back and
back through the years as the bus climbed the Slug, years like
the rustle of falling leaves, dreams by night and dim turnings
in sleep, and you were again that quean in the sleet, all the
world and living before you unkenned, kisses and hate and
toil and woe, kisses at night when the byre-stalls drowsed,
agony in long deserted noons, hush of terror of those

moon-bright nights when you carried within your womb seed of men—for a minute they seemed no more than dreams as you drowsed, a quean, in the smore of the sleet. . . .

But now below, creeping out of the heat, the Howe left behind, came Banchory shining in its woods and far away the long flicker of the ribboned Dee that went down through the fine lands to Aberdeen. On the sky-line the mountains marched snow-covered, lifting white faces to the blink of July, in great haughs the fir-woods bourouched green, red crags climbed the northwards sky to peer, hands at their eyes, at Aberdeen. Sometimes a body would get off the bus, sometimes it would stop by a tottering gate and a slow, canny childe climb grinning aboard, or a sharp-faced woman, Aberdeen, thin-voiced, thin-faced, with a quick ferret look around, from Chris to Ewan, Ewan to Ellen, syne to the driver, syne up to the roof, syne out of the window, syne folding her lips and her hands, the world well and respectable and behaving itself. And Chris sat and watched the comings and goings, happy and happy and sweir to the bone.

Then at last here was Ewan shaking her: *Chris. Where are we going?—to Aberdeen?* She said goodness no, she didn't hope so, though the tickets were for there and 'twas a pity to waste them. And then she looked out and saw flash by a word white-painted on a cross-roads sign, a word and a place she had long forgotten. *We'll get out at Echt and wait the bus back*.

So they did, Echt snoozing white in its stour, bairns playing about the doors of the houses, Ewan went into a shop and bought pieces, Chris went to help: loaf, butter and milk, some cakes and a knife, they looked loaded down for a feast or a famine, or tinks on the road, fair shocking Echt. Ellen showed her bit English mettle at once, no pride, she caught up the loaf and the bottles, some of the bairns cried after them, she laughed and didn't mind, kitten not cat. Then Chris led them off on the ploy she'd planned.

The Hill of Fare towered high in the sun, scaured and red, the flow of heather like a sea of wine, leftwards, dark, the Barmekin haunted even in July's sun-haze. Chris cried *Oh, wheesht!* to the others and they stopped, looked at her, listened, and heard through the sun, lonely, unforgotten, never-stopping that plaint, the peesies flying over Barmekin. Twenty-three years and they never had stopped. . . . And Chris thought half-shamed, in a desperate flyting: *Losh, but their throats must surely be dry!*

And at last through the litter of the wild-growing broom choking the upward track, they came to the croft of Cairndhu where Chris had been born, rank thistles all about, the windows were shuttered, grass crept to the door, another and bigger farm long syne had eaten up the land and the implements. They poked their heads inside the out-biggings, the barn musty with a smell of old hay, rats scampered there in the sun-hazed gloom, Chris wandered from place to place like one seeking that which she wouldn't know—maybe something of that sureness mislaid in the past, long ago, when she was a quean. But here was nothing, nothing but change that had followed every pace of her feet, quiet-padding as a panther at night.

When she turned away from the biggings at last she found Ellen and Ewan sitting on the mill-course, speaking low and clear to each other, not to disturb her, cat-like the two of them, unheeding the sun, haunted by no such memories as hers. Daft not to have known from the first that this meant nothing to them, ruined biggings on a little farm: her old frere the land was nothing to them, children of touns by love or by nature, Ewan born in a croft in Kinraddie knew little of the land, cared less, not his job—that was stoking a furnace in Gowans and Gloag's!

He asked where now, and said Chris was the guide, and she pointed up to the Barmekin shining high and flat in the air against the tops of the further hills: *I haven't been there since I was a bairn.* Ellen said *Well, you don't look as though that was long ago,* and Chris asked *Am I as bairn-like as all that?* and Ellen flushed and said she hadn't meant that—*it's just you don't possibly look as though Mr Tavendale here were your son.* Chris smiled at him. *But he is, worse luck,* Ewan nodded, a kindly joke in his compass: *The luck's all mine. Come along then. Carry your parcel, Chris?*

Chris said shortly she'd manage it herself, she wasn't in her second childhood, either; and they laughed and went up and left the road and waded through the whins and the broom and over fences and up steep braes, steep so's you'd to clutch up step by step with handfuls of heather and grass for holds, Ellen flinched with stung legs and Ewan slipped on smooth shoes, Chris laughed back at both of them, shinning the slopes light and free and sure of her hold, she looked back from the uppermost ledge and waved to them, poor fusion-less creatures her father would have called them—her father who all his years in Cairndhu had never (that she knew) climbed Barmekin, over-busy with chaving and slaving his flesh, body and soul and that dark, fierce heart, into the land to wring sustenance therefrom. So the whirlimagig went round and on: Father, now Ewan, the hill little to either, only to her who came in between and carried the little torch one from the other on that dreich, daft journey that led nowhither—

But, standing up there, with the wind in her hair, the thought came to her that THAT didn't much matter—daft the journey, but the journeying good. And she looked at the slopes gay in their gear, useless and meaningless but fine fun to climb. . . . The other two thought the same when they came, Ellen with smooth braids tangled a bit, a damp lock over Ewan's high forehead, they laughed and said things about Excelsior, young and sexless both, like the angels, dark angels, folk of an older stock than Chris's, intenter and sharper, not losing themselves in heather dreams or the smell of broom. Ewan said he was hungry,—*aren't you, Miss Johns?* and Miss Johns said *Aren't I? Hungry as hell.*

So they made their way in the brush of the broom along the outer wall of the old Pict fort built by the men of antique time, a holy place before Christ was born, Chris said they'd find shade from the sun in its lithe. Syne they came on a thing they had little looked for, Ewan swore, his old passion for old times rekindled—men had been here, a great gang of them, had torn down the walls and flung them aside, deep ruts showed where the carts had been driven: and within the inner walls of the fort were the char and ash of a great foolish fire.

Some celebration, Chris thought, not caring, Ewan did, he said it was a filthy outrage and justified nothing that had happened in Aberdeen since they told the first of their filthy stories—that was probably before Christ's coming as well. Chris had never seen him so angered, she herself wasn't, they were only rickles of stone from long syne raised up by daft childes who worshipped the sun. Ewan said *That's rot. You know nothing about it*, and Chris gave a laugh and sat down on a stone, clasping her knees, not caring a fig one way or another. Miss Johns said *I agree with Mrs Colquohoun. What does it matter what happens to this rubbish? There are things more in need of worrying about.* Ewan turned his grey granite glance upon her: *I didn't expect that* YOU *would think different.*

So they sulked a bit, sitting each side of Chris, and she didn't laugh, but looked fearsomely solemn. Then Ewan opened the milk-bottles and got out the bread and Ellen spread out the papers for a tablecloth, two sleek black heads under Chris's gaze; and they fed her solemn, though Ellen peeped at Ewan through those dangerous lashes—she'd trip on them some time. But he wasn't thinking of her at all, his mind far off with his ancient men, he began to tell them of that time that had been, how close in the generations these men were, how alike ourselves in the things they believed, unessentials different—blood, bone, thought the same. For if history had any lesson at all it was just that men hadn't changed a bit since the days of the folk in the Spanish caves who painted the charging aurochsen—except to take up civilization, that ancient calamity that fell on the world with gods and kings and culture and classes—Ellen cried *But then you're a Socialist!*

Ewan looked blank, smooth boy face, angel-devil eyes, suddenly dragged from his ancient Picts: *What's that to do with it?* And Ellen said *Everything. If there was once a time without gods and classes couldn't there be that time again?*

Ewan said *I suppose so. I don't much care. It won't come in our time. I've my own life to lead*—and at that the slim quean seemed to forget all her hunger, curling lashes and dimpled ways, she said Mr Tavendale was talking rot, how could anyone live a free life in this age?—capitalism falling to bits everywhere, or raising up classes of slaves again, Fascism coming, the rule of the beast—

Ewan sat and munched bread *They won't rule me. I'm myself.—You're not. You're a consequence and product as all of us are. If we're all the children of those old-time men that you've told us about do you think for a moment we aren't more the children of our fathers and mothers and the things we've read and depended upon? Just silly to say that we're not.* And Ewan asked what had that to do with it?; and they lost their tempers; and Chris fell asleep.

When she woke they were nowhere in sight; far off, drowsy, a ring-dove crooned in the little woods scampering down to Echt, remoter still a peesie cried. The sun had wheeled to afternoon, red on the nearer mountain cliffs, blue far in the upper heights. Mountain on mountain: there was Bennachie ahint which the tired folk went in song. Sitting with her hands so propping her, Chris found herself aching, sun-wearied and sad, in the bright day's glister curiously lost though she knew that Ewan and the English quean couldn't be far off, they'd come if she cried. Call?—behave like a frightened old wife?

She lay back again in the heather bells, and under her ears heard whispers unceasing, sounds soft and urgent and quieter than mice, the little world of the little beasts about its existence of sowing and harvest, feeding and fighting and a pridesome begetting, moral and urgent and dreadfully unsweir, pelting through lives as brief as a blink as though the blink lasted a hundred years. It felt like God so to lie and listen—so long's the beasts didn't come climbing up a stalk and mistake one's ear for heaven.

When she rose and went to look for the others she found them close on the ruined dyke, not sitting and kissing as they might have been (some sense in that, said her mind, still sleepy), Ewan perched on a stone, hands clasping his knees, looking down at Ellen sitting clasping hers, nice knees and long legs and the lot forgotten, talking, still talking—about history and Socialism and freedom for people in the modern world. And Ewan was saying *Yes, that seems sense and I'll look it up. I've always thought Socialism just a measly whine, MacDonaldish stuff and politicians' patter. Different when you think of it as history making, the working class to be captured and led: all right, I'll give the keelies a chance.* Ellen said *And don't be so horridly superior; you'll never lead if you can't be an equal. . . . Oh, there's your mother. Coo-ee, Mrs Colquohoun!*

It seemed that their talk had run them clean dry, quiet enough in the afternoon quiet gathering up the papers and burning them, carrying the milk-bottles down the hill, the sun was dimming and all about bees homing like drunken men from a pub, one came bumbling against Chris's face and tangled itself in her hair. She brushed it aside, quickly and quietly, and Ellen shivered *I couldn't do that!* Chris asked *What?* and Ellen said *That bee—I'd have jumped and hit it and it would have stung me. I'm a ghastly coward,* and shivered again. Ewan didn't notice, far off in thought, treading down from the breach in the Pictman's fort to seek the like in the crumbling castle that prisoned the men of his time.

Alick Watson said *Och, let the sod a-be. He gave me as good as I gave him;* and Norman Cruickshank said *He gave you a mucking sight more; who'd have thought a toff Bulgar had a punch like that?*

So they wouldn't have anything to do with the plan of Wee Geordie Bruce to send a bit note, insulting-like, to Tavendale's address when he bade at home nursing the broken head he'd gotten in that fight with Alick in the yard—Christ, the place was splottered in blood, wee Geordie went out and glowered all about it and nearly got down on his knees to lick it, with his wee shrivelled face and shifty eyes, awful keen on blood and snot. Alick said *You're not right in your head, you wee whoreson,* he seemed hardly right himself all that week, snapping a chap's head off if you spoke to him praising him a bit how he'd bashed the toff Bulgar.

Norman wasn't much better, they both worked like tinks

doing Tavendale's furnace as well as their own, trying to stick in with the foreman, were they? They got little thanks if that was their hope, Dallas came down and glowered *God Almighty, is that the way to work at Gowans and Gloag's?* Alick said to him *Ach, away to hell. We're doing the work of a dozen here—if that doesn't please you, gang off and clype.* The foreman looked a bit ta'en aback, *We've all to do more than our shift in Gowans, so give's none of your lip, you Cowgate brat.* And Alick said when the foreman had gone what he'd like to give the bastard was one in the guts, syne dance on his face with tacketty boots.

For Gowans and Gloag were fair in a way, they'd sacked a dozen from Machines that week and were trying to cheese-pare all over the shops, they'd been on to Dallas and gotten out his rag. The apprentice chaps in the dinner hour sat out in the yard and swore at them, and smoked, and watched through the haze from the Docks the swinging cranes that loaded the ships, or the bridges open and a laggard trawler creep in from an antrin night on the sea, lost in the fogs of the Dogger Bank. And Alick said by Christ if he had the guts he'd run off from it all and take to the sea, a fine bit life if it wasn't that on a ship a common chap was near starved to death. And Norman said that he'd like a farm: and he'd near as much chance of getting that as of wee King Geordie making him his vallay.

Well, you couldn't but wonder what Tavendale would do when he got back to Furnaces on the Monday morning, stuck up as ever, and acting the toff he looked when he came down and took up his shovel, you keeked sideways and saw he'd no sign of a bandage, froze up and don't-touch-me-I'm-awful-grand. Syne the work started, all at it hell for leather till the hooter went, no larking or jookery-packery, Alick and Norman not looking at the toff, they were maybe a bit feared he'd reported them.

And then as you all climbed up to the yard the toff turned round to Alick *Hello!* and Alick gave a kind of a start *Hello!* and they laughed, and Norman went dandering over *Hello!* as well, and a fag to the toff Tavendale. You'd never seen him smoking before, but he took it: *I'm going down to the Docks to eat my dinner. Coming, you chaps?*

Now Alick and Norman never left the yard, they would bide there all the dinner hour and raise hell with pitching stones at old tins, telling bit tales of their Saturday nights, they were both of them awful Bulgars with the queans, Norman had gotten a tart into trouble, and laughed when her Ma came after him chasing him with a bit of a broken bottle from the Gallowgate half through Paldy Parish; and they'd tease Geordie Bruce, the dirty wee devil, and get him to do the dirtiest capers, rouse hell's delight and have a fair time. But now they just looked a bit tint and surprised, and Alick said *Och, ay*, as though he couldn't help it, and Norman Cruickshank gave a bit nod, and away the three of them went together.

That was the beginning of a gey queer time, it wasn't only the apprentices noticed it, the toff didn't go out of his way to be friends but if he came on you, joking-like, he'd sit down and listen and smoke a fag-end and give a bit nod, and he wasn't so bad, not looking at you now so that a childe felt his face was all wrong and his sark gey clorted up at the neck and he hadn't ta'en the trouble to wash that morning. Some said that his bashing had done him good, he'd gotten scared of the working chaps; but Alick Watson said that that was damned stite, *Ewan Tavendale could tackle any Bulgar here.* And had he gone clyping to the management?

He was in and out of the shops all the time, and Norman's father, in the Grindery, took him down to a meeting of the Union branch, Norman didn't go, he couldn't be bothered, he said to Tavendale *They just claik and claik and grab your subscription and never give anything, they're a twisting lot of sods in the Union. But the old man's aye been keen on them.* And looked a bit shamed, *He's Labour, you see.*

Tavendale said *There are lots of chaps that, my step-father was,* and you all cheered up, sitting on buckets in the furnace room, a slack hour, and having a bit of a jaw, you were none of you Labour and knew nothing about politics, but all of you had thought that the Bulgars of toffs were aye Tory or Liberal

or this National faeces. And somehow when a chap knew
another had a father who'd been Labour you could speak to
him plainer, like, say what you thought, not that you thought
much, you wanted a job when apprenticeship was over and a
decent bit time and maybe now and then a spare bob or so to
take your quean to the Talkies—och, you spoke a lot of stite
like the others did, about the queans that you'd like to lie
with, and the booze you'd drink, what a devil you were, but if
you got half a chance what you wanted was marriage, and a
house and a wife and a lum of your own. . . . Wee Geordie
Bruce said *The Tories have the money, they're the muckers for the
working man;* and Norman said *Blethers, the Bulgars have
money, but they take good care to keep it for themselves or spend it
on their lily-fingered whores, what's the good of Tories to us, you
neep?* Alick said that maybe the next Labour Government
wouldn't be so bad as the last had been, they were working
folk themselves, some of them, though they'd birns of the
rotten toffs as well. . . . And you all said what you thought,
except Ewan—funny, you'd started to call him Ewan—he
just sat and listened and nodded now and then, as though he
couldn't make up his own mind: well, that's what a chap with
sense would do. And when one of the chaps in the Stores said
to you: *I hear you're all sucking the young toff's anus* you nearly
took him a crack in the jaw, the daft sod, young Ewan was as
good as he was and a damn sight cleaner in the neck and the
tongue.

Well, Ewan went to the Union meeting that night, next
morning chaps asked him what he'd thought o't, and he said
there hadn't been much on at all, there'd been less than a
dozen members there—*I suppose you can't blame a union if the
chaps who belong to it won't attend its meetings.* Norman asked
what the hell was the good of attending, the Union had sold
the pass time and again, the heads of the bloody thing down
in London were thick as thieves with the viscounts and earls.
Ewan said that was rotten if it was true, why didn't the Union
give them the chuck? And Norman said he'd be Bulgared if
he knew.

Alick Watson said that his Ma's new lodger, a chap called

Selden, and he was a Red, was aye saying the unions should chuck out the leaders. And everybody laughed, you knew well enough what Reds were like, daft about Russia and its Bolshevists—tink brutes, it made you boil to think the way they mis-used the ministers there, the *Daily Runner* had pages about it and the Pope had been in a hell of a rage at atheists behaving near as bad as Christians.

And you all sat by the Docks, you'd go down there now and look at the two or three ships in the harbour sleeping an hour in the still July, smoke a slow pencil plume from the derricks, a dead cat or so floating under your feet, far off through the brigs you could see the North Sea fling up its green hands again and again and grab and scrabble at the breakwater wall—and you blethered about everything you could think of, Ewan wouldn't talk much unless Alick made him, Alick'd slap him on the shoulder, *Come on, man, tell us*. But he'd say *I don't know any more than you chaps—less, it's only stuff out of books*.

Well, wasn't that a lot? And you'd ask him about it, did *he* hold with this ongoing of the Bolshevists in Russia, closing down kirks and chasing ministers all to hell for just preaching, like? He said he didn't know anything about Russia but he thought the time of kirks was past. *But you surely believe there's Something, man?* and Ewan said *Maybe, but I don't think it's God*.

And you couldn't make out what he meant by that, funny chap, fine chap, you liked to go home with him, he called you Bob as you called him Ewan, and was awfully interested in everything, where you'd been born, and gone to school, and the stuff they'd taught you in Ecclesgriegs. And you felt a bit shy to invite him, like, the old man's house was a hell of a soss, but you'd like him to tea some Saturday night. And he said *Right, thanks. I'd like to come;* and you went home and maybe boasted a bit till your sister, the silly bitch, said *Tavendale: isn't that the toff that you couldn't stick?*

And out of the fragments of days and nights Chris saw her life shape to a pattern again. Getting up and working and going to bed—it had never been anything else in a way she thought as she scrubbed the floors, tidied the rooms, and helped Ma Cleghorn cook the meals or young Meg Watson wash up at the sink. Meg had come back and was fair subdued, looking at Chris with a frightened eye, afraid, poor lass, she'd be somehow blamed over that fight at Gowans and Gloag's. But Chris wasn't so daft as pay heed to that, Ewan could heed to himself, she thought, he was growing up with his own life to lead. And she had hers, and sleep, and food, work, and meikle Ma Cleghorn to laugh at—and what else was there a body could want?

Ma said B'God she should marry some childe, fair going to waste, a lassie like her. And Chris asked who she should marry—Mr Piddle? and Ma gave a snort, she'd said marry, not martyr, he'd never get up from the marriage bed.

Chris said she thought that was fair indecent, drinking tea and pulling a long face; and Ma shook her meikle red face at her, Life was damn indecent as both of them knew. The first time she'd lain with a man, her Jim, she couldn't make up her mind to be sick or to sing. But there was more of the singing than sickness for all that, even though it felt awful like going to bed and being cuddled by a herring-creel, not a man. But mighty, a lassie when she was a lass just bubbled for a childe to set her on fire. But now they were all as hard and cold and unhandled as a slab of grey granite in a cemetery. Look at that teacher-creature, Miss Johns, whipping in and out the house like a futret, with books and papers and meetings to attend, never a lad to give her a squeeze. Chris said *You don't know, she's maybe squeezed on the sly*, Ma said *Not her, she'd freeze up a childe. Not but she isn't bonny in a kind of a way, though I never could stick they black-like jades with a bit of a mouser on the upper lip.*

Chris thought of the faint, dark down on the lip of a downbent face, and the long lashes, curled, soft and tender, blue in the sun. And she said that she thought it rather bonny, and Ma said *Bonny? You've an awful taste. Though the Cushnie and Clearmont think the same, they near eat her up at breakfast time. I suppose the most of the queans about are all such*

*a pack of scrawny scarts that a sleek pussy-cat like our
Really-Miss-Johns just sets a childe fair a-tingle to stroke her.*

Chris had noticed how Ellen woke up the breakfast,
though she herself didn't seem to know it, canty and trig,
with her braided hair and her cool, blue eyes, John Cushnie
would pass the marmalade, and blush, and habber a bit of
English, making an awful mess of it above his tight-tied tie,
Mr Clearmont would give his cheerful guffaw and fix his
round baby eyes on this titbit—*Coming to the Saturday
Match, Miss Johns, Students and Profs, it'll be great fun?* And
Miss Johns would shake her head, *Too busy*, and Archie's
face would fall with a bang. Even Mr Quaritch forgot his
books, the pussy-cat had snared him as well, he'd waggle his
thin little beard at her and tell her stories of the *Daily Runner*,
and start to explain the Douglas Scheme, the Only Plan to
Save Civilization by giving out lots and lots of money to every
soul whether he worked for't or not. *Who would be such a fool
as work at all then?* Miss Johns would ask, but she'd ta'en it
up wrong, Mr Quaritch would marshal bits of bread to prove
the Scheme again up to the hilt, and Miss Johns would say it
sounded great fun, she knew there was Relativity in physics,
this was the first time she'd met it in maths. Mr Piddle would
say, *He-he! Fine morning. And how is Miss Johns today,
yes—yes?* And Feet the Policeman would curl his mouser, a
Sergeant, and give her a bit of a stare like a cod that wanted its
teeth in a cat, instead of the other way round, as was usual.
Chris would smile at the coffee-pot and meet Ellen's eyes,
demure blue eyes with an undemure twinkle.

She and Ewan were indifferent, polite, Chris thought them
too much alike to take heed of each other. But Miss Lyon
couldn't abide her at all, and would sniff as she watched her,
Just a Vulgar Flirt, she didn't let men take Liberties with *her*.
She told this to Chris after breakfast one day, didn't Mrs
Colquohoun think the Johns girl Common? And Chris
smiled at her sweet, *I don't know, Miss Lyon. You see I'm
awfully common myself.*

The first bit of scandal on the pussy-cat Chris heard was
brought by Miss Murgatroyd, *she* had heard it up at the

Unionist Ladies—it was awful, and Miss Johns looking Such
Genteel. And what the Tory women had been saying was that
the new teacher in the Ecclesgriegs Middle was being
over-quick with the strap, strict as could be, maybe not a bad
fault. But worse than that she was telling the bairns the
queerest and dirtiest things, Mrs Colquohoun, drawing
pictures on the blackboard of people's insides and how their
food was digested and oh—And Miss Murgatroyd coloured
over with Shame, and dropped her voice and nearly her
cup—*the way that the waste comes out, you know.*

Chris said she thought that was maybe good and the bairns
would be less constipated. Miss Murgatroyd tweetered like a
chicken in the rain, and then bridled a wee, *Well, of course I'm
Single, and don't know much about things like that.* Chris
wanted to ask, but didn't, if being Single meant that you
never went to the bathroom; but a question like that
wouldn't have been Such Fine.

But more was to come, as she heard soon enough, the
Unionist Ladies in an awful stew, and hot to write the
Education Authority. Miss Johns had been explaining the
Bible away, the whole tale told to Miss Murgatroyd by Mrs
Gawpus, the wife of Bailie Gawpus, she said her little niece
had come home and said there wasn't a God at all, the new
teacher had said so or as good as said so, He was just a silly old
man the Jews worshipped and the world had really begun in a
fire. . . . Just Rank Materialism, wasn't it, now?—And who
would think it of a girl like Miss Johns?

She told the same story to Ma Cleghorn that night, but got
feint the much petting for her pains. *Well, damn't, there's
maybe some sense in her say, Miss Murgatroyd, the Bible's no
canny. Mind the bit about Lot and his daughters, the foul
slummocks, him worse, the randy old ram? It's better to speak of
beginnings in fire than let the weans think it began in a midden.
Ay, there's more in the lass than meets the eye, I'll have to see how
she's getting on.*

Chris met Ellen Johns a week after that, coming up the
stairs, her dark face pale, she smiled at Chris, a tired-looking
lass and Chris said she looked tired. She said so she was,

though not with the teaching, and then told she'd been summoned before the Authority and reprimanded for telling the Duncairn kids a few elementary facts about themselves. —*So I've to leave off physiology and it's Nature Study now—bees, flowers, and how catkins copulate. Won't that be fun?* But she didn't wait an answer, just smiled in the sleekèd way she had, dark and cool and wise, a mere slip, a little quean playing about with fire, and went on up the stair to the room next Ewan's.

Jim Trease had planned the march for the Friday, Broo day, with all the unemployed of Paldy and contingents from Ecclesgriegs and Footforthie and a gang of the chaps on the Kirrieben Broo. The main mob marshalled up in the Cowgate, the Communionists crying for the folk to join up—*we'll march to the Council and demand admittance, and see the Provost about the* PAC. And a man'd look shamefaced at another childe, and smoke his pipe and never let on till Big Jim himself came habbering along, crying you out by your Christian name, and you couldn't well do anything else but join—God blast it, you'd grievances enough to complain of. The wife would see you line up with the other Broo chaps, looking sheepish enough, and cry out *Will!* or *Peter!* or *Tam! Come out of that—mighty, it'll do you no good.* And a man just waved at her, off-hand-like, seeing her feared face peeking at him. But a bit of a qualm would come in your wame, thinking *Och well, she'll be all right. We're just marching down to the Castlegate.*

Syne the drum struck up and off you all marched, some gype had shoved the handle of a flag in your hand, it read DOWN WITH THE MEANS TEST AND HUNGER AND WAR, the rest of the billies made a joke about it, they would rather, they said, down a bottle of beer. Right in front was Big Jim Trease, big and sappy in his shiny blue shirt, beside him the chap he'd been helping of late, Stephen Selden that had been an emigrant to Canada and come back from the starvation there to starve here. The two of them were in the lead of the march, wee Jake Forbes waddling behind, banging the drum, *boomroomroom*, he could play a one-man band on his own, a Red musician, and played at the dances with his meikle white face that had never a smile. And on and up you rumbled through Paldy, clatter of boots on the calsay stones, the sun was shining through drifts of rain, shining you saw it fall on the roofs in long, wavering lines and floodings of rain, queer you'd never seen it look bonny as that.

But now all the chaps were lifting their heads as they marched, and looking as though they hadn't a care in the world, not showing their qualms to the gentry sods. Bobbies had come out and now marched by the column, a birn of the bastards, fat and well fed, coshes in hand, there was the new Sergeant, him they called Feet—Christ, and what plates of meat! *Boomr-oom* went the drum and you all were singing:

> Up wi' the gentry, that's for me,
>   Up wi' the gentry fairly,
> Let's slobber on King and our dear Countree—
>   And I'm sure they'll like me sairly.

And a lot more like that, about Ramsay Mac, stite, but it gave a swing to your feet and you all felt kittled up and high by then and looked back by your shoulder and saw behind the birn of the billies marching like you, you forgot the wife, that you hadn't a meck, the hunger and dirt, you'd alter that. They couldn't deny you, you and the rest of the Broo folk here, the right to lay bare your grievances. Flutter, flutter the banner over your head, your feet beginning to stound a wee, long since the boots held out the water, shining the drift of the rain going by. And now you were all thudding into step, and beyond the drum saw Royal Mile, flashing with trams, thick with bobbies: and here out from the wynds came the Ecclesgriegs men and the fisher-chaps from Kirrieben, they looked the worst of the whole caboosh. And Big Jim Trease cried *Halt a minute*, you all paiched to a stop while the other chaps drew in and formed fours.

Watching that you minded your time in the army, the rain and stink and that first queer time your feet slipped in a soss of blood and guts, going up to the front at Ypres—Christ, long syne that, you'd not thought then to come to this, to

come to the wife with the face she had now, and the weans—
by God, you would see about things! Communionists like
Big Jim might blether damned stite but they tried to win you
your rights for you. And all the march spat on its hands again
and gripped the banners and fell in line, and looked sideways
and saw the pavements half-blocked, half Duncairn had
heard of the march on the Town House—and och, blast it if
there wasn't the wife again, thin-faced, greeting, the silly
bitch, making you shake like this, the great sumph, by the
side of those oozing creashes of bobbies, shining their capes
in the rain.

But now you'd wheeled into Royal Mile, a jam of traffic,
the trams had slowed down, flutter, flutter the banners, here
the wind drove, your mates shrinking under the sleety drive,
Woolworth's to the right, where all the mecks went, and
there the big Commercial Bank and the office of the *Daily
Runner*, the rag, it had tried to put a stop to this march, the
sods had said you never looked for work, you that tramped
out your guts day on day on the search—to the Docks, to the
granite works, the country around, as far to the north as
Stonehyve. *Boomr-oomr*, wee Jake'll brain that damn drum if
he isn't careful, God, how folk stare! A new song ebbing
down the damp column, you'd aye thought it daft to sing
afore this, a lot of faeces, who was an outcast? But damn't,
man, now—

　　Arise, ye outcasts and ye hounded,
　　Arise, ye slaves of want and fear—

And what the hell else were you, all of you? Singing, you'd
never sung so before, all your mates about you, marching as
one, you forgot all the chave and trauchle of things, the sting
of your feet, nothing could stop you. Rain in your face—that
was easy to face, if not the fretting of the wife back there (to
hell with her to vex a man's mind, why couldn't she have
bidden at home, the fool?).

She'd take no hurt, you were all of you peaceable, the
singing even in a wee died off, they'd shooed the traffic to the
side of the Mile, a gang of the Mounted riding in front, their
fat-buttocked horses swaying away, well-fed like their riders,

the rain sheeting down from their tippets, the Bulgars, easy for them to boss it on us—

What the devil was up down there?

The whole column had slowed, came bang to a stop, more Mounties with their wee thick sticks in their hands strung out there across the Mile, rain-pelted, the horses chafing at the bridles, impatient, Christ, rotten to face if a brute came at you. And a growl and a murmur went through the column, what was wrong up there, why had they stopped? Chaps cried *Get on with it, Jim, what's wrong?* Syne the news came down, childes passing it on, their faces twisted with rage or laughing, they hardly bothered to curse about it, the police were turning the procession back down into Paldy by way of the wynds. It wasn't to be let near the Town Hall at all, the Provost had refused to see them or Trease.

And then you heard something rising about you that hadn't words, the queerest-like sound, you stared at your mates, a thing like a growl, low and savage, the same in your throat. And then you were thrusting forward like others— *Never mind the Bulgars, they can't stop our march!* And in less than a minute the whole column was swaying and crowding forward, the banners pitching and scudding like leaves above the sodden clothes of the angry Broo men. Trease crying *Back! Take care! Keep the line!*

And your blood fair boiled when you heard him cry that, a Red—just the same as the Labour whoresons, no guts and scared for his bloody face. And above his head you saw one of the bobbies, an inspector, give his arm a wave, and next minute the horses were pelting upon you hell for leather, oh Christ, they couldn't—

Ewan was down in Lower Mile when the police tried to turn the unemployment procession down the wynds to the Gallowgate. He'd just come from a bookshop and was forced to stop, the pavements black with outstaring people. And then they began to clear right and left, the shopman behind cried *Come back, Sir. There'll be a hell of a row in a minute*, he was standing on a pavement almost deserted. Then he saw the mounted policeman wave and the others jerk at their horses' bridles, and suddenly, far up, the policeman of Segget, the clown that the Segget folk had called Feet, not mounted, he'd come by the side of the column—saw him grab a young keelie by the collar and lift his baton and hit him, crack!—crack like a calsay-stone hit by a hammer, Ewan's heart leapt, he bit back a cry, the boy screamed: and then there was hell.

As the bobbies charged the Broo men went mad though their leader tried to wave them back, Ewan saw him mishandled and knocked to the ground under the flying hooves of the horses. And then he saw the Broo folk in action, a man jumped forward with a pole in his hand with a ragged flag with letters on it, and thrust: the bobby took it in the face and went flying over his horse's rump, Ewan heard some body cheer—himself—well done, well done! Now under the charges and the pelt of the rain the column was broken, but it fought the police, with sticks, with naked hands, with the banners, broken and knocked down right and left, the police had gone mad as well, striking and striking, riding their horses up on the pavements, cursing and shouting, Ewan saw one go by, his teeth bared, bad teeth, the face of a beast, he hit out and an old, quiet-looking man went down, the hoof of the horse went plunk on his breast—

And then Ewan saw the brewery lorry jammed by the pavement, full of empty bottles; and something took hold of him, whirled him about, shot him into the struggling column. For a minute the Broo men didn't hear or understand, then they caught his gestures or shout or both, yelled, and poured across the Mile and swamped the lorry in a leaping wave. . . .

That evening the *Runner* ran a special edition and the news went humming into the south about the fight in the Royal Mile, pitched battle between unemployed and police, how the Reds had fought the bobbies with bottles, battering them from their saddles with volleys of bottles: would you credit that, now, the coarse brutes that they were? The poor police had just tried to keep order, to stop a riot, and that's what they'd got.

. . . . .

The Reverend Edward MacShilluck in his Manse said the thing was disgraceful, ahhhhhhhhhhhh, more than that, a portent of the atheist, loose-living times. Why hadn't the police called out the North Highlanders? . . . And he read up the *Runner* while he ate his bit supper, and called in his housekeeper and told her the news, and she said that she thought it disgraceful, just, she'd heard that a poor old man was in hospital, dying, with his breast all broken up: would he be a policeman, then, would you say? The Reverend MacShilluck gave a bit of a cough and said Well, no, he understood not— *Ahhhhhhhhhhhh well, we mustn't worry over much on these things, the proper authorities will see to them.* And gave the housekeeper a slap in the bottom, well-fed, and said *Eh, Pootsy, tonight?* And the housekeeper simpered and said *Oh, sir—*

Bailie Brown, that respectable Labour man, was interviewed and was awful indignant, he said that he fought day in, day out, the cause of the unemployed on the Council, none knew the workers better than he or the grievances they had to redress. But what good did this senseless marching do?—the Council had to impose the PAC rates the National Government laid down for it, you could alter nothing for a three or four years till Labour came into power again. The unemployed must trust the Labour Party, not allow itself to be led all astray—And he shot Mr Piddle out on the street, in a hurry, like, he'd to dress for dinner.

. . . . .

Lord Provost Speight was found in his garden, stroking his long, dreich, wrinkled face; and he said that this Bolshevism should be suppressed, he put the whole riot down to Communist agents, paid agitators who were trained in Moscow, the working-class was sound as a bell. If they thought they could bring pressure to bear on the Council to alter the rates of the PAC, by rioting about in Royal Mile, they were sore mistaken, he'd guarantee that—

. . . . .

Duncairn's Chief Constable said it wasn't true the police had run, they'd just given back a wee till reinforcements came and by then the crowd had dispersed, that was all. No, they'd made only one arrest so far, the well-known agitator Trease. And the old man who had died in the hospital had been struck down by one of the rioters—

. . . . .

And the men came back to their homes in Footforthie and Paldy Parish and Kirrieben, some of them walking and laughing, some glum, some of them half-carried all the way, with their broken noses, bashed faces, it made a woman go sick to see Peter or Andrew or Charlie now, his face a dripping, bloody mask, his whispering through his broken lips: *I'm fine, lass, fine.* Oh God, you could greet if it wasn't that when you did that you would die. . . .

And all that night they re-fought the fight, in tenements, courts, this room and that, and the bairns lay listening how the bobbies had run, of the young toff who'd appeared when Trease was knocked down and shouted *Break down the lorry for bottles!* and led them all off when the bottles were finished, him and Steve Selden, and told them to scatter. By God, he'd lots of guts had that loon, though, toff-like, he'd been sick as a dog of a sudden, down in the Cowgate when binding a wound. You wanted more of his kind for the next bit time. . . . And the wife would say *What's the use of more bashing?* and you said a man had to die only once and 'twould be worth while doing that if you kicked the bucket with your nails well twined in a bobby's liver—

. . . . .

A week later the *Daily Runner* came out and announced that after a special sitting the Council had raised the PAC rates.

Ma Cleghorn heard the story from Chris: *Ah well, if that's how your Ewan feels. I'd never much liking for bobbies myself, though maybe the meikle sumph, you know, was doing no more than his duty, like.* Chris said *His duty? To bash a young boy—before the boy had done anything to him?* And Ma said

Well, well, you're fair stirred up. I'll think up some sonsy lie as excuse, and tell him the morn to look out other lodgings.

And next morning Ma tackled the sacking of Feet, he'd spluttered a bit and put on the heavy as she told Chris when she came back to the kitchen. But she'd soon settled up his hash for the billy, telling him his room was needed for another, a childe they'd promised it a long while back. He'd told her she'd better look out, she had, and not get in ill with the Force, they'd heard things in headquarters about that quean Johns and were keeping an eye on the house already—

Ma had fair lost her rag at that and told him she didn't care a twopenny damn though all the bobbies in Duncairn toun were to glue themselves on to her front door knocker, the meikle lice—who was he to insult a decent woman who paid her rent and rates on the nail? *If my man had been alive, he'd have kicked you out, sergeant's stripes and all, you great coarse bap-faced goloch that you are.* Feet had habbered *I wasn't trying to insult you*, and Ma had said *Give me more of your lip and I'll tackle the kicking of your dowp myself*, and left him fair in fluster, poor childe, hardly kenning whether he stood on his head or meikle feet, fair convinced he was in the wrong, and packing up his case to get out of the house.—*So there you are, lass, and we're short of a lodger.*

Chris said she was sorry, she'd try and get another, and Ma said Och, not to worry about that, some creature would soon come taiking around. Chris thought the same, not heeding a lot, though it was a shame to lose Feet's fee. But he couldn't have bidden in the house at all after that tale that Ewan had told her—Ewan with a pale, cool angry face, stirred as she'd never seen him stirred.

She was thinking of that when the postman chapped, Ma Cleghorn went paiching out to the hall and silence followed till Ma cried up *A letter for you, Mrs Robert Colquohoun.*

When Chris got down to the hall there she stood, turning the thing this way and that, all but tearing it open and reading, Chris nearly laughed, she was used to Ma. *It's from Segget*, Ma said, and Chris said *Is't now?* and took the thing and opened it and read, Ma giving a whistle and turning away and dighting with a duster at the grandfather clock, making on she was awful ta'en up with her work. And Chris read the long straggle of sloping letters and was suddenly smelling, green and keen, sawdust, sawn wood—queerly and suddenly homesick for Segget:

We've a new lodger coming on the Monday, Ma. A man that I used to know in Segget, Ake Ogilvie the joiner, he's gotten a job as a foreman up at the Provost's sawmills.

Chris started awake. The fog had re-thickened, blanketing Duncairn away from her sight as she stood here dreaming like a gowkèd bairn. Her hair felt damp with the pressing mist veils and the weight the bag on her arm was lead—funny this habit she aye had had of finding some place wherever she bade to which she could climb by her lone for a while and think of the days new-finished and done, like a packman halting hill on hill and staring back at the valleys behind. She minded how above the ploughed lands of Blawearie this habit had grown, long syne, long syne, when she'd lain and dreamed as a quean by the loch in the shadow of the marled Druid Stones, and how above Segget in the ruined Kaimes she had done the same as the wife of Robert. Robert: and Ake Ogilvie was coming from Segget with his long brown face and his rangy stride. How would he take with a place like Duncairn? How had he gotten the job with the Provost?

Autumn coming down there in the fog, down in the days you no more could glimpse than the shrouded roofs of Duncairn at this hour. . . . And Ewan—what was happening to Ewan? Once so cool and cold, boy-clear, boy-clever, a queer lad you'd thought would never be touched by any wing of the fancies of men, grey granite down to the core—and now?

In the mirror she saw her face, dim in mist, and smiled at it with a kind dispassion. And what to herself?—just the trauchle of time, the old woman she'd believed herself at first in Duncairn—as she still did sometimes at moments of weariness—or that other quean that refused to die, that moved and looked and stole off her thoughts, and dreamed the daftest of old, lost dreams, blithe as though twenty, unkissed and uncuddled?

Well, time she went into those mists of the future. There was ten o'clock chapping from Thomson Tower.

TWO

Sphene

AS THE DAY awoke great clouds had come out of the North Sea over Duncairn, with them the wind rose and rose, snarling at the gates of the dark, waiting to break through with the first peep of light. And now as that peep came glimmering, far off, beyond the edge of the Mounth, the storm loosed itself over the toun, sheeting down a frozen torrent of water. Sometimes the sleet was a ding-dong fall, and again the wind would whirl and lift, pitching great handfuls into your face though a minute before you had been in the lithe. The Windmill Steps were sheeted in slush, twice Chris slipped and nearly fell as she ran for the shelter of the mirror ledge, low below a first shrouded tram wheeled, moaning, and took the road to the Mile, the lights were going out one by one as the winter morning broke on Duncairn.

In the lithe of the mirror Chris stopped and panted and beat her frozen hands together, hatless still but muffled in a scarf to the ears for that last silly journey down to the doctor's. She'd finished with him, done everything proper, and now there was surely nothing else. And she felt—oh, she could sleep for a month—like a polar bear, with the sleet for a sheet—

Her hair faint-sprayed by the sleet that went by, not touching the rest of her, she raised her eyes and saw it, half in the dark, half in the light, strange, a strange blind glister and drift high in the lift, a bannered attack going by in silence though you heard the shoom of the spears far down. Stamping her feet to bring them to warmth, she rested a minute, closed her eyes, yawned over-poweringly and achingly, and ceased from that to stare sombre-eyed down at

63

the breaking of the sleet-hunted light. Whatever next? Whatever next?

How could she have known that day in July when she rested here and wondered on things that *this* would come, that she'd stand here appalled, that she wouldn't know which way to think or to move? Her mind shrank in a passion of pity a minute, strangely linked with a desire to laugh. . . . And she shook herself, no time to stand here, with the house above wakening and waiting her—

Oh, let it wait, let it rest awhile while she caught her breath and tried to make out where she'd mislaid that security hers and her own only a short six months before:

Long-mousered, green-eyed, with his ploughman's swagger, it had seemed to Chris six months before that Ake Ogilvie's coming had brought to Duncairn something clean and crude as the smell of rain—crude and clean as she herself had been once before a playing at gentry enslaved her, like turning round in a lane at night and meeting one's own lost self and face, lost a long fifteen years before, smiling with cool and sardonic lips. Not that Ake had anything very young about him, or old-like either, he was one of the kind that seem to stick to one age all their lives, swagger and pipe and clumping feet, met on the stairs as he carried up his kist that Monday morning from the taxi below.

Ay, Mrs Colquohoun, you look bonny as ever. And Chris said that was fine, but why was he carrying the kist? The cabman would surely have given him a hand. And Ake said he'd just had an argy with the billy and sent him off with a flea in his lug, by God he'd wanted a whole half-crown for bringing them up from the Central Station.

Chris said that was awful, cabmen were like that, but Ake wouldn't be able to carry up the kist on his shoulder further, the stairs drew in. So he lowered it down and syne shook hands and looked her all over with his swagger green glower. *Ay, you've fairly ta'en with Duncairn. D'you miss the Manse?* Chris said *Not much. Shall I give you a hand?*

Ake looked a bit doubtful, he thought of her still as the

wife of Robert in Segget, she saw, genteel and neat and fine and frail—she said *Come on!* and took hold of an end and Ake did the same, up they went to his room, made ready, and put down the kist in the corner for't. Syne Ake looked round and out at the roofs: *A hell of a place for a man to bide, the toun, though the room looks canty enough. You'll be gey busy here, no doubt then, mistress?*

Chris nearly cuddled him, calling her that, so long since a soul had called her mistress: *I've a lot to do, same as other folk. But we'll have a crack on Segget some time.—Ay, faith we will.* He had turned away, no frills or unnecessary politeness with him: *I'll be in to my tea, but not to my dinner. I've to gang up and see the Provost man.*

Chris said that she hoped he'd get on fine, and he said *No fear of that. Ta-ta.*

He made himself at home from the first, sitting arguing in the sitting-room with Mr Neil Quaritch, thin, with his little tuft of a beard and his Douglas Scheme (that Ewan called the Bourgeois Funk-Fantasy), Ake beside him looking like a shorthorn bull taking up its spare time on a gossip with a goat. He looked over-real sometimes to Chris to be real as she'd meet him coming in at the door, slow and yet quick, throwing down his feet with a fine and measured stride, the earth's his, yielding the wall to none in Duncairn. And he'd clump up the stairs and into his room without a sideways look or a thought, he'd paid his fee and the room was his, would he creep up quiet for any damned body?

Chris never saw him at ease in his room. Rousing the first morning after he came she'd thought to make him a cup of tea and take it to him the same as to others. But while she was moving about with the cups and the kettle was singing and Jock the cat purring away for dear life by the range and the caller air of the August dawn coming up the Steps and into the house, she heard a pad of feet on the stairs, and there was Ake at the kitchen door, his mouser fresh-curled, in his waistcoat and breeks, no slippers, his kind never did have slippers Chris minded back to her farmhouse days: *Ay, mistress, I thought it would maybe be you. This'll be your kitchen place, no doubt.* Chris said it was—*Come in and sit down.*

And in he came and sat by the fire and gave the cat Jock a bit of a stroke, and sat and drank the tea that she poured him, not offering to help her as Quaritch would have done, God be here it was a woman's work, wasn't it now, who'd ever heard of a man who sossed with the cups? And Ake drank the tea through his curling moustache, and wiped that, and nodded *Ay, that's a good brew. I think I'll taik down every morning for one.* Chris said *There's no need to do that, Mr Ogilvie, I take up cups to the folk that want them.* And Ake said Oh to hell with that, he wasn't a cripple and could come for his own. Besides, he was used to getting up with the light and hadn't a fancy for stinking in bed. Chris thought *And suppose I've no fancy for you sitting about in my way in the kitchen?* But she didn't say it, just went on with her work, watched by Ake sitting smoking his pipe—Ay, God, she looked a bonny lass still, a bit over-small for her height, you would say, but a fine leg and hip, a warm bit quean. She'd fair set a-lowe and burned up Colquohoun in her time, you wouldn't but wonder; and maybe had never yet had a man to handle her as she needed handling.

So he got in the way of coming to the kitchen and sitting drinking his tea every morning, Ma Cleghorn heard and said to Chris that she'd better look out, for they weren't to be trusted, childes with curling mousers like yon. And then sighed: *Though, God, there's no need to warn you, I keep forgetting you're gentry yourself, a minister's widow, not for common folk.* Chris asked what Ma wanted her to do with him—or thought he was likely to do with her? And Ma said that if Chris couldn't guess about that there were other folk than the Virgin Mary had had their immaculate conceptions, faith.

Chris laughed and paid her but little heed, Ake as far (she knew) from such thoughts as herself, funny in a way to have him about, it wiped out the years, all the gentry in her, she was back in a farm kitchen again and the man sitting douce and drinking his tea and she getting ready the meat for him. . . . And Ake would give his bit mouser a curl and tell the latest tale of the Provost.

Chris asked how he'd gotten the job and Ake said by the skin of the teeth and the will of the Lord, he'd been at school with the laddie Speight a thirty-five years or so back, they were both of them of Laurencekirk stock. Well, he'd been a gey dreich and ill-favoured loon, and Ake had ta'en him a punch now and then to kittle him up and mind him his manners. The result was he'd fair ta'en a liking to Ake and would follow him about like a cat a fish-cadger, right through their schooldays and a wee whilie after, when they'd gotten long trousers and cuddled their bit queans. Syne they'd tint one another, Ake had gone drifting south as a joiner, to the feuching stink of the Glasgow yards, to that windy sods' burrow, the capital, Edinburgh, syne drifted up to the Howe again, he'd never felt much at home, as you'd say, outside the cloud-reek and claik of the Howe. And that was how he had come to Segget, not near so dead in those times as now, the joiner's business with still enough fettle to brink a man a bit meal and drink.

So he'd settled down there, as Mrs Colquohoun knew, till the place was fairly all to hell, with unemployment and all the lave; and after her good man died and so on Ake fair got sick of sitting about in his shed and looking for custom to come, scribbling a wee bit of poetry the while, and glowering up at the Trusta heuchs and wishing to Christ that something would happen.—And Chris said *Oh yes, I mind your poetry. You still write it, do you?* and Ake said *Ay. Bits. It would hardly interest you. Well, as I was saying*—and went on to say that one day he was having a bit look through the paper and what did he see there but that young Jimmy Speight, him that he'd gone to school with long syne, had been made the Lord Provost of Duncairn toun. At first Ake could hardly believe his own eyes, he'd thought that talent must be fairly damn scarce to make Wabbling Jimmy a Lord Provost, like. He'd heard about him afore that, of course, how he'd been ta'en into his uncle's business and heired when the old uncle wore away a fine sawmill and a schlorich of silver. But he'd never much bothered about the creature till he read this notice of him being Provost.

Well, damn't, that fairly moved Ake a bit, if Wabbling Jimmy was all that well off he'd surely scrounge up a job for a body. So Ake locked up his place and put on his best suit and got on the morning train for Duncairn, and took a tram to the Provost's house, out in Craigneuks, a gey brave-looking place with fal-lal ornaments forward and back and a couple of towers stuck on for luck like warts on the nose of Oliver Cromwell. A servant lass came tripping and held the door open, *What name shall I say to the Provost, please?* And Ake said *My name's Ake Ogilvie, tell him, and ask if he minds the time in Lourenkirk when I gey near drowned him in a stone horse-trough.* Well, the lass went red and gave a bit giggle, as a young quean will, and went off with the message, and into the room in a minute came Jimmy, gey grand, but dreeping at the nose as ever. And damn't, he'd come in fair cocky-like but syne a funny thing happened to him, it just showed you what happened when you were a bairn—if you got a rattle in the lantern then you might build a battleship in later life and explore the North Pole and sleep with a Duchess, but you'd never forget the lad that had cloured you, you'd meet him and feel a bit sick in the wame though it was a good half-century later.

Well, something like that came on Wabbling Jimmy, he dropped his politeness and his hee-haw airs, and Ake took his hand and cried out loud: *Ay, Jimmy lad, you're fair landed here, with all these queans to see to your needs, at door and table and no doubt in your bed.* And the Lord Provost went as yellow's a neep: *Wheesht, Ake, wheesht, the wife's on the prowl.* And Ake said he didn't know that he'd married— *d'you mind what happened to Kate Duthie long syne?* . . .

Now, that had been just a kind of blackmail, as Ake knew right well but didn't much care, in a minute poor Wabbling Jimmy was ready to offer him half his worldly possessions if only Ake would keep quiet on the subject of Kate. Ake said that he was on the look for a job, what about this sawmill that Jimmy owned? And Jimmy said he seldom interfered, he'd a

manager, and Ake said he hardly wanted *his* job, though he'd
tackle a foreman's he'd manage that fine. So Jimmy in a stew
howked out his car and in they got and drove to the Kirrie, a
fine sawmill, and they weren't there long afore the manager
came over to ask if Jimmy had yet ta'en on a new foreman in
place of a childe that had gotten the sack. And at that what
could poor Jimmy do but go a bit blue about the neb and say
Ay, I have; and this is him.

So that's how he'd collared the Duncairn job, not that he
was over-keen on the thing, *D'you ken now, mistress, what I've
aye wanted?—Losh, a job on a ship at sea, the fine smell and the
pelt of the water below you, there's fine carpentering work to be
done on ships.* And Chris, with the teacups cold on the tray,
said she thought it a shame he'd never got it, maybe he'd get a
job like that yet. Ake nodded, fegs, and he might, not likely,
better to hang on the Provost's tail, old Wabbling Jimmy that
was feared at his past. *Not that poor Jimmy's an exception in
that: We're all on leading strings out of the past.*

For days you couldn't forget that scream, tingling, terrified,
the lost keelie's scream as that swine Sim Leslie smashed him
down. Again and again you'd start awake, sweating, remembering that from a dream, Duncairn sleeping down Windmill
Steps, all the house in sleep, quiet next door, that kid Ellen
Johns not dreaming at all. Luck for her and her blah about
history and Socialism: she hadn't a glimpse of what either
meant. . . .

Oh, sick of the whole damn idiot mess, drifting about
nowadays like a fool, couldn't settle to anything, couldn't
read a book, caught in the net of this idiot rubbish. Your head
had softened like a swede in the rain ever to be taken in with
the rot—rot about leading new life to the workers, moulding
them into History's new tool, apprehending a force more
sure and certain than the God poor Robert had preached in
Segget. . . . In the workers?—Rats, what was there in them
that wasn't in the people of any class? Some louts, some
decent, the most of them brainless, what certain tool to be
found in crude dirt? You'd dug deep enough to make sure of

that, playing the game as a keelie yourself, fraternizing with the fauna down at the Works—hell, how they stank, the unscrubbed lot, with their idiot ape-maunderings and idiot hopes, their idiot boasts, poor dirty devils. They took you for one of themselves nowadays, so you'd almost become as half-witted as they.

Finished with it all quite definitely now. What have the keelies to do with you—except to make you feel sick? They don't like the same things, haven't the same interests, don't care a hang for the books you read (mislaid those text-books this last week somewhere). And you pretending an interest in horses—dog-racing—football—all the silly kid-games that excite the keelies—find History's beat in their drivelling blah!

. . . That ghastly house that Bob took you to—father unemployed for over five years, mother all running to a pale grey fat like a thing you found when you turned up a stone, one of the brothers a cretin, rickets—sat giggling and slavering in a half-dark corner, they couldn't afford to have the gas on, a dead smell of dirt left unstirred and unscrubbed, disharmonic heads and moron brains; and outside the house as you came away: streets on streets, the fug of the Cowgate, keelies on the lounge in the gutter, in the dirt, their ghastly voices and their ghastly faces—

They DON'T concern you. BREAK with it all.

So when Alick and Norman that Saturday asked if you were coming to the Beach Pavilion, Snellie Guff the Scotch Comedian was On, you said *No, sorry, I've reading to do*, and saw their faces fall, damn them, they'd just have to learn as you had to learn. But when you got home and had finished dinner and been caught by that ghastly old bore Ake Ogilvie who thought himself God's regent on earth because Christ had been of the same trade as himself, and heard his lout swagger on this and that, you felt too restless to rout out the books. Damn nuisance, August blazing outside, birds high up in the Howe today, a bus would take you to Segget in an hour. . . . If only it could take you back over a year!

And you thought of the times when you'd haunted the

Howe, as a schoolboy, seeking the old-time flints, Neolithic stuff, passable collection: you'd forgotten it since you'd come to Duncairn. Where could it be?

And in chase of that you went down to the kitchen and knocked and looked in, Chris and Ma Cleghorn and Meg the maid, they all looked up and you said *I'm sorry. Chris, d'you mind where my flints went to?*

Chris said she thought you had finished with them, they were up in the box-room under the eaves. Ma called as you turned away *Ewan man, why aren't you out at a game this weather? Or out with a lass?—that'd be more your age than bothering about with a rickle of stones. Your mother showed me them and I thought 'What dirt!'*

You said *Oh, really?* funny old hag, another keelie trying to keep you in the gutter—games and street-crawling and their blasted girls. Her face fell a bit when you spoke like that, the old fool should heed to her own damned business. Chris looked at you with her nice, cool eyes, a long time since you'd kissed her, she had a nice kiss. Then you went up the stairs to your flints.

They were thick with dust, lying higgledy-piggledy in the press, tortoise-cores and a scraper or so, you took them out and turned them about, and saw the wavery lines of the knapping done long ago in the hills of the Howe, some day three thousand years before. Some careful craftsman had squatted to knapp, with careful knee and finger and eye, looking up now and then from his work on the flakes to see the grey glister of the Howe below, the long lake that covered the Low Mearns then, with sailing shapes of islands upon it, smoke of fires rising slow in the air from the squatting-places of the Simple Men, deer belling far on the hills as the sun swung over to the hazes of the afternoon, things plain and clear to anyone then—you supposed: was that no more than supposing?

But at least they had made the things they desired, finely and surely and lovely as these, long long ago. Still, things no lovelier than the shining giants that whirred and spun in Gowans and Gloag's, power-dreams fulfilled of the flint-knapping men. . . . And at that the little warmth they had brought you quite went, you were staring down at a dusty stone, chipped by someone no shape at all, a dim shadow on dust, meaning nothing, saying nothing: and down there in the heat of this August day the festering wynds of Paldy Parish—

You closed the press and went down the stairs, out of the house, down Windmill Brae, idiot-angry to escape your soft self. Turning up to Royal Mile you went slower, wondering what you could do at this hour. A thin little gallop of Autumn rain came pelting down the street as you wondered, and you looked up and saw the Library near and beside it the Museum Galleries.

Inside there, breathing from running from the rain you debated a minute to stay or go out, the place as usual dingy and desolate, old chap in uniform yawning at a table. Then you went past him into the hall and stood and looked at the statues around, poor stuff the most of it, you'd seen it before.

Plaster-cast stuff of the Greek antiques, Discobolus, blowsily mammalian Venus, Pallas Athene—rather a dirty lot they had been, the Greeks, though so many clean things survived. Why did they never immortalize in stone a scene from the Athenian justice-courts—a slave being ritually, unnecessarily tortured before he could legally act as a witness? Or a baby exposed to die in a jar?—hundreds every year in the streets of Athens, it went on all day, the little kids wailing and crying and crying as the hot sun rose and they scorched in the jars; and then their mouths dried up, they just weeked and whimpered, they generally died by dark. . . .

There was a cast of Trajan, good head; Cæsar—the Cæsar they said wasn't Cæsar. Why not a head of Spartacus? Or a plaque of the dripping line of crosses that manned the Appian Way with slaves—dripping and falling to bits through long months, they took days to die, torn by wild beasts. Or a statuary group of a Roman slave being fed to fishes, alive, in a pool. . . .

You turned and went up the deserted stairs to the picture galleries, dusty and dim, drowsily undisturbed but for one room you passed where a keelie was cuddling a girl on the sly, sitting on a bench, they giggled a bit, dried up as you looked and stared and stared. You looked away and about the room, flat seascapes and landscapes, the deadest stuff, why did people make a fuss of pictures? Or music? You'd never seen anything in either. You went and sat down in the Italian room, on the bench in the middle, and stared at a picture, couldn't be bothered to find out the painter, group of Renaissance people somewhere: soldiers, a cardinal, an angel or so, and a throng of keelies cheering like hell about nothing at all—in the background, as usual. Why not a more typical Italian scene!—a man being broken on the wheel with a club, mashed and smashed till his chest caved in, till his bones were a blood-clottered powdery mess?—

Passed in a minute, that flaring savage sickness, and you got to your feet and went on again: but the same everywhere, as though suddenly unblinded, picture on picture limned in dried blood, never painted or hung in any gallery—pictures of the poor folk since history began, bedevilled and murdered, trodden underfoot, trodden down in the bree, a human slime, hungered, unfed, with their darkened brains, their silly revenges, their infantile hopes—the men who built Münster's City of God and were hanged and burned in scores by the Church, the Spartacists, the blacks of Toussaint L'Ouverture, Parker's sailors who were hanged at the Nore, the Broo men manhandled in Royal Mile. Pictures unceasing of the men of your kin, peasants and slaves and common folk and their ghastly lives through six thousand years—oh hell, what had it to do with you?

And you bit your lip to keep something back, something that rose and slew coolness and judgment—steady, white-edged, a rising flame, anger bright as a clear bright flame, as though 'twas yourself that history had tortured, trodden on, spat on, clubbed down in you, as though you were every scream and each wound, flesh of your flesh, blood of your blood. . . . And you gave a queer sob that startled yourself: Something was happening to you: God—what?

*

Ma said, coming down to Chris in the kitchen after collecting the lodgers' fees, she went round each room of a Sabbath morning before the breakfast time or the kirk: *The Murgatroyd creature's fair in a stew, her dividends are all going down she says and she hardly knows how she'll Pay her Way. She's a bittie of a shareholder in Gowans and Gloag's and there's not a cent from the firm this year. Aren't they brutes to mistreat a respectable woman?*

Chris asked if that meant that she'd have to leave, and Ma shook her head, Oh no, not her, she'd a bit of a pension as well as an income, a three hundred pounds a year from a trust. Chris stared: *Then what's coming over her?* and Ma sighed that Chris didn't understand and hadn't a proper sympathy, like, with financial straits of wealthy folk—like herself and their wee Miss Murgatroyd. What the old bitch really wanted of course was her runkled old bottom kicked a bit and turned out into the streets for a night hawking herself at a tanner a time. . . .

And Ma sat down and paiched a bit, smoothing out the pounds and the ten bob notes, and said that Mr Piddle was short again, him that banked nearly every meck that he got. Ma'd told him she'd need the balance on Monday—and not to *he-he!* at her like a goat. *Four, five, two halves, a one and ten silver, that's our little bit English pussy-cat. Sitting up there and reading a book—can you guess what the book is about now, lass?*

Chris looked in the range and over at the clock, and shook her head, only half-heeding Ma's claik.—*Well, then, it's a Manual of Birth Control. What think you of that and our Ellen Johns, with her little mouser and her neat long legs?*

Chris was over-surprised a minute to say anything, then asked if Miss Johns tried to hide the book? Ma said she hadn't, neither showing off nor hiding: *Ay, a gey keek our Ellen, with all her quiet ways. And it's all to the good of the trade, anyhow.* Chris asked *How?* and Ma said *Why, she'll be able to sin as she likes and go free, with no need to marry the gallus childe. So we'll be able to keep her our lodger. . . . Twelve, thirteen, ten, Ake Ogilvie's—ay, faith he's made of the old-time stuff. If I'd been a ten years younger or so I'd be chumming up to him, a bonny man, well-shouldered and canty, it's a pity you're gentry.*

Chris had heard this before and now hardly smiled, if it was gentry to know her own mind, the things that she liked and the things that she didn't, well then, she was gentry down to the core. And Ma had been watching her and cried out *Hoots, now don't go away and take offence. I'm just a coarse old wife and must have my bit joke.* Chris laughed, half-angry, *Well, don't have it on me*, and Ma said she'd mind and went on with her counting, Miss Lyon's Boss had fined her two shillings, Awful the way that they treat Us Girls, the Clearmont laddie was all a-blither and a-clatter over his Rectorial election, fegs, what was this Nationalist stite that had got him?

Chris minded back to her days in Segget and said that this Nationalism was just another plan of the Tories to do down the common folk. Only this time 'twas to be done in kilts and hose, with bagpipes playing and a blether about Wallace, the English to be chased across the Border and the Scots to live on brose and baps. Ma said *Fegs now, and are we so, then? Then I'm for the English. Eighteen, nine and six, the lot for this week and we're doing fine. Did I ever tell you when I wanted a partner my niece Izey Urquhart wanted to come in?*

Chris said she didn't know Ma had a niece, Ma nodded, worse luck, a thrawn wee skunk that lived away down in Kirrieben. Ma couldn't stick the creature at all but she was her only living relation and kenned that when Ma pushed off at last she'd get what bittie of silver there was. That might be so, but Ma had made up her mind she wasn't to have the long-nosed sniftering wretch skeetering around while she was alive; and maybe when Ma died holy Izey would find a bit of a sore surprise to meet—*I'm fond of you, lass, and I'm sending next week for my lawyer man to alter the will. What's in the house and all things I have would be better in your bit keeping, I think, than as miser's savings in Kirrieben.*

Chris said sensibly that Ma shouldn't be silly, it was likely that she would outlive them all. And Ma said she hoped to God that she wouldn't, if there was anything that cumbered the earth it was some old runkle of a woman body living on with no man to tend and no bairns, a woman stopped living when she stopped having bairns. And Chris laughed at that and said *What about men?* and Ma said *Och, damn't, they never live at all. They're just a squeeze and a cuddle we need to keep our lives going, they're nothing themselves.*

And Chris went out in the Sunday quiet to the little patch of garden behind and worked there tending the beds of flowers she'd put in early in blinks of the Spring, sooty and loamy and soft the ground, clouds were flying high in the lift beyond the tilting roofs of Duncairn, the hedge by the house next door was a-rustle, soft green, with its budding beech, far off through the hedges some eident body was at work with a lawn-mower, *clinkle-clankle*, a bairn was wailing in a bairn's unease as Chris dug and raked, watered the flowers, pale things hers compared with Segget's. And somehow Ma's daft words bade in her mind, those about a woman having finished with things when she finished having bairns, just an empty drum, an old fruit squeezed and rotting away, useless, unkenned, unstirred by the agonies of bearing a bairn, heeding it, feeding it, watching it grow—was she now no more than that herself?—a woman on the verge of middle age content to trauchle the hours in a kitchen and come out and potter with weeds and flowers, all the passion of living put by long ago, wonder and terror and the tang of long kisses, embracing knee to knee, the blood in a stream of fire through the heart, the beat and drum of that tide of life that once poured so swift in those moments unheard—never to be heard again, grown old.

And, kneeling, she stared in woe at the fork in her hand, at the prickly roses that leaned their pale, quiet faces down from the fence: well, was she to greet about that? She had had her time, and now it was ended, she'd to follow the road that others took, into long wrinkles and greying hair and sourness and seats by the chimney-corner and a drowsy mumble as she heard the rain going by on its business in a closing dark. Finished: when her heart could still move to that singing, when at night in her bed she would turn in unease, wakeful, sweet as she knew herself, men had liked her well long ago, still the same body and still the same skin, that dimple still holding its secret place—Och, Ma would say that she wanted a man, that was all about it, as blunt and coarse as a farmer childe that watched his cattle in the heats of a Spring.

But there was more to it than that, some never knew it, but real enough, an antrin magic that bound you in one with the mind, not only the body of a man, with his dreams and desires, his loves, even hates—hate of Ewan, a wild boy's hate, passionless coldness of Robert in shadow, they'd given you hate with their love often enough, tears with such white tenderness as even now you might not unfold in memory,— here, at this moment, kneeling here, still, the August sun on your hair, dreaming and dreaming because Ma Cleghorn had blithered on the curse of a woman growing old, because you had heard a baby nearby wailing soft in a baby's unease!

And, suddenly remorseful at her terrible sweirty, she bent and dug and smoothed out the earth, raked it again to a loamy smoothness around the wide feet of the Michaelmas daisies, they looked a bit like Sim Leslie the bobby. Babies? (said her mind, though she tried to still it)—hadn't she had Ewan, perfect enough, grown up though he was, distant and cool? And wasn't he fine enough to have made with a little help from his father long syne? And she minded that other baby who had died in the days of the General Strike, he came over-soon that night she ran to warn the strikers who were out by the railway to blow up Segget High Brig. Oh, long since she'd minded that baby at all, the baby Michael, she'd never seen him, he'd died within an hour of his birth, killing something in Robert as he died, killing the last of the quean in herself she had thought through the long drowse of years in Segget, my bairn, the lost baby who might have been mine—

She heard light footsteps hesitating on the path and shook the mist from her eyes a minute before she looked up to see who it was, Ellen Johns, slim, sweet in a summer frock, a blue cloud her hair in the August day, soft dark down on her

lip, blue eyes like pansies, dark and wet, looking at Chris
queer, half-poised like a bird to turn about and fly off.

I'm sorry, Mrs Colquohoun, I didn't know—

Chris said *That I was weeping a bit? Old women often have a
weep, you know. Coming to help, or only to watch?*

Ellen said *I'll help* and squatted on long, pointed shoe-
heels and began to weed with long, pointed fingers—*I was
sick of sitting indoors and reading.*

Chris minded the book that Ma had seen and looked at her
with a little smile: *You were reading something about Birth
Control?*

And she didn't blush and didn't look up, just went on with
the weeding, quick and calm, intent, and nodded: *Yes. I
suppose I'll need it some time. Can't find out much and it sounds a
mess, but it's a thing that's got to be learnt. Don't you think so?*
and Chris nearly laughed, but didn't, *Yes, I think it has. But
you'll want a baby sometime?*

Ellen shook her head and said she didn't suppose so. There
were thousands of unwanted babies already and most of *them*
should never have been born. . . . *Can I have the fork to have a
go at those weeds?*

Thank Creeping Jay for the change at last, the six of you
turfed out of Furnaces, three to Stores and two to Machines,
Alick and Norman the lucky sods, they would be, they gave
more lip to old Dallas, they two, than any half-dozen in the
whole of Gowans and Gloag's: and he seemed to like them the
better for't!

Not that Stores was bad, a fine change from the Furnace,
your own bench and lists and pigeon-holes, rows on rows of
the tools and castings, birns of stuff to unload for the Shops,
finished with being a damn kid in the Works, though the
older sods that had been there awhile looked gey glum when
you got your shift. And they'd something to look glum about,
poor muckers, for afore the change had been a week over
there were six of the older hands got the sack, on to the Broo,
och, hell, you couldn't help it. It was just the way that things
were run.

Ewan Tavendale had been moved to the manager's office, blue-printing, they liked his prints in the shops, a clever young Bulgar as you'd found out in Furnaces. You didn't see much of him the first week or so, but syne he came into the Stores one morning and started talking to the foreman chap, wee Eddie Grant, he listened awhile and said *Ach to hell, I'll have nothing to do with it. Look out yourself, you'll be getting in the faeces.* But Ewan, he looked fairly the toff again, clean hands and suit, hair trig and neat, just nodded, *All right, if you feel like that. But maybe it'll be your turn next for the sack.* Wee Eddie burbled *Me? What the hell! And who's to take MY place I'd like to know? Another of you whoreson apprentice sods?*, and Ewan said nothing, just nodded to you, *Hello, Bob!* and walked out, what the hell was he up to now?

Well, it was soon all over the works what it was, he was trying to stir up the Union men to threaten a strike if Gowans and Gloag carried on with the plan they'd had year in, year out—taking on apprentices and sacking the old ones, they saved a fair sum on the weekly wage.

You knew it was Ewan had started the thing, every body knew, and the story came down to the Stores that the manager had had him on the carpet for't, Ewan hadn't denied it and the manager had asked if he knew what would happen to him, stirring up trouble? And Ewan had said Oh yes, he knew well, he'd be sacked when his apprenticeship was done. And the manager had roared *Well then, less of it. You've had your warning, you won't get another.* And Ewan had said *Yes, thanks, I've been warned.*

There was nothing else for a chap to say, the Union wouldn't move a foot in the business, it was crammed with Broo folk to the lid already; and the stour died down; and the gleyed Stores mucker who had sneered afore at Ewan as gentry said *What do you think of your toff sod now?* and you said *He'd the guts to try something, anyhow, more than a sheep like you ever would.*

Then Norman came round in the dinner hour with a funny like story you could hardly believe, he said that Ewan'd ta'en up with the Reds, Jim Trease and his crowd, and was going to

their meetings. And you said *Away, he's not so daft*, and
Norman said *Ay, hell, but he is. What's the use of the Reds to
any body? They just get out the Broo men and march down the
Mile and get their heads bashed in in the end*. Well, surely Ewan
knew that as well; why was he taking up with them, then?
Norman said he was damned if he knew, some rubbish about
all working parties co-operating, Ewan had asked him to go
to a meeting but he'd said he wouldn't, he wasn't so soft, he'd
a quean to take out on a Sunday, him, not mess about with a
lot of Reds who were just damned traitors to the Labour
Movement. Not that *it* was worth a faeces either. As for
Alick, he'd gone skite, same as Ewan, anything Ewan said
went down with *him*.

Well, hell, that was coarse enough to hear, but whatever
made Ewan take up with the Reds? Him a gentleman, too, as
you all knew he was though he tried to deny it and that time at
your home when he came to tea had acted so fine, you'd all of
you liked him, it had been nearly worth spending the day
before scrubbing out the place, and hiding the twin, the
daftie, and getting in cakes for the tea. So you went now and
looked him up in the office, making on you wanted a chit for
some tools, he was sitting at his desk among the office
muckers, all with their patted hair and posh ties, young
college sods no better than you though they tried on their airs
if you didn't watch.

Ewan cried *Hello, Bob!* and you said *Hello*, and *Ewan, I'd
like to speak to you sometime*. And he said *Right, let's get out a
minute*, and out he came and you asked him point-blank. And
he said *I didn't know you'd be interested*, and you said *Hell, I'm
not*, and he said *Yes, you are. Look here, come along to the
Saturday meeting, in the Gallowgate, 3 Pitcarles Wynd*. And
afore you well kenned what it was you had done you'd
promised to be there—oh, sod the whole business!

But there you were at the chapp of seven, a little bit room
with maybe twenty in't, chaps and some queans all much of
your age, chairs and a table and a chair for the chairman and a
picture of a chap above the table that had cheated the barber
from birth by his look, that awful coarse old billy Marx. Then

Ewan came along and made you sit down, and went back to the table to sit by a lassie, a stuck-up bitch with black hair, fine legs, she'd a pen and a lot of papers afore her. And there was a piano up in the corner with a lad sitting at it, and he started to play and you all got up and sang about England arising, the long, long night was over, though the damn thing had barely yet set in, Christ, what a perfect fool you felt not knowing the words, a quean next you pushed a book in your hands, smirked at you, trying to get off, would you say? So you made on to sing, glowering about, there was Alick Watson, bawling like a bellows, if England didn't awake she must be stone deaf, and another chap you'd seen down in Gowans, an older apprentice out of Machines. Syne the singing stopped and down you all sat, and Ewan looked at the stuck-up get and said *Miss Johns will now read the minutes.*

It was only as the quean was doing that that you knew she was English, Haw-Haw-Really-Quite, and found out what the blasted meeting was about, Ewan and some others were getting up a party for the young in Duncairn, neither Labour nor Communist nor yet in opposition, but to try and keep the two of them working in harness for the general good of the working class, get rid of the cowardice and sloth of Labour and cut out the nonsensical lying of the Communists, the older generation in the workers' parties had made an idiot mess of things, it was up to the young to straighten things out, join this new workers' league in Duncairn. You said to yourself you'd be damned if you would, Christ, they'd have you out with a banner next. But then Ewan stood up and started to speak, quiet, not bawling blue hell like the Reds or cracking soft jokes like a Labour man, but just in an ordinary voice and way, telling what he thought this young league could do to waken up all the young workers in Duncairn, get strong enough till the time might come when it would take over Duncairn itself. First, the membership: they'd twenty or less, what they'd now to discuss was a big drive for members: *Six minute speeches, not a minute more, and practical suggestions, not oratory, please.*

A red-headed kid of a quean got up, near gave you a fit with what she wanted done—the whole lot go out and march down the Mile with flags and collecting boxes, just, and hold a meeting in the Castlegate. That was the way to win new members and serve the workers. . . . And you thought she was daft, had she never seen a worker? The Bulgars would laugh and tell her what she wanted was some chap to serve her in another way. Then the lad from Gowans and Gloag's got up and said what they should do was smuggle a lot of leaflets inside the Shops, and pass them round quiet, you'd get interest that way. And the quean who had given you the glad eye like a Garbo got up and said in a he-haw voice, Christ, another of the bloody toffs, *What's wanted is to advertise the meetings and then hold readings from the great revolutionary poets, beginning with the greatest of all, William Morris*. And after that every body was over stunned to say more, except young Ewan, who'd been staring at the roof.

He got up and said it wasn't much use marching down the Mile, they'd only get their heads smashed in by the bobbies. Leaflets in the factories wouldn't help much, no body read leaflets, there were too many about. And the comrade who had suggested reading William Morris had surely meant the Dundee *Sunday Post.*. . . . What was needed was something light and attractive.

And at that the English quean beside him, ay, a nice leg, got up and said what they wanted was a tanner hop—she said just that, fair vulgar-like, though you'd heard by now that she was a school-ma'am. She said that would bring in members thick and the dances would pay for themselves twice over.

Ewan asked if he'd put that as a resolution? And the schoolteacher said *Yes*, and Ewan put it, and you heard yourself saying *I second that*, your ears near burning off your head with shame, Creeping Jay, you were in for it now. And only as you were coming away from the meeting did it dawn on you with a hell of a shock that now you were some kind of ruddy Red.

Ellen waited for Ewan to lock up the room, the air was a stagnant unstirred pool, out by the Crossgate the autumn night lay low in pale saffron over Footforthie. As they turned from the door they could see far down through the winding corridors of the Gallowgate the smoulder of the sun as it lost itself in the smoking lowe of Footforthie by night. Ewan said there was night-work again at the shipyards, even Gowans and Gloag's were looking up a bit, didn't look much, did it, like capitalism's collapse?

They were trudging together up through the streets, half-lighted, smell of urine and old food seeping out from dark doorways, sometimes a grunt as a man would turn in his sleep in the heat, sometimes a snuffle of wakeful children. Ellen said nothing for a little while and Ewan had half-forgotten her when she asked of a sudden: *Are you losing heart?*

He said *Eh?* and then *Oh, about capitalism? Losing heart would do a lot of good, wouldn't it?*

She said then something, queer kid, he was to remember: *Anyhow, your heart's not in it at all. Only your head and imagination.*

—*And I'm not in much danger of losing either. You don't quarrel with History and its pace of change any more than you quarrel with the law of gravitation. History's instruments, the workers, 'll turn to us some time—even though it's only for a sixpenny hop. You or I to see to hiring the hall?*

Ellen said she thought it had better be him, the only one suitable was the Lower School, and they didn't trust her too much there already. And Ewan looked at her, pale kid, tired kid, and felt an indifferent touch of compassion. Where else might she be if it wasn't for this belief she'd smitten on him?—at a dance, at the pictures, in a pretty dress. And he dropped the thought, with indifference again. Much better as she was, seeing she wasn't half-witted.

They were into the Lower Cowgate by then, ten o'clock and the pubs were spewing out the plebs, raddled with drink, kids crying in the gutter, Ewan saw a man hit a woman in the jaw, she fell with a scream and a bobby came up and an eddy of the crowd came swirling around, and they couldn't see more, going up Sowans Lane. But half way up they came on a woman pulling at the coat of a man who was lying half in a doorway, half in the gutter. *Och, come on home, you daft Bulgar*, she was saying, *or the bobbies'll damn soon land you in the nick*. But the childe wasn't keen to go home at all, he was saying what they wanted was a little song—*Come on, you bitch, and give's a bit tune*. And the woman said of all the whoreson's gets she'd ever met he was the worst: and what song did he want then, the neep-headed nout? And he said he wanted the songs his mucking mother sang, and Ewan and Ellen didn't hear more, they were out of the Sowans Lane by then, on to the Long Brig where it spanned the Forthie, and stopping to breathe from the Gallowgate fug.

And then, as Ewan stood there and whistled under-breath, indifferently, far away in his thoughts, he became aware of Ellen Johns by his side wiping her eyes in helpless mirth: *History's the funniest of jokes sometimes. If we'd had the courage of our convictions do you know what we would have done back there?*

He said *No*, and stared a cool surprise.

—*Why*, STOPPED AND SANG HIM SOME WILLIAM MORRIS!

Ma Cleghorn had taken Chris to the Talkies, to get out of the stew of the house for a while, she said she was turning to a cockroach, near, and Chris to an earthworm out in that yard. Meg would see to the tea for the folk, wouldn't she, eh? and Meg said she would, Meg had kittled up a lot of late, Chris thought as she went to her room to change. When she came down Ma was waiting for her, dressed all in her braws with a big black hat, with beadwork upon it, and a meikle brooch pinned in under one of her chins. *There you are, lass, though, God be here, you're wearing so little I can see your drawers*. And Chris said *Surely not*, and stooped to see *Anyhow, I can't wear more than I'm wearing*. And Ma said maybe but it was a damned shame to go about with a figure like that, half-happed and stirring the men to temptation. And they'd better get on, near the time already, what in Auld Nick's name were they gossiping for?

So they got on the tram and soughed down Royal Mile, and up Little James Street to the Picturedrome; and paid for their seats and went in and sat down; and Chris felt sleepy almost as soon as she sat, and yawned, pictures wearied her nearly to death, the flickering shadows and the awful voices, the daft tales they told and the dafter news. She fell asleep through the cantrips a creature was playing, a mouse dressed up in breeks like a man, and only woke up as Ma shook her: *Hey, the meikle film's starting now, lassie, God damn't, d'you want to waste a whole ninepenny ticket?*

So Chris had to stay awake and see that, all about a lassie who worked in New York and was awful poor but awful respectable, though she seemed to live in a place like a palace with a bath ten feet in length and three deep, and wore underclothes that she couldn't have afforded, some childe had paid for them on the sly. But the picture said No, through its nose, not her, she was awful chaste but sore chased as well, a beast of a man in her office, the manager, galloping about the screen and aye wanting to seduce the lassie by night or by day. And instead of letting him and getting it over or taking him a crack in the jaw and leaving, she kept coming home in tears to the bath, and taking off her underthings one by one, but hiding her breasts and her bottom, fair chaste. Syne she met with a man that managed a theatre, though he looked from his face as though he managed a piggery and had been born in one and promoted for merit, a flat cold slob of a ham of a face with little eyes twinkling in the slob like currants, he was the hero and awful brave, and he took the lass to the theatre and made her sing that the skies were black and she was blue, and something that rhymed with that, not spew, and all the theatre audiences went wild not with rage, but joy, they'd been dropped on their heads when young: and the lassie became a famous actress and the film did a sudden close-up of her face with a tear of gratitude two feet long trembling like a jelly from her lower eyelid. And she and the slob were getting on fine, all black and blue, my lovely Lu, when along came the leader of a birn of brutes, a gang, and kidnapped the lass, grinding his teeth in an awful stamash to sleep with her; and took her away to an underground den; and was just about to begin at last, and Chris was just thinking it fairly was time, would they never get the job over and done?—when in rushed the hero and a fight began and chairs were smashed and vases and noses, and the lass crouched down with her camiknicks showing, but respectable still, she wouldn't yield an inch to anything short of a marriage licence. And that she got in the end, all fine, with showers of flowers and the man with the face like a mislaid ham cuddling her up with a kiss that looked as though he was eating his supper when the thing came banging to an end at last.

Ma said God be here, now wasn't that fine? It must be a right canty place, this New York, childes charging about like bulls in a park trying to grab any lass they saw—even though the creatures were all bone and no breast and would give a man as much joy in bed as a kipper out of an ice-box, you'd think. Ay, she'd fair made a mistake a twenty years back when she stopped her Jim emigrating, faith. He'd been keen as anything on going to America, a man had loaned him a bit of a book about Presidents being just plain working folk, born in cabins and the queerest places; and maybe Jim thought that he had a chance, he'd been born next door to a cabin, near, his mother was bairned on the trawler *Jess*. But Ma'd put him off, like a meikle fool, to think she might now have been out in New York with big Jews chasing her in motor-cars and offering to buy her her undies free. . . . And God, the bit show was over, it seemed.

But she wouldn't have it that they should go home, they'd have tea at Woolworth's in the Royal Mile. And in they went in the Saturday crush, full of soldiers and bairns and queans, folk from the country, red and respectable, an eident wife with a big shopping bag buying up sixpenny tins of plums and her goodman standing beside her ashamed, feared he'd be seen by a crony in Woolies, and she'd be telling him, *Look, Willy, such cheap! Mighty, I'll need a pound of that;* and buy and buy till he'd near be ruined. And hungry Broo folk buying up biscuits, and queans with their jingling bags and paint, poor things, trying on the tin bits of rings, and mechanic loons at the wireless counter, and the Lord alone knew who wasn't in Woolies, a roaring trade and a stink to match, Ma fought her way through the crush like a trawler taking the tide from Footforthie and Chris followed behind and felt sorry for a man who'd left his feet where Ma's came down, he cried *Hey, you?* and Ma said *Ay? Anything to say?* and he said *Ay, I have. Who do you think you are—Mussolini?* And Ma cried over her shoulder *Faith, I could wear his breeks and not feel ashamed. You never had a thing under yours, you runt.*

So up at last, sitting down in the tea-room, Ma ordering eggs and scones and pancakes and butter and honey in little jars, Chris gasped *But whatever's all the feast for?* Ma said Och, she was sick of cooking herself, and the sight of those feeds that they had in America fairly stirred up a body's stomach. Losh, wasn't it fine to think of the lodgers sossing on their own?—*though your Ewan and our Ellen, the sleek wee cat, are out again together the day. Would you think the two of them are getting off?*

Chris said not them, they had just gone Socialist as young folk would, some plan they had to link up the Labour folk with the Reds. Ma nearly choked on a mouthful of egg, God be here, whatever did they want to do that for? Chris said for good—or so the two thought, and Ma said they'd think mighty different soon, the Reds were just awful, look what they did in Russia to that poor Tsar creature back in the War—shot him down in a cellar full of coal, and buried the childe without as much as God bless you. Chris said she didn't know anything about it though it sounded as though it maybe messed up the coals, as far as she knew neither Ellen nor Ewan had yet shot anybody, even in a cellar. Ma said No, but she wouldn't trust Ewan, a fine loon, but that daft-like glower in his eyes—*Och, this Communism stuff's not canny, I tell you, it's just a religion though the Reds say it's not and make out that they don't believe in God. They're dafter about Him than the Salvationists are, and once it gets under a body's skin he'll claw at the itch till he's tirred himself.*

Chris said she supposed she thought the same, had always thought so, but that didn't matter, if Ewan wanted God she wouldn't try and stop him; there was plenty of mess to redd up in the world on the road to where He was maybe to be found. Ma said she didn't believe there was, this daft Red religion was maybe needed in places where there was a lot of corruption, coarse kings that ran away with folks' silver and prime ministers just drunken sots. But where would you find the like in Duncairn? . . . *Now, don't start on me, we'll just away home. Eh me, to think of those New York childes tearing after the women like yon! Where would you see the like in Duncairn?*

With one thing and another it was late that night afore Chris went up the stairs to her bed, Ewan had looked round the kitchen door and cried good night a good hour before, Ma had gone off to dream of New York, the rest of the lodgers were sound in their beds. And Chris was taking off her clothes, slow, tired to death with the evening's outing—why did folk waste their time in touns, in filth and stour and looking at shadows when they might have slipped away up the Howe and smelt the smell of the harvest—oh! bonny lying somewhere on a night like this! . . . And just as she sat and thought of that, not sad but tired, she heard a commotion above her head, the clatter of footsteps, and syne a door bang, a woman's voice—for a minute she was back in the Picturedrome, watching and hearing that shadow-play that was never limned in a toun like Duncairn—And then as a bigger stamash broke out she opened the door and ran up the stairs.

Ake Ogilvie told the tale the next day to Ma Cleghorn, Ma lying at rest in her bed, she'd gone to bed with a steek in her side and was lying fair wearied till Ake looked in. He said *Ay, woman, I hear you're not well?* and Ma said his hearing was still in fair order—*sit down and gie's a bit of your crack. How are you and your Provost creature getting on?*

So Ake filled up his pipe, sitting sonsy, green-eyed, with

his curling mouser and Auld Nick brows, a pretty childe as Ma had thought often. And he said the Provost's bit influence had been fairly heard in this house last night, hadn't the mistress been waked by the noise? And Ma asked *What noise? Was the Provost here?* and Ake said No, God, the lass escaped that, it was only one of his Bacchic chums.

Syne he started to tell of the Saturday outing of the Duncairn Council to High Scaur Hill. Ma knew of the new waterworks built there?—Ay, she'd known, faith, or at least her rates had. Well, the official inspection had been billed for the Saturday and the Provost had come to Ake at the sawmill and said that he'd want him to join the bit outing, he'd want his opinion on the timber-work. And Ake had said Ay, he didn't much mind, though he'd little liking for councillors and such. *Still, the poor Bulgars have to live somehow, haven't they, Jimmy?* and the Provost grinned sick and said he was still the same old Ake.

Well, the whole lot set out on the official treat, Speight, Bailie Brown and the Dean of Guild, all the Bailie billies and a wheen hangers-on, two coach loads hired with the Duncairn rates to give a treat to the City Fathers. And who should the *Daily Runner* send but the wee Mr Piddle, like a snake on the spree, he squeezed into the back of the Provost's coach, *he-he!* and sat down by the side of Ake with his little note-book fluttering, grinning like an ape, the City Fathers all brave in their braws. And off the jing-bang had rolled to the Scaur.

Well, they got out there at the dinner-time, the staff all drawn up ready for inspection, and Puller, of Puller and Grind's, the contractors, was there with the finest of feeds made ready for the Duncairn Council and afore you could wink the contractor had wheeled in Jimmy the Provost and all his tail and sat them down to a four-course gobble, specially made and sent up from the Mile, with wines in plenty—they needed them after the heat of the drive. Mr Piddle nipped in and sat by Ake and wolfed into the fodder like a famished ferret, with his wee note-book held brisk at hand for words of wisdom from the City Fathers. But they'd hardly a word, Provost Jimmy or the lot, they'd gotten such an awful thirst to slock.

That was about noon; about three the Fathers made up the mischances they called their minds to go up at last and look at the works. Jimmy Speight stood up and started a speech about how these works were a fine piece of work (aye, a habbering gawpus with his words, poor Jimmy), and carried through in every particular a credit to Duncairn and Puller and Grind. He might have gone on for God knows how long but that Ake beside him pulled the old sod down and whispered *You haven't seen the thing yet.* And Jimmy said *Neither we have; that's suspicious,* and turned on Puller with a gey stern look, but got suddenly mixed in a yawn and a hiccup. When Ake had slapped his back out of that they all set out for the new waterworks.

It was nearly a quarter of a mile from the shed where Puller had spread them their brave bite of lunch, hot as hell the sun; and the first man to fall by the wayside was Labour's respectable Bailie Brown, he sat down and said he would take it on trust, the workers knew that he was their friend, he was awful tired and would need a bit sleep. So they shook him a bit and syne left him snoring like a pig let loose overlong on a midden, and went on a bit further till the Dean of Guild, he'd been swaying a bit with his meikle solemn face, suddenly wheeled round on wee Councillor Clarke and told him he'd never forgiven him, never, for that time he had voted an increase in the tramwaymen's wages the last year of the War—September, it was. And wee Clarke said the Dean was a havering skate, it wasn't the last year, but the year afore; and they started to argue the matter out till wee Clarke had enough, he punched the Dean one, all the folk around you may well be sure looking shocked as hell and enjoying themselves, the Dean sat down of a sudden on the path and looked solemner than ever and syne started to sing; and the Lord Provost who'd been looking on at it all, very intent, but with both eyes crossed, got fairly as mixed in his mind as his eyes and thought he was down at the Beach Pavilion adjudicating on the Boxing Finals, and started a speech about

the manhood of Duncairn, how pleased he was to see the
young men were taking up the manly art of defence, and not
rotting their minds with seditious doctrines. And Ake,
standing by and wondering quiet what the hell they'd do if
they ever met in with a real booze-up, he himself was as
drouthy as a lime-kiln, near, saw Mr Piddle, with a fuzzy bit
look, taking it all down in his little note-book with a carbon
copy for the *Tory Pictman*; and they left the Dean singing
that his Nannie was awa', and resumed the trek to the High
Scaur works.

Well, believe it or not, they never got there, Puller had the
wind up by then just awful, he saw he'd drammed up the
Councillors over-much, if he took the boozed Bulgars up to
the works they'd more'n likely fall head-first in. So he
rounded them back to the lunch-shed again, Ake dandering
behind with a bit of a laugh, Jimmy Speight stopping every
now and again for another bit speech, he was fair wound up.
Puller tried to sober them up with coffee, two of the
workmen carried the Dean, they found Bailie Brown had
started to crawl home and when they tried to get him to stand
he said he was only playing at bears, couldn't a man play at
bears if he liked?

Ake saw Mr Piddle taking that down as well, he was just a
kind of stenographic machine by then. But the Council
wouldn't have much of the coffee, the Dean said if Puller and
Grind expected them to pass the new water-works, the works
in the disgraceful state they were in, they were sore mistaken
he could tell them that. And Jimmy Speight started his
seventeenth speech, this time about corruption rearing its
ugly head like the sword of Damocles in every avenue. So
Puller called to the waiter childes to bring in the whisky
bottles again, they might as well go home soaked as go home
soft.

So our City Fathers lay the afternoon there, soaking up
truly, but Ake drinking cannily—*and I guess if a pickle of
those Communist childes had been there they'd have got enough
propaganda to start a Soviet the morn's morning*. It was seven
o'clock before Mr Puller could get the soaked whoresons

back in their coaches. Then he routed out Mr Piddle from a sleep in the grass and told him he expected he'd say nothing of this, and Mr Piddle took that down in his note-book as well, but said *he-he* he knew discretion, he was a man of the world as well. And old Puller muttered something about Christ help the world and then dosed Mr Piddle with a dram or so to put him into a right good tune and bunged him in aside Bailie Brown; and off they all drove back to Duncairn, the coach-drivers were told to take it slow and see they didn't get back till dark.

Well, they halted up at the top Mile rank and pushed the Councillors into taxis; but Ake and Mr Piddle made for a tram; and were soon at their lodgings in Windmill Place; and syne the bittie of trouble began.

Ake took the creature along to his room, and took off his boots and gave him a bit shake, and went off to his own bed, thinking no more on't. But it seemed that the outing to the High Scaur works had fair let loose the ill passions of Piddle, he made up his mind to go up the stairs and pay his respects to little Miss Johns.

So, forgetting he'd taken off most things but his breeks, he padded up the stairs and knocked at the door, and went in, *he-he!* Miss Johns was in bed, the lass sat up and asked what he wanted and he closed the door and giggled at her, soft, it doesn't seem she was frightened, much. But she nipped out of bed as Piddle came nearer, and called out *Ewan!*; and a minute later there was a hell of a crash.

Ake was taking off his boots when he heard that crash, and he tore from his room just as Mistress Colquohoun tore out of hers, she'd less of a wardrobe on than he had and fair looked a canty bit dame for a man to handle, he couldn't but think. Ake cried *What's up, up there, would you say?* and she laughed in her cool-like, sulky way *Sounds more as though the ceiling was down;* and up the two of them ran together and there Ake set eyes on as bonny a picture as he'd seen for long, Mr Piddle lying over the bed like a pock, the lassie Ellen Johns in a scrimp of a nightie, all flushed and bonny, red spot on each cheek, and young Ewan Tavendale looking at Piddle—the two young creatures with their earnest bit faces and their blue-black hair a sheen in the light looking down at Piddle like a couple of bairns at a puzzling and nasty thing on a road.

Ake cried to the quean *Has he done you harm?* and she answered back cool, *Not him. He's just drunk*, and looked at Ewan that was standing beside her: *You shouldn't have hit him; that was quite unnecessary.*

Syne they all looked at Ewan's knuckles and saw they were skinned and dripping blood, it seemed he hadn't known himself, he looked kind of dazed and now wakened up. *Yes, sorry. Damn silly thing to do. Ake, will you help me carry him down?*

So the two of them carried him off like a corp leaving the women to redd up the soss, the Piddle childe slept through it all like a bairn. Ake said to Ewan as they laid Piddle in bed that he'd given the poor sod a gey mishandling, and Ewan said so it seemed, he knew little about it. He'd heard Miss Johns call and then things had gone cloudy—interesting, supposed it was much the same thing happened to stags in rutting time.

Ma said B'God 'twas the best tale she'd heard since a gelding of her father's at Monymusk had chased a brood mare into a ditch—*why didn't you let on to me about it?*

This was to Chris after dinner that day, Chris shook her head, it wasn't worth mention. Mr Piddle had made a fool of himself, there was no harm done, he was only a bairn.

Ma said *And what about your Ewan, then?* and Chris said she thought that that had been straightened, Ewan had told Mr Piddle he was sorry and Mr Piddle had asked him *He-he! What for?* he'd had no memory of the happening at all. Now Ma mustn't worry, she was just to lie still, the house would be fine and all the things in't.

Ma shook her head: *And to think of me lying flat on my back when there's all these fine stravaigings about! Speak of New York—damn't, it's not in't!*

October came in long swaths of rain pelting the glinting streets of Duncairn. Going up and down the Windmill Steps with her baskets of groceries Chris would see the toun far alow under the rain's onset move and shake and shiver a minute like an old grey collie shaking in sleep. The drive of wind and rain cleared the wynds of the fouller smells; down in the Mile, shining in mail, the great houses rose above the wet birl and drum of the trams, buses creeping about like beasts in a fog, snorting, and blowing the wet from their faces, Duncairn getting out its reefers and bonnets, in drifting umbrella'ed afternoon tides the half-gentry poured down the Mile every day. Up in the house it was canty and fine, the wind breenging unbreeked into room after room whenever you opened a shutter a bit, Miss Murgatroyd thought it was Such Rough, and John Cushnie came home from Raggie Robertson's store and said they were doing a roaring trade, him and Raggie, in selling a new line in raincoats. Jock the cat shivered so close to the range Chris wondered he didn't get in and look out.

Ma got up the second day of her illness, she said it was no more than sweirty, just, she must redd out the kitchen press today. But half-way through she gave a bit groan, Chris caught her as she tottered and turned white, Meg was at hand and lended a hand, they got her to sit in a chair in a minute. Then Chris said *It's back to your bed for you, my woman*, and back to it they took her, Ma puffing and panting, *God Almighty, lass, don't look feared about a small thing like this. There's more old folk than me in their time been ta'en with a bit of a paich, you know. Get out for a bit of fresh air yourself.*

Chris went for a walk to fetch the doctor, a thin young country childe with pop eyes, he came in his car and looked at Ma and gave her a prod and listened to her lungs and said what she wanted was quietness and rest and not to excite herself on a thing. But to Chris he said she'd a swollen heart, serious enough, she'd have to look out. Chris asked what she'd better do, then? and the doctor asked were Ma's relatives near, and Chris remembered about the niece, only she didn't know where she bade. The doctor said that it couldn't be helped—*try and find out without fearing the old wife.*

So Chris waited till Ma was sleeping again and then went and took a bit look through her desk, beside the great curtain, worm-eaten, old, bundles of papers tied in neat pilings, a fair soss of ribbons and cards and circulars, paid bills and bits of tow and old brooches and safety-pins and a ring or so, and some letters fading off at the edges, Chris didn't read them or heed to them except to peer at the writer's name. She found no trace of the niece's address in the pigeon-holes, Ma sleeping as the dead in the bed out under the shadow of the patterned wall. So she opened the lower drawers, old clothes, old papers, a bundle of photos, a little pack tied up in tape which came away in her hands as she looked, she stared at the thing a puzzled minute.

It was the photo of a little lad with Ma's nose and eyes and promise of her padding, keeking at something the photographer did, no mistaking Ma's face in his. And below was written 'James at 2' and inside the package two other things, tawdry and faded, a hank of bairn's hair, brown soft, dead and old, it had lost its shine, and a crumpled scrap of ancient crape. Long, long ago it all had happened. Why had Ma never told she'd a son?

And Chris stood with the things in her hand in a dream looking at the faded, puctured face of the little lad who had died, she supposed, when he was no more than a little lad, he'd finished quick with a look round about and gone from Duncairn and gone from Ma, queer that such things should be—all the care and heed and tears of pain that had once been given this little childe far back there in the years where he twiddled his toes. And he'd ceased with it all, a mistake, a journey he would not make, no rain to hear or grow to knowledge of the dark, sad things of life at all, no growing to books and harkening to dreams, like Ewan—no growing to be a queer young man far from Ma and all she had hoped, only leaving her a searing memory awhile and then a quiet glow that lasted forever. Not leaving an unease that washed as a tide through one's heart, unending . . . dreaming on Ewan.

How she hated the splatter of the driving rain!

*

As that rain held on and pelted Duncairn with the closing in of the storm-driven clouds, great cumulus shapes that came wheeling down from the heights of the far brown lour of the Mounth, the roof-tops glistered in the lights of the Mile and far and near the gutters gurgled, eddied and swam, piercing down to a thousand drains, down through the latest Council diggings, down to dark spaces and forgotten pools, in one place out through an antique tunnel that the first Pict settlers had made and lined with uncalsayed stones, set deep in earth, more than two thousand years before. And far and near as the evening came under the stour a thousand waters by gutters and wynd and the swollen Forthie, dark, brimming, wheeled down through the darkling night to seek the splurge and plunge of the sea pelting beyond the dunes of the beach. Ellen heard its cry long ere they reached it, harsh, soft, the patter of the rain on the waves.

Then Ewan and she had climbed through the Links and up the railings to the desolate front, wet-shining, with hardly the glimmer of a light. Here the rain caught their faces in swaths, warm rain, like corn felled in a reaper's bout, some Reaper high in the scudding lift. Ewan said _There's a shelter further along. Let's run for it_, and caught her hand and they ran together, both hatless, both wet, and gained its lithe and sat on the bench, panting, staring out at the dark.

Ellen closed her eyes and leaned back her head and stretched out her nice legs, she knew they were nice, and lovely and tingly, and put her hands up behind her wet hair. That run was fun, hard to believe that this was Duncairn, here in the darkness with the forgotten sea.

She peeped at Ewan, sitting near, queer Scotch boy, solemn and not, wonder if he's ever kissed a girl? And she thought not likely and was angry with herself behaving just like an idiot shop-girl. She'd been tired and drowsy tonight with that long, stuffy meeting of the League, Semple had come and talked for the Reds, she'd thought him a catty and smelly bore. So when it finished and they came out into the rain flooding the Crossgate she'd said to Ewan _Let's go a walk before we go home_, half-expecting he'd snub her, he could do that easily. But instead he'd said *Yes, if you like, where'll we go?* and she'd said *The Beach* and he'd said *Right-o*, not thinking her silly as any other would, Duncairn had stopped going down to the Beach now that Snellie Guff and his Funny Scotch Band had finished their season assassinating music. So down through the squelching Links they'd come and here they were, and there, a creaming unquiet, the sea.

And Ewan said suddenly out of the darkness *This would be a splendid night for a bathe.*

Ellen turned to the glimmer of his face: *What, now?—Why not? The rain's warm enough and I'm sticky still with the Crossgate heat.* The glimmer grew blurred: *I'm going to. Shan't be out long.*

Ellen said *You can't. You haven't a bathing-dress—or towels—or anything.*

—*That's the beauty of it. Nothing at all.*

And supposing he caught cramp down there alone? Ellen swallowed: *It might be fun. I'm coming in as well.*

As she threw off her coat and unbuckled her shoes she saw him about to go out of the shelter. Funny the tingle that touched her then, cool enough though she was: *There's plenty of room for both of us, isn't there?*

He called *I suppose so*, and stripped in like haste with herself, it was cold in the shelter, a long pointer of wind stroked Ellen's back as she wrenched off her stockings, Ewan asked suddenly out of the dark if a girl always took off her stockings last?

Ellen raised her head and saw him a white glimmer, goodness, shouldn't look; but why shouldn't she? He was looking at her, she supposed, thank goodness couldn't see much. She said *Yes, I think so. I've never noticed. Oh, hell, it's cold!*

Ewan said *It's not. Come on. Can you swim?* And Ellen said she could or was trying to say it when the rain-laden wind whipped the words from her mouth, on the promenade they were caught and twirled, she thought in a sudden panic, *This is mad we'll never get back*, and next minute found Ewan had caught her wrist: *Down together. I know the way.*

They ran. The way lay over the sand, soft and wet and slimily warm, the pelting on the water drew their feet, they forgot Duncairn and the lights behind, all the hates and imaginings that drowned those sad children lost from the winds and tides, rain at night, sting of flesh smitten under rain. Suddenly Ellen's legs seemed stroked with fire: they ran out into the play of the sea.

Beyond the shore-beat they met a great wave, Ewan tried to cry something, failed, dived, vanished, Ellen felt herself lost, laughed desperately, dived as well. Ewan suddenly beside her: *Let's get back. Over-rough*, and she turned about, she seemed sheathed in fire, saltily grainily slipping through water, she fought off cramp, struggled, and found her feet abruptly on the shore again. . . . Idiots! Goodness, what idiots!

Next minute, wading, she gained the wet sand, saw a glister beside her, Ewan Tavendale, head bent and wiping the water from his hair. Then he whispered *Sh—look at that!*

Ellen peered up at the promenade and her heart peered up in her throat. The shelter had squatted dark on the slope but now it was lighted with a moving light: Some man or other had gone in there and found their clothes, he'd switched on a torch—

Ewan whispered there was nothing else for it but to tackle him, and they ran up, the wind in Ellen's hair, she thought *I don't care, it's fun*, she felt warm, suddenly tingling from head to heel. Ewan glimmered in front: at the sound of the pelt of their feet on the sand the light switched about and Ellen for a moment saw Ewan, she thought *He's nice hips*, and at that the light vanished, Ewan had caught it and flung it down the Beach.

Now then, now then, what's this that you're up to? Do you know you're assaulting the police, my lad?

Ellen nipped past and caught up her clothes, struggled into her vest, into her knickers, the bulk of the bobby hiding Ewan from her. He was saying *You'll come along to the Station with me, the two of you, there'll be a bonny bit charge, public indecency down at the Beach.*

Ellen gave a gasp, Ewan said nothing, she could see him move quickly and dimly, getting in his clothes, he was dressing more quickly than she was, she knew, her shift stuck to her, it didn't matter, yet she felt cold now, her mind a tumult. Oh, they COULDN'T charge anybody with THAT, just for nothing—

Come along, you're all ready. Mind, none of your tricks. Here you—this to Ewan—*have you matches on you?*

Ewan made on that he hadn't heard, the bobby swore and made to come between them. It was then that Ewan acted, Ellen saw the play, an instant, dim as a bad-made film, the bobby vanished, there came a crash and a slither from below, Ewan had said *There's a match for you*, and flung him from the top of the high Beach steps.

He grabbed her hand *Run like hell!* and they ran like that till she gasped that she couldn't do more, else she'd burst. He told her not to do that, it would be a mess, and released his hold, and halted beside her.

Out in the Links they stood listening: Nothing, nothing but the far cry of a seabird desolate about the turning tide, forward the glimmer of Duncairn in the rain warm and safe and all unaware. Ellen asked with a sudden catch of breath: *What if the bobby has been badly hurt?* and Ewan said *Let him hurt, it will do the swine good,* cool and unperturbed, she felt sick a moment. *It was only that half-wit Sergeant Sim Leslie who used to dig with my mother, you know.*

Things were fair kittling up at Gowans and Gloag, a lad had to keep nippy with the new tools that came, packing and storing and wondering about them, damned queer frames for new castings, too, nobody kenned what the bits were for. But there were orders enough to hand and the management was taking on folk again, it just showed you the papers were right what they said—that the Crisis was over and trade coming back.

And meeting Ewan Tavendale outside the office you cried to him, *Ay! Ewan, what about the collapse of capitalism now? Doesn't look very much like it, does it?* He said *No? D'you know*

what the new orders are for? You said you didn't and you
didn't much care as long as it gave a bit work to folk, better
any kind of a decent job than being pitched off on the bloody
Broo.

Ewan said *And better getting ready stuff to blow out another
man's guts in his face than starving yourself with an empty guts?
Is that what you think? Then your head's gone soft.*

You'd never seen him look angry before, you felt angry
yourself and damned hurt as well, you asked who the hell he
was calling names and he said *Clean your ears and you'll hear
quick enough. Bob, be up at the League room tonight. There's a
meeting on of all the chaps I can bring.*

Who the hell did he think he was ordering about? But you
went to the meeting all the same, a fair birn of the Gowans
and Gloag chaps there, half the young lads from Machines
and Castings and that thin-necked Bulgar who worked in the
Stores, Norman and Alick and wee Geordie Bruce. No
League folk and thank Christ no queans, Ewan sat behind
the chairman's table alone and banged it and stood up and
began to speak: and afore he'd said much there was such a
hush you'd have heard the wind rumble in the belly of a flea.

He said they'd all noticed the new orders coming into
Gowans and Gloag's. Did they know what the orders were
for—the new machinery, the new parts they made? Especially had they noticed the new cylinders? He could tell them:
he'd found out that morning. They were making new
ammunition parts, bits of shells and gas-cylinders for
Sidderley, the English armament people.

Somebody cried up *Well, hell, does it matter?* and Ewan
said if a man were such a poor swine that it didn't matter to
him he was making things to be used to blow Chinese
workers to bits, people like himself, then it didn't matter.
But if he had any guts at all he'd join the whole of Gowans and
Gloag in a strike that would paralyse the Works. Gas-cylinder
cases: he hadn't been at the War, none of them had, but
they'd all read and heard about gas-attacks. Here was an
account by a hospital attendant that he'd copied from a book:

I RECEIVED AN URGENT MESSAGE FROM THE

HOSPITAL TO BE IN ATTENDANCE IMMEDIATELY.
I HURRIED THERE AND ALMOST AT ONCE THE
STREAM OF AMBULANCES WITH THE UNFOR-
TUNATE PRISONERS BEGAN TO ARRIVE. AT FIRST
SCORES, THEN LATER HUNDREDS, OF BROKEN
MEN, GASPING, SCREAMING, CHOKING. THE
HOSPITAL WAS PACKED WITH FRENCH SOLDIERS,
BEATING AND FIGHTING THE AIR FOR BREATH.
DOZENS OF MEN WERE DYING LIKE FLIES, THEIR
CLOTHES RENT TO RIBBONS IN THEIR AGONY,
THEIR FACES A HORRIBLE SICKLY GREEN AND
CONTORTED OUT OF ALL HUMAN SHAPE—

There was plenty more, but that gave you a taste. Well,
that's what he'd summoned this meeting for. What were they
to do about it in Gowans?

Christ, you'd felt sick at that stuff he'd read, but then wee
Geordie Bruce at the back of the hall sounded a raspberry and
everybody laughed, high out and relieved, you laughed
yourself, only Norman and Ewan didn't. Ewan said if the
chap at the back had anything to say let him get up and say it,
and at that wee Geordie Bruce stood up and said *Ah, to hell
with you and your blethers. What do you think you're trying to
do?—play the bloody toff on us again? It doesn't matter a faeces
to us what they're going to do with the wee round tins. If you're a
Chink or a Black yourself, that's your worry.* And other chaps
called out the same, who the mucking hell did Tavendale
think he was?—daft as all the bloody Reds. And afore you
could wink the place was in a roar, Ewan you could see sitting
at the table, listening, looking from this side to that. Then he
stood up and said that they'd take a vote—*those in favour of a
strike hold up their hands.*

The noise quietened away a bit at that, you looked round
about, nobody had a hand up, and och to hell suddenly you
minded the stuff that Ewan had been reading about chaps
caught in gas, and you felt fair daft, up your hand shot, and so
did Norman's, and so Alick's, and Ewan was counting:
For—three. Those against?—But there was never a real
count, chaps started whistling and stamping, raspberrying

and banging out of the room and knocking over the chairs as they went. You sat where you were feeling a fair fool, in a minute there was only the four of you left.

Syne Ewan called out: *Bob, close the door. We've to make ourselves into a Committee of Action.*

At half past five it happened again. Running down the stairs Chris met Ake Ogilvie who'd newly letten himself in at the door. *Ake, Ma Cleghorn's ta'en ill again. Will you run for the doctor?* and Ake said *Eh? Oh, ay, I'll do that*, and asked the address and nodded and went stamping out into the dark, Chris glanced from the window and saw it coming down, dark early now the winter was near. Syne she turned and ran up to Ma's room again to ease her out of her stays, poor thing, lying black-faced and gasping and swearing like a soldier.

The doctor came as he'd done before, had another look, gave another sniff, and said that Ma must be kept fell quiet. Chris told him she'd found out the relative's address, should she send for her? The doctor pulled at his lip and said *Oh no, just keep the address by handy-like. And don't worry too much, Mrs Colquohoun. I'll send up medicine*, and off he went. Chris went down to the kitchen to get ready the tea, Ma ill or Ma well folk would need their meat.

She went to bed dead tired that night. But she couldn't sleep, getting up every hour or so to look in Ma's room, after midnight the breathing grew easier. It had grown cold and looking out of the window Chris saw that snow had come on, soft-sheeting, the early soft seep of November snow whitening the roofs in a spilling fall. And she stood and looked at it a little while in the still, quiet house above the stilled toun, in a cold no-thought till the clock struck three—suddenly dirling beside her head.

Far away through the snow beyond Footforthie the lighthouse winked on the verge of the morning, and a feeling of terrible loneliness came on her standing so at that hour, knowledge of how lonely she had always been, knowledge of how lonely every soul was, apart and alone as she had been surely even at the most crowded hours of her life. And she

went up the stairs in a sudden fear and listened outside
Ewan's room a minute and heard his breath, low and even. In
the next room the door hung open unsnecked, she'd have to
see to that lock tomorrow. Closing the door she saw Ellen
Johns a dim shape curled like a baby in sleep, and stood, the
snow-hush upon the panes, looking at her in a kind of
desperation, half-minded to waken her up to talk.

Then that daft thought went from her, she went down the
stairs and into the kitchen, cold even there, the fire in the
range had drooped to ash, she stirred it a little and Jock the
cat purred a drowsy greeting a minute, grew silent; she sat
and stared in the fading ash, alone and desperate—what
would she do?

It was plain enough Ma wouldn't last long. And then—
Chris hadn't enough money to carry on the house herself and
whoever heired Ma mightn't want to come in with her. So out
again, looking for some other thing in this weary life of
Duncairn, seeking out some little shop, she supposed,
somewhere where she and Ewan could bide and trauchle and
fight with the going of the years, he wouldn't earn money of
account for years. And so on and on, streets all about,
slippery with slime, the reeking gutters of Paldy Parish, the
weary glint of shop-fronts in the Mile—till she grew old and
old and haggard, thin—who would have dreamed this for her
long syne that night she wedded Ewan in Blawearie, just a
night like this she minded now, lights, and Long Rob and
Chae at the fiddle, dancing, warmth, the daftness of being
young: they'd seemed eternal, to outlast the hills, those
moments when Ewan had first ta'en her in his arms, naked,
unshielded, unafraid, glad to be his and give and take for the
fun and glory of being in love . . . all far away in the snowing
years down the long Howe on Kinraddie's heights.

And she thought of the croft in the north wind's blow, of
the snow driving about it this night lashing the joists and
window-panes, the fly and scurry of the driving flakes about
the Stones high up by the loch, the lost rigs sleeping under
their covering, the peesies wheeping lost in the dark. Oh
idiot, weeping to remember that, all things gone and lost and

herself afraid and afraid and a morning coming she was feared to face, lost and alone.

And again she got to her feet and wandered through the hush of the sleeping house, and stood in her own room, with the sickly flare of the gaslight behind her and looked at herself in the mirror, hands clenched, forgetting herself in a sudden wild woe that wouldn't stop though her mind clamoured it was daft, things would redd up in time, she wasn't hungry or starved, she had friends, she had Ewan. . . . SHE HAD NOTHING AT ALL, she had never had anything, nothing in the world she'd believed in but change, unceasing and unstaying as time, light after light went down, hope and fear and hate, love that had lighted hours with a fire, hate freezing through to the blood of one's heart—Nothing endured, and this hour she stood as alone as she'd been when a quean in those wild, lost moments she climbed the heights of Blawearie brae. And she covered her face with her hands and sat down and so stayed there awhile and then rose and put on her clothes, coldly, mechanically, looking at the clock. . . . Trudging in the track of those little feet as a tethered beast that went round and round the tethering post in the midst of a park—

The Young League dance was fair in full swing, chaps had gone flocking to buy up tickets at Gowans and Gloag's and all over Footforthie, a tanner hop was a good enough chance to take your quean to on New Year's Eve. And she'd said *But aren't those creatures Red?* and you said you were Bulgared if you knew, did it matter? And she said Reds were awful, they believed that women—och, stuff that you wouldn't speak about. And you said you wouldn't but these Reds were different, the head of them was a toff kind of sod, Ewan Tavendale—

And your quean said *Bob!* or *Will!* or *Leslie—don't use those kind of words to me*, and you nearly went off your head at the runt, trying to make a lad speak genteel. But she turned up ready to go to the dance down in Long Hall, and there was that Tavendale, you'd never spoken to him, standing at the door and taking the tickets and nodding to folk; and up on the platform Jake Forbes's band that was wee Jake Forbes all on his own, hard at it banging out the Omaha Pinks, Jake tootling away with his big white face like a bowl of lard on the melt by a fire, queans and chaps all over the floor, your quean looked the bonniest and awful posh, how the hell did queans manage to dress up like that?

Then the Pinks struck up and you gave her a grab, she hadn't on stays or much else below, and off you all went, slither and slide, one foot in and another out, like a cock with concussion, tweetle the flute. And Jake stood up and hit the drum and banged the bell and clattered the cymbals and looked as though with a bit of encouragement he'd have kicked hell out of the nearest wall. Christ, what a row: but it kittled you up.

It was cold outside but the chaps didn't heed, you took out your quean for a squeeze between dances, cold though it was, she breathed *You mustn't, not here*—to hell, she liked it. Then she'd fix up her dress and back you'd go, New Year coming fast, some of the chaps nipped over to the pub and brought back a gill of the real Mackay, kittling everybody up, you forgot you'd got sacked the day before, and father was cursing like hell and said he'd have to keep you on the PAC . . . or that your job was a bloody stalemate with no chance of earning a penny piece more. Funny how fine your quean felt and smelt, other queans as well as you changed with chaps. And there was that toff Ewan Tavendale, only he didn't look a toff a bit, just one of the lads, he was dancing like hell when Jake put on a Schottische. Every body cried *Hooch!* and wakened up more, a daft old dance, not up to date, but you fair could swank and give a bit prance, in and out, now on your own quean's sleeve, now on that of the schoolteacher folk said was Red, only a kid, she was dressed in red, with black hair and a flaming skirt, she laughed and cried *Hook!* not *Hooch!*: she was English.

Jake quietened a minute to wipe his fat face and Ewan carried him something to drink; and Ewan called *The New Year dance is next. Just a word to you all before it comes on. You know who're the people who've got up this dance. They say we're some kind of Reds: let them say. We're workers the same as all of you are and as fond of taking a girl to a dance and giving her a cuddle on the sly as the next. In fact, that's why we believe what we do—that every one should have a decent life and time for dancing and enjoying oneself, and a decent house to go to at night, decent food, decent beds. And the only way to get those things is for the young workers of whatever party to join together and stop the old squabbles and grab life's share with their thousand hands.* And he stopped and looked down at the chaps and queans, all kittled up as they looked, with flushed faces, the lasses bonny in that hour though they came from the stews of Paldy and Kirrieben and Footforthie, their thin antrin faces soft in the light: *And isn't it worth grabbing? And that's all the speech.*

And as they cheered him and cried his name, the dirty, kind words of mates in the Shops, a great chap that Ewan, just one of themselves . . . it seemed to Ewan in a sudden minute that he would never be himself again, he'd never be ought but a bit of them, the flush on a thin white mill-girl's face, the arm and hand and the downbent face of a keelie from the reek of the Gallowgate, the blood and bones and flesh of them all, their thoughts and their doubts and their loves were his, all that they thought and lived in were his. And that Ewan Tavendale that once had been, the cool boy with the haughty soul and cool hands, apart and alone, self-reliant, self-centred, slipped away out of the room as he stared, slipped away and was lost from his life forever.

And then Ellen Johns was pulling at his arm: *Ewan, you look funny, is there anything wrong?* and he moved and came out of that dreaming trance, and smiled at her, and Ellen's heart moved, not the cold smile at all, it might have been that of any kind boy. *Hello, Ellen. You look lovely tonight. Can I have the next dance?* and she said, wide-eyed, *You can have them all if you want them, Ewan.*

And he took her hand and drew her close and waved to Jake and Jake started it up, *tooootle* the flute, *claboomr* the drum, off they all went in the wheel of a waltz, winkle the lights and Ellen's head close under Ewan's shoulder as they spun. And he looked down and suddenly smelled her hair, strange and sweet, and felt dizzy a minute, at the tickle of it up under his chin, at the touch of her up against him close, breast and belly and legs, soft, sweet, something ran with a torch and fired all his body. And Ellen looked up and saw his face, white, and suddenly knew what she'd always known, that she was his for as long as he liked, and *she* would like that till the day she died.

And she knew then that all the old stories were true, while they wheeled together, while they paused and rested, standing together so that they just touched, her hand touched his and his fingers closed on it, quick and glad—troubling fingers—Oh, all true that they'd sung in the olden times in this queer Scotland that had felt so alien, the dark, queer songs of lust and desire, of men and women and this daftness of love, dear daftness in soft Scotch speech, on Scotch lips—daftness like this that she felt for Ewan, and it didn't matter what he thought or did, whatever he might do or say or believe, the glory of it would last her forever. . . .

Jake cried *A last one ere Ne'ersday comes. What'll it be?* and they cried back *A reel!*, all the chaps smiling by then to their queans, the queans that had lost their clipped, frightened looks, their distrusts of men and hands and lips, forgetting the dark and the cold outbye and those dreary dawns that haunted Duncairn, thinking only of touches kind and shy, weak faces they loved, a moment to snatch when all this was over, somewhere, anyhow—to hell with risk when you liked him so well! And they flushed at their thoughts and said flyting things; and all lined up for the last of the reels; and Jake crashed out the tune, walloping the drum till it boomed like a bittern, tankle the melodeon, tootle the flute, and off they all went. Round and faster and faster still, Ewan with Ellen and holding her so she was frightened and struggled a wild-bird moment, Ewan lost in a queer, cruel flame of wonder, desire, and—heart-breaking—a passion of pity. Play on, Jake, play on, never stop, Ellen and I, Ellen and I. . . .

And far away Thomson Tower clanged midnight across
the toun and into Long Hall, the long dark hall where the
League had its dance; and Jake stopped in the middle of his
clatter of playing and they all stopped and laughed the queans
pulled at their dresses, and Tavendale stood with the
schoolteacher close, close as though glued, jammed up
against Alick and Norman and their queans; and Jake cried
out *Join hands—here's New Year*:

So here's a hand, my trusty frere,
And here's a hand o' mine—

And Ellen wished the mist would go from her eyes; and
then they'd all stopped and the music was done and queans
were being pushed into their coats, and coddled, and
everybody crying goodnight. *A happy New Year! Goodnight, then, Ewan. Goodnight to your lass—what's her name?
—Ellen? Ta-ta, Ellen.* And she cried *Ta-ta*, standing
by Ewan, the mist quite gone, alive and tingling not heeding at all that some cried back *Hell, it's snowing like
Bulgary!*

They left Jake to lock up the hall and went out, snow
sheeting down on the snow-rimed streets, all around the
lighted wynds of Ne'ersday, first foots and greetings and
drams poured in tumblers, the bairns crying *Is't time to get
up?* and their mothers, tired, happy, crying back to them:
*Mighty be here, get into your beds. You'll get all your presents on
New Year's Day—*

But the streets were nearly deserted as they hurried, Ellen
and Ewan, from the Cowgate's depth across the Mile and the
Corn Market, the cold air blowing on Ellen's face, Ewan
looked down and saw her face a winter flower and wanted to
sing, wanted to stop and say idiot things, to stop and go mad
and strip Ellen naked, the secret small cat, slow piece on
piece, and kiss every piece a million times over, and hit her—
hard, till it hurt, and kiss the hurts till cure and kisses and
pain were one—mad, oh, mad as hell tonight!

And she tripped beside him, sweet, slim and demure in act
and look, dark cool kitten, and inside was frightened at the
wildness there. So up Windmill Steps through the sheet of

the snow, a corner with a mirror, here the snow failed, Ewan halted panting while she made to run on.

But he caught her arm and drew her down, she wriggled a little, the light on her face, startled, eyes like stars and yet drowsy, he drew her close to him and they suddenly gasped, with wonder and fear and as though their hearts broke and were shattered in the kiss, sweet, terrible, as their lips met at last.

Thin and lank, with a holy mouth and shifty eyes, she sat in the kitchen and had tea with Chris: *Eh me, and you think she won't last the night?* And Chris said, *No, I don't think she will. Another cup of tea, Miss Urquhart?* and Ma's niece Izey sniffled through her nose, godly, and pecked at her eyes with a hanky: *Have you had the minister up to see her?*

Chris said No, she hadn't, Ma had told her in a wakeful moment that day she didn't want any of them sossing about, if St Peter needed a prayer for a passport he'd be bilked of another boarder, fegs. And Niece Izey held up her hands in horror, *But* YOU *don't believe that, do you, now?* and Chris said more or less, she didn't care, and Miss Urquhart drew in her shoggly mouth, prim: *I'm afraid we wouldn't get on very well. I believe in God, I've no time for heathen.* And Chris said *No? That must be a comfort. Try a cake, Miss Urquhart,* and sat watching her eat, she herself couldn't, over tired with running up and down the stairs and seeing to the lodgers' meals as they came, they needed something special on New Year's Eve, and letting Meg go early though she'd offered to stay. . . . And suddenly the lank Izey said *I suppose you know that I heir it all?—the share in the house and the furniture?*

Chris said she'd heard that and knew it to be true, whatever intention Ma had once had of altering her will to surprise Niece Izey she'd never had the time to carry it out. And Miss Urquhart pursed up her holy-like mouth and said she would realize her share, she'd no fancy for the keeping of lodgers herself, not a decent work, she'd always thought. Maybe Mrs Colquohoun would buy her out?

Chris said *I've no idea what I'll do. But I'm dead tired now.*

Will you watch by your aunt? Niece Izey gave a kind of a shiver: *Oh, but I don't know a thing about nursing. You won't leave me alone with her, will you?*

Chris looked at her in an idle pity, too tired to hate the poor, fusionless thing, a black hoodie-crow scared of a body not yet quite a corpse but ready to pick out its eyes when it died. *I'm going up to rest in my own room a while. If there's any change you can run up and tell me.*

Without taking off her clothes she lay on the bed and drew the coverlet over her, not intending to sleep, only rest and lose her aches in the dark. But afore she knew it she was gone, sound, the last whisper she heard the fall of the snow pelting Duncairn in its New Year's Eve.

She woke from that with a hand on her shoulder, the lanky niece had lighted the gas, she was all a-dither and the long face grey. *I'm feared she's gey ill, and Oh, how you were sleeping. I thought I would never waken you.*

Chris got off the bed and tidied her hair. And as she did so she heard from Ma's room an antrin sound—a blatter of words, then a groan of pain. She was down the stairs and into the room, Izey trailing behind in a lank unease, and saw that it couldn't be very long now, she had better send for the doctor at once.

Ma Cleghorn was fighting her last fight with the world she had jeered at and sworn at throughout her life, gallant and vulgar, untamed to the end, her arms beating the air in this battle. Chris wiped the spume from the swollen lips, the smell of death already in the air, and did not move as she sat by the bed, the niece went out of the room to be ill, down in Duncairn a late tram tootled; and the dreich fight drew to its close, begun a sixty years before, ending in this—what for, what for?

And suddenly Ma's lips ceased to twist and slobber with their blowings of brownish spume, her hand in Chris's slackened with a little jerk; and she stepped from the bed and out of the house and up long stairs that went wandering to Heaven like the stairs on Windmill Brae. And she met at the Gates St Peter himself, in a lum hat and leggings, looking awful stern, the father of all the Wee Free ministers, and he held up his hand and snuffled through his nose and asked in GAWD'S name was she one of the Blessed? And Ma Cleghorn said she was blest if she knew—*Let's have a look at this Heaven of yours.* And she pushed him aside and took a keek in, and there was God with a plague in one hand and a war and a thunderbolt in the other and the Christ in glory with the angels bowing, and a scraping and banging of harps and drums, ministers thick as a swarm of blue-bottles, no sight of Jim and no sight of Jesus, only the Christ, and she wasn't impressed. And she said to St Peter *This is no place for me*, and turned and went striding into the mists and across the fire-tipped clouds to her home.

The sleet had ended. Looking up in the lift Chris saw it lighten and the cumuli clear, a stiff wind blowing the New Year's Day into the eyes of Duncairn below, wakening down there and about her, wakening while she stood here frozen like—oh, like a corpse, like Ma up there in the blinded room, if Ma *was* there, no day for her, just the dark, no snow, sun never again or shadow or cold.

Long ago Robert would have been able to put in fine words the things that you felt—or could even Robert? Could he have put in words both your pity and desire to laugh— laughter because death was so funny and foolish?

. . . And whatever next—oh, whatever next?

And then, as always at breaking point, she felt cool and kind and unworried no longer, brisk and competent, unwearied, she whistled a little as the sleet went by.

No worry could last beyond the last point, there was nothing awaiting her but her life, New Year and Life that would gang as it would, greeting or laughing, unheeding her fears.

And she went up the steps to death and life.

THREE

Apatite

COMING DOWN THE steps of Windmill Brae in the blaze of the late May afternoon Chris paused at the mirror, dust-sprinkled in summer's beginning, and looked at her blithe self with a cool curiosity. If finery made fine birds, she thought, she'd peacocks beaten to the likeness of sparrows, new hat and dress, new shoes, new gloves, new-bathed—oh, new to her skin at least!

And, so she supposed, behind this newness and those cool eyes in the mirror, the fugitive Chris was imprisoned at last, led in a way like the captives long syne whom men dragged up the heights to Blawearie Loch to streek out and kill by the great grey stones. Caught as they were: she, who had often lain down in the shadow of the Stones—oh, daft to blether in her thoughts like this, when all that was happening to her today was as common a happening throughout the world as getting up, getting down, sleeping and waking. . . .

Sleeping—

Even the cool amusement behind which she shielded could not restrain that shudder of disgust, goodness knew why, what was disgusting about the business? Going back to a life again full and complete from a half-life, unnatural, alone and apart. But she pulled off her gloves and stared at her fingers in a sudden, unreasoning spasm of panic. Oh, however had she come to betray herself so? Better the sleet and the grey despair of that five months ago when she last climbed here, no road or vision before her at all—

When young Alick Watson taiked home one night to the Cowgate in the middle of January and told the news that a strike was on, there was no going back to Gowans and Gloag's till they'd stopped the making of shell-cases and cylinders,

Meg Watson asked *And what does that mean?—that a lot of tink brutes like yourself'll gang idle?*

Alick said that it meant she could give him less of her lip, Christ, wasn't there even a cup of tea? And him on picket the morn's morning.

Meg was wearied from her work at Windmill Place, she said he could get the tea for himself, he'd have plenty of time for cookery classes now he was out on his half-witted strike. And who did he expect would keep him, eh? Father or herself or that Red sod Selden? She'd aye known that Alick was a silly gawpus, she could bet they hadn't ALL come out on strike.

Alick said she could bet herself blue in the face, they'd all come out that had any guts excepting a few of the sods in the office. Meg said she was glad Mr Tavendale and his like had more sense, Alick stared at her and then gave a laugh: *Ewan Tavendale? Why, you silly bitch, it's him that's organized the whole mucking strike—he's been going it for weeks now, him and his League. They'd never have brought off the strike at all if it hadn't been for the speeding-up as well—chaps doing double work in the same spread of time. And we're all out the morn and the whole damn business led by your Mr Tavendale, see?*

Then he said in a minute he was awful sorry—*I didn't mean to vex you, Meg.* And she snuffled and dabbed at her eyes, making out she'd a cold, she hadn't—what had he said, what was wrong with her? And he glowered at his sister in the littered, cold room, with the rags on the beds and the rickety chairs, something about her looked queer to a chap. . . .

Why should she greet when he spoke about Ewan?

Stephen Selden, the lodger, came in at that minute, Alick told him the news, he was fair delighted. He said that the Communist local would help, they'd take over the running from this daft young League. Alick asked what the hell it had to do with the Communists—or Tavendale's League, if it came to that? It was only the concern of the Gowans chaps. But Selden said it was every worker's affair that another was fighting for his livelihood and to put down the manufacture of armaments. He himself would be along at the picketing the morn.

And there sure enough he was at the gates with a birn of others when the morning broke, a crowd of Broo chaps from all over Duncairn standing about easy and looking at the gates and watching the half-dozen men on picket. Folk took a bit dander across the calsays and cried out to ask what the strike was about? The pickets said there was a statement to be issued soon, they'd nothing to say until that was done. And they stood and gowked at the gates, damned cold, or looked back up the streets to the fug of Footforthie, Alick and Norman and the new Stores chap, Bob, two old men who worked in Machines, and a young chap who looked like a toff, folk thought, 'twas said he was a gent who worked in the Office. Whatever could he be doing on strike?

At nine o'clock, with the crowd gey thick, two bobbies came barging through the press and stood up on either side of the gate, one a young constable childe from the country, that everybody liked, a mere loon, with no harm and a cheery smile that he couldn't hide though he tried to look solemn as a sourock now, standing under the eye of his sergeant, the big ugly sod that had come to Footforthie, some called him Feet and some called him worse, Leslie his name, a heavy-looking brute with bulging eyes and a grind of a voice. *Stand back there!* he cried to the folk round about, and somebody sounded a raspberry, and everybody laughed.

Then folk looked round and saw that a car was coming, the manager's car, slow, Sergeant Leslie opened the gates and gave it a wave in. But one of the pickets, the young toff, held up his hand, every body stared, Christ, didn't he know the manager?

But the car slid to a stop and Ewan went forward and talked a minute to the manager, he said *You is it, Tavendale? Yes, I've heard all the story. This'll mean one thing certain enough, anyhow:* YOU'LL *not come back to Gowans and Gloag's.* Ewan said they would see about victimization when the strike was over: what about the manager himself coming out? And the manager reddened and said to his chauffeur

Drive on! and Sim Leslie caught Ewan's shoulder: *Stand away there, or I'll have you ta'en in!*

A fair growl went up from the folk at that, no body could stop strikers picketing their works. Who did the fat sod think he was—Hitler? And two loons at the back threw a handful of clinkers over a baulk, they splattered all about the big sergeant's helmet and his meikle red face, like a sow's backside, went a mottled grey: *Stand away there!* though not a soul stood within ten feet. Some chaps cried *Let's pitch him into the Dock*, Broo chaps that had nothing to lose anyway, and God knows the mischief that mightn't have happened but that some of the older folk with sense cried out to the young ones not to haver, where the hell did they want to land —in the nick? And the young toff nodded to the bobby; Feet: *We've a legal right to be here to argue with anybody who tries to get into the Works. . . . Lads, here's the first of the blacklegs coming.*

Sure enough they were, a dozen of the muckers, the most of them foremen like old Johnny Edwards, dandering along in a bouroch, fair hang-dog, though laughing out loud and gey brassy, fair brave if it wasn't for the wamble of their eyes and hands. They pushed through the stir, syne the picket tackled them, there rose a surge and a stour so that folk couldn't see. Then the gates were opened and in they all went, the dirty blacklegging lousy scabs. Why the hell hadn't the Reds flung them into the Dock? What the hell were Reds for but to take up a row?

Alick Watson pushed through to relieve Ewan Tavendale, Ewan said he didn't think more would come, the lot for the day, but the morn—well, there'd be a stamash, for the Union wasn't supporting the strike and there'd be no strike pay unless they could raise it. . . . Then he said *You look fearfully solemn, Alick*, and smiled at a body that way he had, dark and kind, like a bit of a quean. Alick went a bit red and said *Don't haver.* And then: *That silly bitch, my sister, seemed awful concerned about you last night.*

Ewan said *Meg? Oh yes, I know her. Works at our house— she's a nice leg, Meg. But you wouldn't know, being only her*

brother. Bye, bye, I'm off to the committee rooms. Trease is to
raise a fund for the strikers.

He came home soaked to the skin that night with tramping
the rain and helping the Reds to raise an unofficial strikers'
fund. But Gowans had been killed stone-dead for the day,
they hadn't even got the furnaces going. He sat and told this
to Chris in the kitchen, drinking hot cocoa, and then
stretched and yawned: *But you're never bothered about such*
things, Chris. Wise woman. Goodness, I'm tired.

Chris told him he wanted a bath and his bed, and off he
should get; but he turned at the door to ask what next was to
happen to the house? Was Chris to carry on without Ma
Cleghorn?

Chris said she supposed so as Ma was in heaven or at least
in the kirkyard of Kirrieben. Ewan laughed and yawned in a
breath, *Yes, I know. But I meant*—Chris said she didn't
know, she'd see, if he didn't get tirred and into a bath she'd
be carrying on without HIM, anyhow.

He nodded and came back and kissed her, kind, much
slower and kinder than once he'd been, though his mind was
far off with his strike, she supposed. Queer loon that he was,
lovely loon, on even him change working its measure as
sunlight on granite bringing out the gleams of gold and red
through the cold grey glister. For a little while after he'd gone
she stood still, thinking about him, tender, amused, in a
puzzled fear: then sat by the table and thought of herself and
the awful soss that Ma's death had left.

Izey Urquhart had had a valuator in and valued Ma's
things and share of the house at a price that had made Chris
gasp. And Izey had said that unless they were ta'en over,
she'd sell the gear and the house-share as well, *she* had no
fancy for the keeping of lodgings. If the lodgings could have
spoken they might have answered up canty that they had no
fancy for being kept by her, Chris had thought, but hadn't
said it, just nodded, and been given a week to decide.

A week. And when that was over—what?

She went on with washing the supper dishes, Meg she'd

sent home that afternoon, the quean had looked queer and
nearly fainted, she'd almost ta'en Ma's place after her death
and worked like a Trojan, too much for a girl of her size,
Chris had thought—absently, noting Meg filling out a bit,
pale still, but not that slat of a board with a dress tacked on it
that once she'd been.

Ewan met in with Ellen the evening of the next day, going up
to her room, and they stopped close and smiled on the dark
stair's turn. And a queer, sharp pang shot through Ewan's
heart looking down on the sailing thought-shapes in her eyes,
far down deep in the sweet kitten face. And he'd kissed her
only once in his life!

Trembling, he put his hands under her arms, the lights
changed to a hurrying, twinkling flurry, they kissed and
quivered a minute together, and stood breathing, listening,
and kissed again.

He said, mimicking her English phrase *That was fun!* and
she flashed back *I've known worse!* and slipped from him:
looked down from the step above: *Coming out a walk?*

He said he'd just come in; and anyhow it was raining
like—She nodded, *Like hell, but I like the rain. Don't you?*

He put up his hand on hers on the stair-rail and felt the
quiver of blood in her fingers: *I like you at any rate*, and stared
at the fingers so that Ellen whispered *Aren't they clean?* And
pulled them away and ruffled his hair: *There, I'll be ready in
less than a minute.*

She was ready in ten and they went out together to the
windy squall of the February night, a flicker and flow of wet
lights and sounds. He asked where they'd go and she said
Doughty Park, and they made that in a little under twelve
minutes, wide open heath that lay furth of the toun, the great
trees shoomed and pattered to the rain, they passed two
bobbies with glistening capes and came under the shelter of a
strumming beech. Here the lads of Duncairn would take
their lasses on summer nights, fair scandalous, and behave to
them in that scandalous way that first had launched humankind on the globe. But this night was a treey desolation,

rain-pelted, Ewan remembered that night of the year before
when they'd gone that walk to the Beach and stripped and
splashed a mad dip in the sea. He asked Ellen if she minded as
well, she was close beside him, snuggled in the lithe.

*Yes. Goodness, how silly we were! Dirty little tykes. . . . Oh,
Ewan, listen to the wind!*

So he listened, but only with half an ear. That night on the
Beach—what had been dirty about it? Ellen said *Didn't you
want to see me naked? I did you; but I didn't say. That was why
it was dirty, you know.* And thought: *No, I don't suppose you
did, funny Ewan.*

She was silent for a long while after that, leaning up against
him, hearing the rain, content and content, she could stay
there all night. She said so and Ewan said he could as well,
only he mightn't be so funny this time. And at that she said,
sobered, that she didn't suppose he would, it was damnable
for him to have fallen in love, much better to have stayed out
safe and sound so's he didn't much care what she looked, how
she was. And now—

So they began making plans for the future, they'd get
married some time when Ewan had a salary, Ellen would be
forced to leave her school. She asked how much of a salary
he'd get and he said indifferently *Perhaps four pounds*, and
she said *But I get as much as that now—Goodness, we'd have to
stay in the Cowgate!*

He said nothing to that, she thought she had hurt him and
was kind to him a little while, playing a child's game with him
under the patter of the night-blinded trees, kissing him with
eyelids against his cheek, butterfly kisses, rather fun.
Abruptly he pushed her away, cool and quick: *Don't fool,
Ellen*, in his old-time voice, hard, the voice of the student
Ewan that she hadn't heard since New Year's Eve.

She knew he was being only sensible, pity rather, and said
she was sorry, and they didn't stand over-close after that, the
weight of the rain was seeping through the branches and now
a great low gust of wind swept up the park, driving the soft
ground-spray in their faces. Ewan began to talk of the strike,
he said that Selden and Trease and himself had already a good

strike fund in hand though the Union had been trying to force
the men back. Ellen said it was rather a pity to have to work
so closely with the Communist leaders, they'd a horrible
reputation, both of them liars and not to be trusted; and
Ewan said perhaps, he didn't know, anyhow their tactic of
rioting for rioting's sake was pure insanity, it got nowhere, if
a revolution were properly organized it should be possible for
a rising class to take power with little or no violence. But
Trease and Selden were handy in the strike, stiffening it up.
And laughed: *Anyhow, whoever goes back, I shan't. The
manager made that plain enough. Doesn't sound bright for our
marriage, does it? You should have left me alone that day on the
Barmekin and I might have been good and respectable now, not
mixing up with this mess of a strike, but a gent in a bowler,
smoking cigarettes in spats.*

She said if he was sorry he'd mixed up with Socialism he
need never mix up with her, either, then. . . . And flushed
dark in the darkness, but he hadn't tumbled, innocent as a
babe, nice babe. He sat down against the bole of the tree and
patted the dry ground there, and caught her ankle in a gentle
hand: *Sit by me a minute before we go back. You never know
what'll happen to a striker tomorrow!*

As the dozen bobbies cleared the way for the scabs coming
out of the Works, the dark was falling, there came a hell and
pelt of a rush, you were all of you in it, young chaps and old,
one bobby struck at you with his truncheon, missed, you
were past him, slosh in the kisser the scab; and all about you,
milling in the dark, the chaps broke in and hell broke out, the
bobbies hitting about like mad, tooting on their whistles,
scrunch their damned sticks.

And then the fight cleared from its stance by the gates and
went shoggling and wabbling over to the Docks, the dozen
scabs held firm enough, the bobbies bashing to try and get at
them and rescue them. Old man though you were, you
wouldn't have that, you pushed a foot in front of one of the
bastards, down he went with a bang on the calsays, somebody
stepped on his mouth and his teeth went crunch. And there,

in the heave and pitch of the struggle, were sudden the waters of the Dock, dirt-mantled, greasy in oil from the fisher-fleet, the lights twinkling low above it, folk cried *In with them! Dook the scab sods!*

And in they went with a hell of a spleiter, one of them, the foreman old Johnny Edwards, crying *Lads, lads, I can't swim!* Alick Watson beside you gave him a kick: *You can't, you old mucker? Now's the chance to learn*, over he went, your heart louped in your mouth. Then some body cried to look out and run, the bobbies were coming in a regiment, near.

And you looked round and there b'God they were, the calsays clattering under their feet, waving their sticks, Christ, never able to face up to them. Around to the left was the way to take nipping by the timber yard over the brig. All the chaps running helter-skelter you scattered, the bobbies wouldn't spare pickets now except to bash in their brain-caps, maybe, after seeing one of their lot on the ground. B'God, this would be a tale to tell when you got back safe to Kirrieben.

And then the lot of you saw you were trapped, in the flickering light and the scud of the water, a gang of the bobbies had raced across and cut you off, big and beefy, they were crying *We've got you, you sods!*

And you all half-halted a minute and swore and ebbed back a bit, you couldn't see the bobbies' faces or they yours, they wouldn't mind, bash down and bash till their arms grew tired and then haul a dozen of you off to the nick.

Then two of the chaps cried *Come on, lads!* and ran straight for the line of running bobbies, all of you like sheep at their heels, gritting your teeth, nieves ready for the crash. Then you saw the foremost of the running chaps throw up his hand and wave it in front of him right in the bobbies' faces, swish, the other did the same and a yowl went up, bobbies dropping their truncheons and clutching their eyes, you got a whiff running and staggered, and near sneezed your head off. Christ, that was neat, whoever thought of it.

But there'd be a bonny palaver the morn!

And next day the *Daily Runner* came out and told of those

coarse brutes the Gowans strikers, and the awful things they'd done to the working folk that were coming decent-like from their jobs. And all Craigneuks read the news with horror, every word of it, chasing it from the front page to the lower half of page five, where it was jammed in between an advertisement curing Women with Weakness and another curing superfluous hair; and whenever Craigneuks came on a bit of snot it breathed out *Uhhhhhhhhhhhh!* like a donkey smelling a dung-heap, delighted, fair genteel and so shocked and stirred up it could hardly push down its grape-fruit and porridge and eggs and bacon and big salt baps, fine butter new from the creamery, fresh milk and tea that tasted like tea, not like the seep from an ill-kept sump. And it said weren't those Footforthie keelies awful? Something would have to be done about them.

. . . . . .

And the Reverend Edward MacShilluck in his Manse shook his bald head and pursed his long mouth and said to his housekeeper Ahhhhhhhhhhhh, what they needed in Dun- cairn were folk like the Fascists, they knew how to keep tink brutes in trim. And this nonsense about the keelies being on strike because Gowans were making shells and gas-cases— well, wasn't a strong man sure in defence? Wasn't it the best way to avoid a war for a country to keep a strong army in the field?

The housekeeper simpered and said she was sure, that must have been why the last War had happened, those coarse brutes the Germans and Frenchies, like, had had hardly an army to their name, would it be, and that was why the war had broke out?

The Reverend MacShilluck gave a bit of a cough and said *Not quite, you wouldn't understand. Ahhhhhhhhhhhh, a fine thing the War in many a way. Did I ever tell you the story of the nurse and the soldier who was wounded in a certain place, my Pootsy?* And the housekeeper, who'd heard it only a hundred times, standing and sitting and lying down, upstairs and downstairs and ben in the kitchen and once in the bathroom, shook her bit head and made out she hadn't, she'd her living

to look after and she'd long grown used to that look that
would come in MacShilluck's eyes, a look she'd once thought
in a daft-like minute that *stank* with the foulest of all foul
smells. . . .

. . . . .

Bailie Brown said it was that damn fool the Chief Constable,
why hadn't he kept enough bobbies on hand? The workers
were all right, though misled by the Reds, if they'd trusted
their natural leaders, like himself, they wouldn't be in the
pickle they were in, drowning a foreman that had aye been a
right good Labour man, and throwing pepper in the bobbies'
eyes. They should wait till the next Labour Government
came—

. . . . .

The Chief Constable said it was that bloody Inspector, he'd
told him to look out for trouble at Gowans. Pepper flung in
the eyes of the men—by God, you'd find it revolver-shots
next. He was to tell the Council that unless he had powers—

. . . . .

The Provost motored out to his sawmill to get away from the
stir and stew, and wandered around, with his long dreich face
like a yard of bad milk, till he lighted on Ake level-testing a
lathe. And he said *Seen the news in the Runner this morning?*
And Ake asked what news, and the Provost said about the
murder down at the Docks, the strikers drowning the old
foreman Edwards and then throwing pepper in the police's
eyes. Ake said he'd seen it and hadn't wept, a scab was a scab
wherever you found him though 'twas swollen water-dead in
the Duncairn docks or bairning a quean that screamed in a
hedge. . . . And the Provost gave a bit hurried hoast and Ake
thought if ever he was walking alone on a dark-like night and
Jimmy came on him, he with his bare nieves and Jimmy with
a knife, he'd stand as much chance of getting home safe as a
celluloid cat that had strayed into hell. . . .

. . . . .

The sub-editors' room gave a yawn and a grunt Piddle had
done a nippy bit work stealing the photo of that drowned
Edwards bloke. Any chance of a few of the bobbies being

coshed good and proper in the next few days?—half a dozen of them drowned would make a good spread. Damned neat stunt that pepper-throwing, the Chief would blame it on the Reds for sure. Tell the boy to get out Trease's photo, bet he was under arrest by now—

. . . . . .

Chris read the news and thought, far away, *Awful. . . . Three more days to decide on this house.*

. . . . .

The Cowgate read it and a queer sound started, in tenement and wynd and went wriggling on like the passage of a flying train of powder, twisting and glistering and louping to and fro, back to Footforthie, up to Kirrieben, a growl of laughing and cursing, Christ, some Bulgar had dealt with the bobbies fine. And hungry Broo men that had made up their minds to sneak down to Gowans and into the gate and try and steal one of the striker's jobs gave a bit rub at their hunger-swollen bellies—ah well, they must try the PAC again—

. . . . .

Jim Trease the Red leader gave a roar of a laugh and called to his wife to bring him his boots. *They'll be coming for me in an hour or so. Get on with the breakfast, will you, lass, I'll be hungry enough before they finish their questioning down at the Station.* His mistress said *What, are they after you again?* placid as you please, he'd had so much arresting off and on in his life that she thought no more of him marched off to jail than when he marched off to the WC. *And what have your gowks been doing now?*

He told her and she said that sounded gey clever, that pepper business, and Jim Trease puffed *Clever? Some idiot loon has been reading a blood. What we need are the masses with machine-guns, not pepper. . . . To hell, and I suppose if they heard me say that they'd chuck me out of the Communist Party!*

. . . . .

Ewan said to Alick Watson he thought he'd more sense—who'd bought the pepper, Alick himself or that dirty little swine Geordie Bruce?

Ellen met in with Ewan after dinner that day, he'd come up

from watching the pickets at Gowans, the bobbies were keeping them aye on the move, a great birn of folk had been there all forenoon. He told Ellen this as they went out together, she to her school and he back to Gowans, in the clearing weather she looked up in his face, he down at hers—queer what a thrill that faint line of down sent through one, funny biological freak, thought the old-time Ewan that wasn't quite dead—

You can kiss me inside this nook, she said, light-heartedly; and when he'd finished kissed him in return in a sudden terror: *Oh, Ewan, be careful down at the Docks. I'm—I'm frightened for you!*

Making early tea in the kitchen next morning Chris looked out and saw that the rain had cleared, Spring was coming clad in pale saffron—the sun hardly seen all the winter months except through the blanket of Duncairn reek. She stood and looked out an un-eident minute till she heard the sound of feet on the stairs, Ake Ogilvie, big, with his swaying watch-chains and his slipperless feet, swinging into the kitchen: *Ay then, mistress.*

She said absently, her thoughts far away, still looking out at that blink of sun, *Morning, Mr Ogilvie*, her worries forgotten for a lovely minute. Ake sat down and tamped out his pipe on the range: *Well, what are you doing about the bit house?*

She'd told him something of her plight before, and he'd listened, douce, with his ploughman's face, his stare of impudent, grey-green eyes. *Ay, a gey bit fix*, he'd said, and no more, he wasn't much interested; why should he be? Now, she thought with a twinge of resentment against him, did he think it light gossip to be taken through hand in the early morning to pass the time? Pouring him a cup of tea she said shortly *I've no idea. Sell it up, I suppose.*

—*And after that?*

—*Oh, something'll turn up.* She turned away with the brimming tray.

He said *Well, just gi'es a minute of your crack. Let the sweir folk wait for their tea a while.*

Chris put down the tray. *Well, a minute. What is't?*

He sat and looked up at her, drinking his tea, a man from the farms and the little touns, the eternal barbarian Robert had once called him. Now he laid down the cup and gave his mouser a dight: *Ah well, this is it: I've a bit of silver saved myself—about enough to buy the share of the place that Mistress Cleghorn left to her niece. And I'm willing to come in as your partner, like.*

—*Ake! Oh, Ake, you really mean that?*

He said Oh ay, he meant what he said—a habit of his, like. Mistress Colquohoun was willing to take him on, then? He'd look after this lad of hers, Ewan, all right.

Something queer about that: *Ewan—what'll he have to do with it?*

—*Well, damn't, as his stepfather I suppose I'll have more than a bittie to do with him.*

Chris stared: *One or other of us has gone daft. You were proposing to share my house, weren't you, Ake?*

He looked up and nodded, douce and green-eyed: *Ay, lass, and your bed.*

Chris went through that day betwixt anger and laughter, the last would come on her in the funniest way, pour over her in a sudden red, senseless wave. Marriage?—marry a lout like him, lose all that she'd ever gained in her life with Robert, the Manse, Ewan her son? The impudence of him—Oh, the beast, the beast! And she'd stand and suddenly picture him, the sneering, half-kindly, half-bull-like face, the face of the folk of the Howe throughout, canny and cruel and kind in one facet, face of the bothies and the little touns . . . and she'd shiver away from the thought of him, thought of impossible touches, caresses, those red, creased hands and that sun-wrinkled body . . . awful enough to make her feel ill.

At the dinner hour he came back with the others, she served him and them, sitting where Ma Cleghorn once had sat, no faces missing from about the board. And Neil Quaritch looked at her: Neat piece of goods. Sulky and sweet in a breath as one of those damned unbreeked little novelists

would put it. Queer the resemblance between her and Ogilvie
—chips of the same bit of stone in a way—

John Cushnie, sweating, looked over his tie and wondered,
lapsing to keelie-hood a moment, if she were as put-you-off as
she looked. Should start with a woman twice your own age,
he'd heard. . . . And he coloured richly over his pimples, not
decent to think of a woman like that, especially now he'd
ta'en up with that nice girl from an office, real superior, that
he'd met at a dance—

Archie Clearmont thought, switching off Stravinsky,
Lord, what a thrill to kiss her just once!

Ena Lyon thought she was putting on side, as usual, and
her just a Common Servant.

Ellen looked up from her plate at Chris and smiled at her,
dark, and thought she looked nice and queer in a way, as
though newly cuddled.

Ewan had come back from the picket at Gowans, he
thought *Chris looks queer*, and then forgot her, trying to work
out in his mind the balance likely to be left in the voluntary
fund when they'd paid out the first week's pay to the strikers.

Miss Murgatroyd called *Eh me, Mrs Colquohoun, You're
fairly looking Right Well today. Has your lad been sending you a
love-letter, now?* and beamed round the table like a foolish old
hen, all the others looking down at their plates, uncomfort-
able . . . silly old bitch . . . blithering old skate . . . randy dame
. . . silly thing . . . sex-repressed . . . half-witted old wombat.
. . . And a sudden impulse came on Chris, looking down the
table and smiling at Miss Murgatroyd:

*No, though it's something much the same. I had a proposal of
marriage this morning.*

There was a dead silence round the table a second. Ewan
hadn't heard, Chris saw his indifferent face and her heart
sank, on that impulse she'd thought he'd ask *Who proposed?*
and she'd tell the whole table and watch Ake's face. But he
hadn't heard; and the others began a babble: Who was the
lucky man? Was she to accept? Chris laughed and shook her
head and said nothing and the talk passed on to other things.

Ake sat and ate up his meat, calm and sonsy, but biding

when the others had gone. Then he looked up and pushed back his chair, slow, certain: and looked over at Chris.

Ay, mistress, you cook a gey tasty meal. But a word in your lug: try no tricks on me. I'm not your fool nor any body's fool.

Chris looked at him in a curious pity, *It was a silly caper, Ake.*

He said that that was fine, then; and when would she let him know about this partnership business?

Chris said she didn't know, but soon, anyhow; and was moved to a stark curiosity: *Ake, why do you want to marry me so bad? Just to sleep with a woman: that all? I've been married twice already, you know, and it doesn't seem it was lucky for the men.*

He said he was willing to take his risk; and he didn't suppose that Colquohoun or Tavendale had thought themselves cheated, however they ended.

She said she had little mind for any man again, that was the plain truth of it. If she married at all it would be with little liking, necessity only the drive.

Ake nodded: *We'd soon alter that, never fear.* And fear itself leapt in her heart at his look. *There's no woman yet that I couldn't content.*

Trease wouldn't squeal, an old hand him, and the Station Inspector wouldn't let the chaps go into his cell and give the bastard a taste of what he needed, he could raise hell in the courts over-easily, he knew the law inside out and bottom up. So he was letten out, laughed, and went home; and still there wasn't the ghost of a clue to point to the names of the striker sods who'd flung the pepper or drowned old Edwards.

The Gowans gates pickets had a fair dog's life, bobbies badgering them backward and forward, keen to have out their sticks and let fly. The manager had ta'en on a bouroch of blacklegs with a bit of the plant on the go again, but bobbies or no to march by their side the scabs were scared to their marrow-bones to be seen going in or out of the Works.

Sergeant Sim Leslie went to the Inspector and said he wasn't sure, but he had an idea, that the striker at the bottom of most of the business was the young toff Tavendale from the Gowans office. He'd known him back in the toun of Segget, as coarse a loon as you'd meet anywhere.—And the Chief said *Is this a moral homily? or what have you got to say about him?* And Feet habbered a little and then got it out: That assault on him at the Beach last year when he was taking a couple in charge for naked bathing—ay, not a stitch—he was nearly sure 'twas the Tavendale loon; besides, his stepfather had been a Red, a minister that fair demoralized a parish. And the Chief said he wasn't interested in genealogy, had Feet any clue to this Tavendale having drowned Johnny Edwards or thrown the pepper?

Feet said he hadn't; and went back on his beat on the Docks patrol that centred now round the Gowans gates. The picket was dozing away in the lithe from a stiff bit blow of wind from the harbour as Feet came bapping along the calsays. He stopped and looked at the nearest picket, a surly-looking young sod he was, cowering down in the shelter of a barrel. And this picket instead of raspberrying him as most of the impudent muckers would do, looked round about him sly and said low: *Hey, Feet, a word with you, there.*

Feet asked if he knew who he was talking to, and the picket said *Ay, fine that, think I'm blind? Look here, if you want to know who started the pepper business look out for the next birn of pickets that relieves us and spot a long, dark-like chap of my age.*

Feet nearly louped in his meikle boots, but he showed not a sign, just gave a bit purr: *Tavendale, d'you mean?* and the picket said *Ay. The bastard hasn't been able to keep his hands to himself—or other things about his rotten self either. He's done me dirty and it's my turn now.*

Feet said *You'll come and give evidence?* but the picket said *Away to hell with you. Think I'm your pimp, you bap-faced peeler? Find out your evidence for yourself.*

Feet thought of taking him a whack on the head, with his truncheon, like, to teach him manners; but the rest of the picket was getting suspicious and rising to its feet and dandering near, it wouldn't do to rouse the coarse brutes, they might heave even a sergeant into the Docks, they'd no

respect for the weight of the Law. So Feet swung away down
to the Gowans gate to the constable body that was stationed
there; and the picket came up and cried *Hey, Alick, what was
that whoreson gabbing about?*

Alick Watson turned up the collar of his coat, and the
chaps thought it funny he was shivering like that.

Chris stood in her room and looked out of the window at the
quick-darkening February afternoon. It was this day only a
year ago that Robert had died in the pulpit of Segget, the
blood gushing suddenly up on his lips as he preached his last
sermon with a broken heart, Robert, kind, a dreamer, a lover
of men, lover of his Chris once with passion and humour,
sweet and leal and compassionate. And the world had broken
his heart and his mind, his dreams grey ash that had once
been fire. In that last sermon he'd preached for salvation *'A
stark, sure creed that will cut like a knife, a surgeon's knife
through the doubt and disease—men with unblinded eyes may yet
find it—'* not Christianity, or love, or his Socialism, some
dreadful faith that he might not envisage. And then he had
died; and she minded his lips, stained red, bubbly red, and
the curl of the hair on his head, dear alive hair on a head that
was dead. . . .

. . . Oh, less kind to you than I might have been. And I
can't help it now, that's by and put past, nothing helps now,
as little as you can I ever see a way out of all the ill soss. Not
that I think I would look if I could, I've no patience with
crowds or the things they want, only for myself I suppose I
can plan. And I stand in the bareness, alone, tormented, and
you . . . Oh, Robert man, had you stayed to help somehow we
might have found the road together. . . .

Daft old wife to weep over something long by that couldn't
be mended, her nature hers, his his, all chances gone in that
dust of days they'd known together in Segget, in love, in
estrangement, in fear and disgust—all ash with him and
finished forever. And on this day of all she must try to decide
. . . sell herself like a cow, a cow's purpose, in order to keep a
roof over her head.

And abruptly she was minding Robert's study in Segget, the panelled walls black-lined with books, the glint of peat-light on the chairs, the desk, Robert sitting deep in a chair, head in hands, she herself looking down at him in pity and disgust because of that weak God he feared and followed. And with that memory something seemed to blow through the room, blowing out the picture like a candle-flame . . . she had finished with men forever, and could never again stir to a semblance of life that something which died when Robert died. Better a beggar in Duncairn's wynds than sell herself as she'd almost planned.

And so she would tell Ake Ogilvie tonight.

When Alick Watson reached home in the Cowgate after coming off picket at Gowans and Gloag's he met the old woman going trauchling out, away to her afternoon cleaning up for a widow body that bade in Craigneuks. She said *God be here, are you back again? Well, try and do something for once for your meat. Your sister's lying in her bed, no well. If she wants anything, see that you get it her.*

Alick said he could do that without being blackguarded, Meg was his sister, wasn't she? And the old woman said not to give her his lip, the useless skulking striking sod, wasn't he black ashamed to live off his folk's earnings? And Alick said *Away to hell. Did I ask to be born in your lousy bed in this lousy toun?* and brushed past her, swearing soft to himself because of that stricken look in her eye.

Inside he got ready a cup of tea, bread and corned beef, and sat and ate, Meg asleep in the other room, he heard her turn and toss once, and stopped and listened, better to busy himself with souch sounds he needn't think then of what he had done . . . slipped the pepper poke into Ewan's pouch, Christ! if the other chaps ever found out—

And then Meg called *Alick, I heard you come in. Will you bring me a drink of water?*

He carried it to her and put his arm under her, lifting her, she was heavy already though he was the only one of the silly sods that had seen it yet. And because he aye had liked her so

well, as she him, though they'd never let on, he found a sharp
pain in his breast as he held her. Then she pushed him away
in a minute, and was sick.

Alick said that he'd better go get the doctor, and she said
not to talk like a neep-headed cuddy, couldn't a lassie be sick
now and then?

—*Ay, but not that kind of sickness, Meg. When was it you
were bairned?*

She said *Eh?* and then lay still for a minute, staring; he
said it was no good to look at him like that, he'd known a long
time and she might as well tell.

She turned her face to the pillow then, away from him, and
whispered *Six months ago. Oh, Alick!* and began to cry, soft,
in the littered bed, in a misery he couldn't help, could only
stare at helpless. *Where did he do it, the bastard? Up in his toff's
room in Windmill Place?*

She turned her head and stared again, and he saw the
flyting quean in her eyes: Windmill Place? What was he
havering about? The beast was never at the Place in his life.

Alick said *Listen, you bitch, and answer me straight:* and
bent over the bed and caught her wrists, crushing them in
sudden, frantic nieves. *Who's the father? Be quick and tell me!*

When he heard her say *Steve Selden*, he knew he'd been
done, had played the fool. And Oh Christ, Ewan—if Ewan
were caught——

He tore from the room and out of the house, banging the
door behind, down the steps, the old whaler captain was out
in the court, lurching home and singing a hymn, Ake saw his
old wife peering down in fear. But he brushed past the old
carle and ran for the entrance, two chaps that he knew were
entering the court, they tried to stop him, for a joke, and he
flung them aside, and paid no heed as they cried was it
daftness or dysentery? And out in the Cowgate he started to
run, dodging in and out the ash-cans on the pavement, a
black cat ran across the street in front, that for luck, hell,
there was a bobby.

So he slowed to a walk going by the bobby, if a childe were
seen by a bobby running in the Cowgate he was sure to be

chased and caught and questioned. Out of range Alick took
to his heels again and gained Alban Street the same minute as
a tram.

Only as he climbed the steps did he mind that he hadn't
even a meck upon him, and turned to jump off as the tram
with a showd swung grinding down to the Harbour:
suddenly shining in a glint of sun, gulls above it, the guff of
the Fish-Market meeting the tram like a smack in the face, it
grunted and sneezed and galloped on through it. But the
conductor had seen Alick and caught his arm: *Look out, you
whoreson, jumping off here. You'll bash out your brains—if
you've any to bash.*

Alick said he'd found he'd no money on him, he was one of
the strikers at Gowans and Gloag's in the hell and all of a
hurry to get down with a bit of news for the rest of the lads.
He'd jump off here—

But the trammie held fast, a squat, buirdly bird with a face
like a badly-made barn door. And he said Not so fast, wasn't
he Union as well? Here, he'd pay the ticket. Sit down and
wait.

That shortened the run, in a minute the Docks, the
trammie slowed down at a bend where he shouldn't, the
nearest to Gowans, and Alick jumped off and cried his thanks
and took to his heels and ran like the wind.

When the four o'clock picket went on that day there hadn't
been as big a birn as usual of idle folk to look on and claik.
The cold was biting across Footforthie gnawing through the
thin breeks and jackets of Broo men, sending them taiking
off to the Library to read last Sunday's *Sunday Post*, the
racing news and the story of a lassie raped, bairned, killed,
and fried up in chips—Ay, fairly educative, the Scottish
newspapers. . . . But a dozen or so still hung about, not
expecting much of a shindy at all: but you never knew when a
strike was on, there might be a bit of snot flying ere long.

There was only one of the bobbies there, the young
country cuddy, he grinned at the picket and one cried him
the old tale of the bobby whose beat was fair littered with

whores: and a new sergeant came on the beat one night and set the bobby to jailing each whore: but at last the bobby put his splay feet down: *I've run in my sisters and my auntie to please you, my wife and my daughter and my cousin Jean, but I'm damned if I'll run in my mother as well*—

And they all guffawed, they'd no spite against him, he none against them, funny a chap like that should have joined up with the lousy police though you couldn't much blame him, fine uniform to keep out the cold, good pay and a pension and perks for the picking. And you blew your chilled hands and spat in the Docks and were just thinking about dandering away home again when you looked up and saw a half-dozen police coming swaggering down to the Gowans gates, the meikle sergeant, Feet, in the lead. You cleared your throat and spat on the ground to get the stink of their wind from your thrapple, but the birn went by with hardly a look, they were all speaking low and chief-like together: what dirty sodding were they planning now?

The only chap of the picket who stood in the road was the young toff childe folk said was half-Red. He drew back a bit to let the bobbies gang by, but they weren't looking and one of the stots gave a stumble and nearly tripped over the toff. Then, afore you could wink, a queer thing was on, the bobby had grabbed the young toff by the neck and Feet cried out: *What's that—assaulting the police? Right, my lad, you can come on up to the Station.*

Young Tavendale said not to talk rot, the constable had been stumbling all over the street. Some others of the picket came out from the lithe, hanging round the bobbies, and called the same, the cuddy of a bobby had had the staggers, or water on the brain—if he had a brain. But Feet cried *Stand back, or we'll take you as well;* and he asked Tavendale if he'd come peaceable or not and Tavendale lifted his shoulders with a laugh and said he supposed so, he was cool and unfeared: and turned round sudden on the bobby that had bumped him: *I can see that this is a put-up show*—

Afore he could say another word, Christ, what a crack! the bobby had his stick out and smashed him to the ground.

Then he looked to Feet and the meikle swine nodded: *In self-defence, Dickson. All right, pick him up.*

You saw the toff as they carried him past, he was only a kid, his hair dripping with blood, he hung like a sack among their fat hands. The picket tailed after crying that they'd see about this: but at that the rest of the bobbies faced round and in half a minute had cleared the street, Feet said the picket was trying to prevent an arrest.

And off they carted young Tavendale; and just as you were slipping off home yourself to spread the news in Kirrieben you ran bang into a white-faced young fool, panting and habbering, *What's on at Gowans?* You told him, and he cried Oh Christ, he'd never meant it, and you thought he was probably drunk, or daft, or both, and left him to it, he looked soft enough to pitch himself head first in the Docks—

Every movement he made sent a stream of pain down his legs and body, he thought, but wasn't sure, that his right arm was broken where they'd twisted it; and thought again *Not likely, that would show too much;* and fainted off in the fire of the pain.

When next he woke he thought it near morning, his throat burning, he tried to cry for a drink of water. And after a minute the cell door opened, a blaze from the passage on the blaze in the cell, he saw a dim face, big, it floated, and the face said he'd get a drink if he owned up now it was him that had drowned Johnny Edwards and organized the throwing of the pepper at the Docks? And Ewan moved his swollen lips, dull mumble, and heard himself say *You can go to hell!* Then his head went crack on the bobby's boot. . . .

When he'd come-to after that time at the Docks he'd found himself on a bench in the Station, they'd started to ask his name and address and take it down in a big case-book. He'd asked what charge he was arrested on, and the big sergeant at the desk said he'd know soon enough, none of his la-de-da lip here, the bastard. *Right, boys, rape him.*

Two bobbies had taken on the job, in a minute they'd come on a bag of pepper, he'd stared, how the devil had that got there? The sergeant had cried *What say you to that?* and Ewan, half-blind with a headache, had said *Rats. Some groceries I was buying for my mother, that was all,* and the sergeant said by Christ, was that so? If his mother knew him when he finished with the Force she'd be a right discerning woman, she would: *Take him off to No. 3 cell, Sergeant Leslie. See he doesn't try to assault you again.*

He'd thought that a lout joke, suddenly it wasn't, three of them came into the cell behind him. And he'd minded in a flash of a story he'd read of the ghastly happenings in American jails. Rot: this was Scotland, not America, the police were clowns and idiot enough, but they couldn't—

Two of them held him while Sim Leslie bashed him, then they knocked him from fist to fist across the cell, body-blows in the usual Duncairn way with Reds, one of them slipped in the blood and swore, *That's enough for the bastard, he'll bleed like a pig.* Lying on the floor, Ewan had heard a queer bubbling, himself blowing breath through bloody lips.

Then, the cell wavering, they'd picked him up and flung him down on the wooden trestle. *Now, answer up or you'll get the works—*And they'd asked him again and again to declare it was he had caused the drowning of Edwards; and he'd bitten his lips, saying nothing, till their fumblings at last brought a scream shrilling up in his throat, a bit of it ebbed out and the bobbies left off, standing and listening, feared it might have been heard even down this deserted corridor of cells. Then they said they'd leave him alone for a while, they'd be back in a wee to the mucking Red sod. . . .

And still he'd said nothing, setting his teeth, though the pain behind his teeth had clamoured to him to let go, to confess to anything, anything, they wanted, Oh God for a rest from this. But that real self that transcended himself had sheathed its being in ice and watched with a kind of icy indifference as they did shameful things to his body, threatened even more shameful, twisted that body till his self cowered in behind the ice and fainted again. . . . And now, as he thought, the morning was near.

He moved a little the arm he'd thought broken, it wasn't,

only clotted with bruises, the dryness had left his throat, he lay still with a strange mist boiling, blinding his eyes, not Ewan Tavendale at all any more but lost and be-bloodied in a hundred broken and tortured bodies all over the world, in Scotland, in England, in the torture-dens of the Nazis in Germany, in the torment-pits of the Polish Ukraine, a livid, twisted thing in the prisons where they tortured the Nanking Communists, a Negro boy in an Alabama cell while they thrust the razors into his flesh, castrating with a lingering cruelty and care. He was one with them all, a long wail of sobbing mouths and wrung flesh, tortured and tormented by the world's Masters while those Masters lied about Progress through Peace, Democracy, Justice, the Heritage of Culture—even as they'd lied in the days of Spartacus, lying now through their hacks in pulpit and press, in the slobberings of middle-class pacifists, the tawdry promisings of Labourites, Douglasites. . . . And a kind of stinging bliss came upon him, knowledge that he was that army itself—that army of pain and blood and torment that was yet but the raggedest van of the hordes of the Last of the Classes, the Ancient Lowly, trampling the ways behind it unstayable: up and up, a dark sea of faces, banners red in the blood from the prisons, torn entrails of tortured workers their banners, the enslavement and oppression of six thousand years a cry and a singing that echoed to the stars. No retreat, no safety, no escape for them, no reward, thrust up by the black, blind tide to take the first brunt of impact, first glory, first death, first life as it never yet had been lived—

Trease said *Ay, well, we'll do what we can—and a wee thing more. But I wouldn't advise you to come to the court.*

Chris asked why, and the big man with the twinkling eyes in the great pudding face got up from the sofa in the sitting-room and looked at her as though passing a mild comment on the weather: *I'm feared your Ewan'll have been bashed a bit—all in bandages, you know, and a bit broken up.*

Chris stared: *But he didn't try to resist! All the rest of the picket saw his arrest.*

Trease twinkled his little eyes a bit, a mild joke: *Oh ay, but he's a Communist, you see, or he'll be by now, for his fancy League was no more than the dream of an earnest lad. Anyway, the bobbies think him a Red and they aye get Reds to 'resist' at the Station, they generally mash them in No. 3 cell. And this is your Ewan's first go, you know, they try to kill off the Red spirit right off.*

Chris said that was daft, they couldn't do things like that in this country, anybody knew the police were fair and anybody accused got a fair trial. Trease nodded, faith ay, if you were of the middle class and wore good clothes and weren't a Communist. Och, anything else—a sodomist, a pervert, a white slave trafficker, a raper of wee queans—any damn thing that you liked to think of. But if you were a revolutionary worker you got hell. Fair enough, for the Reds weren't out to cure the system, they were out to down it and cut its throat.

He waited while Chris got her coat and hat and left the house to look after itself. At Windmill Brae they found a tram and were down at the court by ten o'clock.

Outside were already a birn of men, down-at-heels, unshaven, they cried *Hello, Jim,* and stared at Chris and came drifting around Trease, unwashed, their stink awful, their faces worm-white, Chris stared at them with a sinking heart. Were these the awful folk that Ewan had ta'en up with?

Bobbies all about the entrance door, one or two had come down in the street, big-footed, and were pushing about, beefy and confident, truncheons out and shoulders squared. Trease stroked his chin and twinkled at the Broo men and strikers: *We'll demonstrate later, lads. You'd better disperse and not raise a row.*

So the two got into the court at last, Chris had never been in one before, panelled in dark wood, with a witness box with a curling bit of wood above it that vexed her because the thing looked so daft. She whispered to Trease, asking what it was, and he twinkled back 'twas the sounding-board, and then leaned back in his bench and yawned, they'd not have her Ewan on for a while, they'd wait till the Bailie got hot up a bit.

They finished at last with the street queans ta'en up, a soldier who'd stolen cigarettes from a stall, a man who'd knocked over a boy with a lorry. But there wasn't much in any of the cases, Bailie Brown, the leader of Duncairn Labour, rapped out his sentences snell and smart, fair a favourite with all the bobbies and giving double the sentences a Tory would have given—to show that he was impartial, like. Then Chris saw an inspector go whisper to him and the Bailie look at his watch and nod; and the far door opened and some body in a bandage came in unsteadily between two bobbies, Chris knew one, Sergeant Sim Leslie of Segget.

And then she knew Ewan, and some body cried *Order!* and Trease gripped her knee so hard that it hurt, left her breathless and she couldn't cry again, couldn't do anything but stare and stare at the bandaged figure pass in front of her and stand in the dock, the bobbies all a-glower. A little neat man got up with a paper, and hitched his gown and gave a quick gabble, talking down his shirt-front low and confidential. Then he asked for a remand . . . death of John Edwards . . . brutal assault on police at Docks . . . incriminating evidence. . . . Violently resisting arrest—

The Bailie nodded and looked up at the clock, *Remanded till Friday,* and then stood up, every body stood, and a bobby grabbed the bandaged figure.

As the bobbies passed by below Trease leaned forward: *Okay, Ewan?*

—*I'm all right. They've got nothing out of me. Hello, Chris. Don't worry.*

Neil Quaritch said he was damnably sorry but he couldn't do anything with the papers about it, he was only sub-ed and book-hound on the *Runner.* Besides, the *Runner* daren't make a comment on a case sub judice. Not that it would make it if it could. Oh, the police were a pretty low set of brutes, but he couldn't believe this tripe about Ewan being tortured—this was Duncairn, not Chicago; just Red blah Mrs Colquohoun could discount. Pity Ewan had been led away by the Reds, if he wanted social change there was Douglasism.

Financial Credit operated as Social Credit would ensure that the products of Real Credit, though privately owned, were not malaccredited—

Mr Piddle said *He-he!* he was dreadfully sorry. Yes, he'd been in the court and seen young Mr Tavendale, and yes, he'd written the story for the *Daily Runner.* No, he hadn't intended to offend anyone, but the public must have its news, Mrs Colquohoun. Could she give him a photo for the *Tory Pictman?* And wasn't it the case that her husband, the late minister of Segget, had also held—*He-he!*—rather extremist opinions?

Jim Trease said plain that of course the Communists would exploit the case to the full—for their own ends first, not for Ewan's. They'd do all they could for him, but Ewan was nothing to them, just as he, Jim Trease, was nothing.

Miss Murgatroyd said Eh me, it was Awful, and young Mr Ewan Such Fine to get on with, right interested in the books on old Scottish magic that she'd loaned him—they were Awful Powerful in magic, the Picts. However had he got in such company?—It was said he'd assaulted the police Just Awful and them so kind and obliging, Too. Ask some of her friends at the Unionist Club to interfere?—oh, she couldn't do that she was feared, it wouldn't be right, now, would it? And they all terrible against the Reds, not that Mr Tavendale was really one, she knew, but there you were, oh, she was terribly sorry—

Archie Clearmont said *Hell, was that Ewan? Didn't know he was Red. So was Wagner. Anything whatever I can do to help—*

John Cushnie said nothing but handed in his notice, he couldn't very well stay on any longer, and him an employé of Raggie Robertson's, you ken—

Ellen Johns said, white, *Anything you want. I'm a Socialist, too, and I started him on it—he's a Socialist, not a Red, it's all a ghastly mistake. Oh, Chris, how did he really look? . . . Oh, Chris, I'm sorry, I'm a fool to cry, he'd think me a fool—*

Ake Ogilvie said to Chris not to fret. He thought he could maybe fix up this business.

★

He went off to his work and bade off the whole day while Chris went about with a mind gone numb, dead brain in her head, scrubbing and cooking and serving the meals, helped by the new maid, a big widow woman who was kind as she could be and never spoke a word about Ewan or the case. The blink of March daylight closed into dark and still Chris worked in a numbing fear; then at last, as it drew to tea-time, she heard the front door open and Ake on the stairs, his slow, independent clump on the stairs. A wee while later he came down again and opened the door: *Ay, mistress, a word with you.*

He sat in the sitting-room, filling his pipe: *Well, you're looking on an unemployed man.*

Chris said *What?* and Ake nodded and struck a match, and took a bit puff, and said Right on the Broo, Jimmy'd finished with him and he with Jimmy. But that was neither here nor there at the moment. The main thing was that Ewan would be safe—or else Jimmy's bit secret would be all over Duncairn as fast as Ewan's Red friends and Ake could spread it abroad. Ay, a great thing, scandal.

Chris gasped *Ake, Ake, is't true?* and he said *Oh ay. There, mistress, don't take on so. He's safe, your loon, they won't push the case—that's the quality of justice we've got in Duncairn. Sit you still a wee bit and I'll tell the tale.*

She realized later he told it her so that she might hide in herself again. But her mind at the time frothed over the telling like a wild thing mad to be out of a cage, trying to think, to think that Ewan—

And Ake said he'd not made the sawmill that morning, but sought out Speight and put it to him that he could get this bit case against the young Red quashed—Ake knew the lad, there was no harm in him, a decent student, and he'd been sore mishandled already by the bobbies. And Jimmy had listened with his long dreich face looking dreicher than ever, and shaken his head, he couldn't interfere, he'd no power to influence the courts or the bailies. Ake had told him for Christ's sake not to talk wet, they were both of them out of their hippens by now, the Lord Provost kenned as well as he did that there was as much graft in the average Scots toun as in any damn place across the Atlantic. Who invited contracts for agreed-on tenders? Who arranged the sale of public land and bought it afore the offer was made public? Who took a squeeze off the water rates, and who made a bit thing from the Libraries? And where did the bobbies, inspectors and sergeants, get their extra wages for houses and motors except by acting as pimps for the whores, living off the lasses and running them in when they wouldn't pay up their weekly whack? And was there a bookie's pitch in Duncairn that didn't pay tribute, week in, week out? Not one.

Speight said that all that was just coarse rumour and scandal, he knew nothing about it, and Ake said *Maybe. And you'll see that this young Tavendale's let off with a caution, or whatever the flummery's necessary?*

The Lord Provost had nearly burst with rage then, he'd said he'd be damned if he'd be badgered and blackmailed in this way any longer, all because of a small mistake in his youth—was he the first young childe to rape a lass in a hedge, with a bit of darkness to hide his identity? . . . And Ake had seen he half-meant what he said, a rat that was fair being driven in a corner, he'd pressed him over-hard and his nerve would gang, the next thing might be Ake himself in the jail.

So he'd laid his proposition in front of Jimmy: if he'd bring this off in the Tavendale case Ake would never again breathe a single word about that lassie raped in a hedge, never a whisper in public or private, nor seek for any advantage on't. And the Provost had said *And you'll leave my sawmill?* and Ake had given a bit shrug and said *Ay. All right, Jimmy, it's ta-ta, then.*

When Alick Watson had settled with Red Steve Selden he looked more like a mess in a butcher's shop than a leader that had once been out in Canada and come back to Scotland all in a fash to see to the emancipation of the working class. They fought it out in a Cowgate wynd, four of the chaps had come to see fair play, in the end they held Alick and said to Selden he'd best give best else he'd get bloody murdered.

Selden coughed and spluttered and stood up again and said

he'd never given any man best, it wasn't his wyte he had bairned the lass and it wasn't his wyte she'd never let on. Alick said *What the hell! You knew all the time!* but Selden swore by Christ he never had, if he'd known he'd have done the decent thing. And all the chaps that were standing around cried out to Alick he might believe that, it was true enough, those daft Bulgars the Reds were as scared and respectable about bairning a quean as though they went to the kirk three times on a Sunday and said a grace afore every meal, there was hardly a one but was doucely married, they never looked near a lass if they were, a damn lot of killjoys a lot of folk said. . . . So Alick had had all his fighting for nothing: and what the hell was his fury for?

Alick said they could mind their own mucking business; and put on his coat and went up to the Slainges Barracks direct and hung about outside the gates a while, half-feared and yet desperate, the sentry looked at him and said *Hello, chum!* And Alick said *Hello. Is this where you 'list?*

The sentry, he was swinging to and fro in his kilt and carrying a wee stick, not a rifle, took a keek at the guardroom and syne round about, and said *For Christ's sake, what's ta'en you?—have you lain with your sister or robbed a bank?* Alick said he'd done neither; and the sentry said not to be a soft sod, then, why join up in this lousy mob? The grub was stinking potatoes, worse beef, seven shillings a week pay and about half of that docked in sports and fines. It was just plain hell when it wasn't hell decorated.

Alick said Ah well, he'd just take his chance; and went in through the gates to the office place, a wheen of poor muckers were wheeling round the square, shoggle and thud, they looked half-dead, punishment drill of some kind Alick knew. And he half made up his mind to turn back, then swore at himself for a yellow-livered sod, they couldn't do worse to him, could they, than the bobbies had done to Ewan?—Oh Christ! And he burst open the door of the office place and went in and they asked who the hell he thought he was, the Colonel, maybe? and closed the door; and that was Alick Watson's end for the Cowgate.

Folk heard the news and took it through hand, he must fair have gone skite, the silly young mucker, wearied no doubt with the darg of the strike. Most knew he'd a hand in the drowning of old Johnny Edwards—well, what of that? More than a dozen had had a bit hand, and a damn good job, the lousy old scab. And *they* didn't run off in a fear to 'list, they marched with the band that Jim Trease got up to demonstrate outside the Central Court where young Ewan Tavendale was coming up on Friday.

Banners and slogans, Jake Forbes with his drum, a cold, dreich, early April day. One or two as they slumped along thought of Alick ticking to another drum now. And what would young Tavendale get, would you say?

Then they heard a bit cheer break out up in front, and the news came flying down the ranks like fire, it was true enough, no it wasn't, yes it was, there he was coming down the steps himself, his head all bandaged: he waved a hand. He'd been letten off with a bit of a fine, his mother had paid it for him at once, there she was behind—*Christ, that his mother? I could sleep with her the morn and think her his sister. . . . Sulky-looking bitch. . . . Get out, she's fine. . . . There's Ewan. Now, lads, give him a cheer!*

Into the procession, Chris never knew how, marching by the side of Ewan up the Mile, *boomr* the drum in the hands of the fat man, big Mr Trease stumping ahead with his grin and his twinkle, Ewan's hand in hers. She wished they'd left her alone with her son, Ake had stood aside as they came from the court, *No, not me,* he had said to Jim Trease. *I'm no body's servant, the Broo folk's or the bobbies',* Chris had liked him for that for she felt the same, had always felt so and felt more than ever that she belonged to herself alone. Except for Ewan: Ewan's hand in hers. And he looked down and laughed, strained, cool from his bandages: *Cheer up, Chris, it'll soon be over and we can slip off and be respectable!*

. . . Come dungeon dark or gallows grim
This song shall be our parting hymn!

The procession halted below Windmill Steps, Trease had seen to that, he did it for her, Chris knew: a little thing that wouldn't hurt his propaganda. And the Paldy folk grabbed hold of Ewan and raised him up on the Steps: *Come on, gi'es a word, Ewan!* and a sudden hush fell, Chris stood back and waited and knew herself forgotten.

And he said in his clear and cool boy's voice that they needn't bother to make a fuss, he'd got no more than any might expect who was out to work for the revolution. One thing he had learned: the Communists were right. Only by force could we beat brute force, plans for peaceful reform were about as sane as hunting a Bengal tiger with a Bible. They must organize the masses, make them think, make them see, let them know there was no way they could ever win to power except through the fight of class against class, till they dragged down the masters and ground them to pulp—

Then he fainted away on the Windmill Steps.

April was in with a wild burst of the bonniest weather, fleecings of clouds sailed over Duncairn with the honking geese from Footforthie's marshes. Out in the little back-garden Chris saw the buds unfolding on bush and twig, and got out her hoe from its winter sleep, over the walls other garden folk were chintering and tamping on the drying earth. And Chris thought in that hour of the bright April day as she hoed round the blackberry bushes and roses—suddenly, with a long-forgotten thrill—what a fine smell was the smell of the earth, earth in long sweeping parks that rolled dark-red in ploughing up the hills of the Howe, earth churned in great acres by the splattering feet of the Clydesdale horses, their breath ablow on a morning like this, their smell the unforgotten stable smell, the curling rigs running to meet the sun. Earth . . . and she sossed about here in a little yard of stuff that the men she'd once known wouldn't have paused to wipe their nebs with!

If Ewan had been as that other Ewan . . . and she paused, bent over the hoe, at the thought. Was he so unalike? There was something about him since that awful time when he'd fainted on the Steps of Windmill Brae that had minded her of his father back from the War—not the Ewan of the foul mind and foul speech, but that darker being she'd not kenned in those days, only later when the tale of his death was brought her: that being who had been the real Ewan imprisoned, desperate, a wild beast seeking a shelter she hadn't provided, a torn and tormented thing seeking a refuge—

Och, she was silly to think that in this case of her little lad whom those beasts had mistreated—though he'd had no great mistreating, he'd told her, he was fine and would soon be about again.

She heard the sound of footsteps coming from the house and looked up and saw, and looked down again. And she thought with a whimsical, cool dismay it was funny she couldn't be letten a-be even out in the yard—a sore-harried body! And the whimsy went, she was cool and kind.

Ay, mistress, I want a bit crack with you.

—Yes, Ake.

He blew out a cloud of smoke, brushed it aside, he was standing with his big, well-blacked boots unlaced, his waistcoat open, his mouser well-curled, undisturbed, unhurrying, she felt his gaze on the side of her face. And he said they'd held up this business of a decision while he'd loaned her the money to carry on the house and ward off Mistress Cleghorn's holy bitch of a niece: but now came an accounting one way or the other: *Are you going to have me, then, as your man?*

And Chris unbent from the hoe and turned to him and that thing that had once been a poet in Ake's heart and was strangled with rage ere it ever reached vision, started sudden within him, oh bonny she was, sulky and gay with her bonny bronze hair. And she said, quiet and sweet, Yes, if he'd have her. She was nothing of a bargain for all that he'd done.

He thought through the dark of every night *Oh God, if only I could sleep!* And sleep came seldom, hour on hour, while he fought to lock back in his memory those pictures: pictures of himself in that prison cell, in the hands of the bobbies while they mauled him about, pictures . . . and he'd cover his face with his hands, bury his face in the pillow to forget the sick shame of it. He, Ewan Tavendale, held like a beast, his body uncovered and looked upon, jeered at, smeared with the foulness of those filthy eyes as battered by their filthy hands, held and tormented like a frog in the hands of a gang of school-kids. His body that once he'd hardly known, so easy and cool and sweet-running it had been: now in the dark it was a loathsome thing that he lay within, a foul thing he didn't dare look upon.

In the grip of that fear he locked his room every night, went about the house swathed up to the chin, Chris was watching, she'd know, Chris or else Ellen. Ellen and he once—sickening to think of, filthy and dirty, lips like hers on his. . . . *Oh, God, please let me sleep!*

Jim Trease called in that day with the news that the strike at last had come to an end, he sat with Ewan in the sitting-room, big, heavy and red, his little eyes twinkling. They'd all gone back and were cheerily at work making their armament bits again—'twas even said that Gowans were to install a gas-loading plant soon. Oh, the strikers had got the speeding up slowed down and a bit of an increase on all the piece-rates, Bolivia and Japan were in a hell of a stamash to get arms: and Gowans were dancing in tune.

—*And I went through what I did—just for that?*

Jim Trease nodded, Ay, just for that. And for just the same kind of result he'd been going through the like things a good fifteen years—living on pay a little better than a Broo man's, working out his guts for those thick-witted sods. . . . He twinkled his eyes and smoked his cigarette, looking like a Christmas pig, Ewan thought, with some foolish toy stuck in its mouth by a butcher. . . . And he'd do it another fifteen years till the bobbies got him down in some bit of a riot and managed to kick in his skull, he supposed—*For it's me and you are the working-class, not the poor Bulgars gone back to Gowans.* And suddenly was serious an untwinkling minute: *A hell of a thing to be History, Ewan!*

And for awhile his words and the image they painted abided with Ewan when Trease himself had gone shambling away across Windmill Place, turning, stout, shabby, to wave ta-ta. A hell of a thing to be History!—not a student, a historian, a tinkling reformer, but LIVING HISTORY ONE-SELF, being it, making it, eyes for the eyeless, hands for the maimed!—

And then he was shrinking back from the window at the sight of Ellen; but she'd seen him; waved. And across his memory there swept again, picture on picture, an obscene film, something they'd stick in him while he writhed, a bobby's hand—

Ewan!

He kept his face buried in his arms, feeling her arms around him, tight, her hair against his cheek, shivering away from the touch of that. And he said to her *Go away!* and she wouldn't, kept close to him, holding him, shaking him: *Ewan, listen, you're to tell me what's wrong with you—what I've done that you avoid me like this. Ewan, do you hate me so much and so suddenly?*

He told her he didn't hate her at all, it was just that he was white-livered, he supposed. And sat up and pushed her away, not looking at her, looking a boy still, with the scar down his temple healed by now. Ewan scarred: last time it had been the keelies, this time the police: who next? and she shuddered as he himself had done. And then in the queerest fashion it came to her that she knew what was wrong, suddenly, she tingled with a blush that spread all over her body, neck, cheek and breast, goodness knew how far, a blush of unbearable shame and compassion: Oh Ewan, poor Ewan!

But she didn't say that, crouched beside him with her chin in her hands looking at him and loving him so that she almost wept; and was desperate while her mind sought round and round for a way to get at him, to help him.

And slowly, with a queer unemotion, she realized the only way—if she'd take it for him.

He'd sat staring out of the window the while, now she ran to that window and pulled open the curtains and stared up at the sky. April was in, the weather would keep all day she thought: *Ewan, what are you doing this weekend?*

He said Nothing. Read a book. Hadn't an idea.

—*I want to go out a long ride on a bus. Somewhere. I get so sick of Duncairn. Will you come with me?*

—*Oh, if you like. I'll be poor enough company.*

She said she'd risk that, she'd go and find out about the buses. Would he be ready in an hour's time?

It felt the most crowded hour of her life, dragging on her hat and running from the house down to the bus-stance in Royal Mile, long lines of buses like dozing dragons, the drivers yawning and staring at the sky, staring at newspapers, buses innumerable, with all signs on them: where would she go? Then she saw a bus with GLEN DYE upon it, and she'd never been there, it was safe enough. So she found out the time when the bus was to start, the conductor said in a fifty minutes—*Don't be late, are you bringing your lad?* And Ellen said *Quite* and smiled at him, a bonny black pussy-cat of a creature, he straightened his tie and looked after her—'Od, keeks of that kind were unco scarce.

But Ellen had scrambled aboard a tram, it shoomed down the Mile as though knowing her haste, she stared in the gaudy windows of Woolies—would that do? for she hadn't much money to waste.

So she hurried in and looked in the trays, at the glitter, at the dull dog eyes of the girl at the counter, and foolishly felt sick, sentimental idiot. No, she wouldn't, she'd get it real, silly though that was!

Out of Woolies and off the Mile and found a passable place in George Street, and went in there, into a great clicking of clocks and watches, glimmer of silver, and bought what she wanted, and came out in the flying sun-scud of Spring. *What next?*—*This'll try your courage, my girl.*

It did, but she stuck it, looking cool as a cucumber, the shopkeeper an elderly, slow-moving man, he listened to her wants in the little shop with the ghastly books and the half-hid door, and said he thought another thing better. Had she ever tried it? And showed it to her, and Ellen said she hadn't, was it really good? And the shopman said Ay, unemotional as a boiled turnip, he could recommend that. And Ellen said *Thanks, I'll have it then. And I'm in a hurry.* And he said *Fine weather.*

Back to the Mile. And now—what else? Rucksacks? She'd one of her own, Ewan hadn't, Woolies again and get one for him. Running up through the crowds she looked at her watch and found she had still a half-hour to spare, saw her face as she whipped into Woolies, flushed and dark, that hair on her upper lip horrid in a way, Spanish and nice in another way. Rucksack and straps and she was digging out the sixpences, three of them, and had the thing tied up in paper. Now for Windmill Place again and see Chris after she'd bought some chocolates and fruit.

Running up the door-steps she peeped through the window and saw Ewan sitting where she had left him, staring out, that nerved her for the thing she'd to do. She ran up to his room and looked quick about and saw the old wardrobe hid in the corner and opened the packet she'd bought from Woolies and stuffed in things from the wardrobe, quick, stopping and listening for feet on the stairs. Then into her own room like a burglar, quiet, panting and working there like a fury, running to and fro and cramming her knapsack, anything forgotten?—Oh Lord, the things from the little shop! Here they were, safe, cheers, that was all.

Chris was making scones in the kitchen when Ellen looked in, looked sweeter than ever, Ellen thought, lovely those tall Scotch cheekbones, nice sulky face.

Hello, Ellen lass, come for a scone?

Ellen said she hadn't, but she'd eat one, though; and sat on the table, eating it, and they smiled one at the other, mistrust long past. And Ellen said *Mrs Colquohoun, Ewan's not well.*

The lovely, sulky face went dark in a minute, like her son's then despite all the differences. *Where is he?—Oh, nothing new happened. But ever since that time in the jail. I want to take him out to the country—somewhere; and I want to know if you'll mind.*

Chris looked at her a minute and then laughed, saying they surely could go where they liked, they were neither of them bairns, Ellen nodded and jumped off the table. *I know. But I don't know if we'll be back tonight.*

And then she thought Ewan's mother understood, her eyes changed and grew darker and glassed over with gold in that way that Ellen had seen before. She said quietly and kindly: *I won't worry. But, Ellen—*

—*Yes?*

—*It's your life and his, but I think I ken Ewan. He's like this for the time, but he won't be long. And when he's once better . . . he's a funny lad. I don't think he'll ever be any lass's lad.*

For a second Ellen felt cold to her spine. True in a way—and she didn't care! Chris liked the gay smile on the scared pussy-face: *We're only going hiking. Bye-bye, Mrs Colquohoun.*

Plodding teams blue steam in the parks as the fat bus grunted up the Hill of Barras, Ellen beside Ewan looked up a moment, he'd just asked, in his soft Scotch voice and as though wakening up, what were a couple of rucksacks for?

She said *For fun. I've brought some lunch.*

Below them all the eastwards Howe lay spread, grey saffron and thinly wooded, cold-gleaming under the quick Spring sun—a bare and wild and uncanny land, she'd never be at home here she thought with a shiver, though she trilled her r's and lived to be a hundred. Hideous country, ragged and cruel . . . but Ewan's shoulder against hers sweet.

And Ewan looked out and saw the Howe and far away high in the air beyond the cold parks and the dark little bourochs of nestling trees under the lithe of the shining hills, the line of the mountains, crested in snow, unmelting, Trusta Peak over High Segget, the round-breasted hills like great naked women waking and rising, tremendous, Titanic. Watching, Ellen saw his face suddenly darken, she said *Headache going?* and he answered her hardly (poor Ewan!) *Yes. I'm all right.*

Down by the Pitforthies and by Meikle Fiddes into the main road winding broad, chockablock with traffic tearing south, loaded lorries and glistening cars, swaying shapes of the great Dundee-Aberdeen buses squattering the ancient tracks of the Howe. Cattle were out from the winter byres, flanks laired in sharn and eating like mad on the thin, lush pastures that couched from the wind under the shelter of the olive-green firs. With a chink and a gleam and a slow, canny stamping the ploughmen faced up against far braes, the dirl of little stones pattered the windscreen as the bus ran through a great skellop of tar, roadmenders resting and giving them a wave, every soul in a fairly fine tune today.

And then, queerly and suddenly, Ewan's heart moved. He said to Ellen: *We're into Kinraddie.*

She'd never heard of it, he'd been born here, away up in a little farm in the hills, they'd see the place in a minute or so. And sure so they did, ringed round with its beech, Blawearie wheeling and unfolding, high, Ewan minded a day as a little lad standing by the side of his mother by the hackstock and watching a man in a soldier's gear going out of the close and not looking back: and his mother paying no heed to the man, the man's hands trembling as he fastened the gate. . . . So bright and near and close was the picture he shook his head to shake it away, he'd never remembered it before. That man—his father, he supposed, in the days of the War, going to the War, had he and Chris quarrelled? . . . Long ago, it had nothing to do with him.

His movement made Ellen ask if he was cold, and he turned and looked into her face, bright, flushed, little beads of sweat along her dark brows, she had opened the neck of her dress, skin warm and olive, he stared at that, looked like silk, maybe felt like it to touch. She asked, peeping a smile, if there was a smut on her nose? and saw the grey-gold eyes lose their dull film a moment. He said *Nice of you to take me out. No, I'm not cold—and there isn't a smut. Devil of a stour this bus is raising!*

The roads were dry and they ploughed a dust cloud in the wake of a wandering bouroch of sheep, maa'ing and scattering, the shepherd waved a canny hand to the driver and the driver wormed a canny way forward. Then the bus picked up and shoggled up through Drumlithie, the steeple still there: tell Ellen the joke.

They both craned out to look up at it, the steeple bell with no church behind; and Ellen's smooth braid of short-cut hair, blue-black, whipped Ewan's cheek like the touch of a bird, swift, with the smell of the Spring.

And his mind at that touch remembered again the Horror: but it was in some way dimmer, queer, as though something were hiding it away. And he sat and puzzled on that while Ellen looked sideways at him and thought in a panic he looked more shut-away and lost than ever, what if she failed?—Oh, she couldn't do that. . . . And again that flush started near the tips of her ears and spread out and under, cheekily, and the bus wheeled on and up into Segget, shining half-dead with its whitewashed walls.

Ewan looked back as they left the place and saw the Manse high up from the toun, and above it the ruined castle of the Kaimes where he'd gathered flints when he was a kid—a million and a half or so years ago. God, what a solemn young ass he had been!

And he minded the rolling drummle of names of those hill-hidden touns through the parks of which he'd searched out the flints—Muir of Germany, Jacksbank, Tannachie, Arnamuck, Bogjorgan, Droop Hill, Dillavaird, Goose-craves, Pittengardener, Cushnie, Monboddo—he could run the list for a hundred more, queer he'd never before seen those names for the real things they were, the lives and desirings of many men, memories of their hopes and possessions and prides though their own names and dates had vanished forever. And he thought of Trease saying that he and the rest of the Reds were nothing, they just worked the will of history and passed. . . . And suddenly Ewan's mind trembled on the verge of something, something that he couldn't name, maybe God, that made this strange play with lives and beliefs: and it seemed a moment that the shambling bus was the chariot of Time let loose on the world roaring down long fir-darkened haughs of history into the shining ways of tomorrow.

They came into Auchinblae, clatter and showd, the mountains near now, and Ewan looked out. Ellen had the tickets: where were they going?

Ellen said she'd taken tickets for Glen Dye but they needn't go there if he'd rather not. And Ewan looked at her shoes and then at his own and said *Let's get out and climb Drumtochty and then go over to Finella.*

Down in the Strath an hour or so later they came into the road through the Garrold Wood, dark the pines, here the sun was lost. Ewan had taken one of the rucksacks and asked again what she'd brought them for? And Ellen had smiled a secret smile at the road—*Oh, for fun!*—slim, like a boy, not feeling like one, and stared up through the woods at the heights of Drumtochty towering far in the April air, dark at this time of the year, the sky behind waiting and watching with a fleece of clouds like an old woman's cap. Ewan looked up when she pointed that out, he said that that was Finella's mutch, had she never heard of Finella?

And they sat and talked on a little bridge, the water below spun coolly and softly down to the hidden Luther water, and he told her the tale of the Lady Finella and the old-time wars in the Howe of the Mearns. And Ellen, sleek head uncovered to the sun, listened and asked were those the Covenanting Times? Ewan said Oh no, they had come long after, funny chaps the Covenanters, he always had liked them—the advance guard of the common folk of those days, their God and their Covenant just formulæ they hid the social rebellion in. They had fought up here in the 1640's and away in Dunnottar Castle the gentry had imprisoned and killed them in scores. . . . And his face grew dark, no boy's face: *There's nothing new under the sun—not even torture.*

She said gently *Ewan, what did they do to you?*

He didn't change colour or alter at all, just turned and looked at her and began to speak, low and steady, she whispered in a minute *Ewan, oh my dear!* and then felt sick, knew she'd faint, gripped herself not to, and felt sick again, she'd fail him completely if she were that. So he went on and finished; in the silence that followed they heard the whisper of the Luther hushaweesh in the reeds and far away in the listening trees—long and contented—the croon of a dove, terrible in its soft and sleepy content.

Ewan took out his handkerchief and wiped his face, and then queerly and tenderly wiped Ellen's, sweat on it as on his own though the wind blew snell. And holding his hand below her chin something lost ran a strange quiver up his arm, he didn't heed it, smiling into the misery of her eyes, speaking Scotch who so seldom spoke it, that blunted and foolish and out-dated tool: *You needn't fash for me. I've been the gypedest of gomerils to let on and vex you so, but I'm better now, I'll forget, we forget everything*.

They left the road and went into the wood and were presently tackling the chave of the slopes, sharp and tart the whiff of the broom, crackling underheel the old year's whins. All the hills and the world in their background stilled except that far off above the ploughed lands that shored red in clay to Drumelzie woods the peewits cried, in a breathing-space they halted and listened, *laplaplap*. Then they took to shinning the haughs again and saw the scrub open in front and far up, ridge on saffron ridge, Finella riding the southern lift.

When they gained the utmost ridge in early afternoon the Howe below was mottled in fog, sun with them here in a little hollow high on the crest where they sat and ate the lunch they had brought. Then Ewan lay flat and looked at the sky, hardly they'd talked in the last hour or so, and talked little now, Ellen squatting beside him said *You need a pillow*, and meant the rucksacks. And then didn't; and was sensible.

His head in her lap he lay quiet, nice head, the weight sent through her a queer delight, foolish and tender, she bent over to speak to him. Then she saw his eyes closed: he was fast asleep.

When he woke he was looking at the westering sun low down in the Howe of Drumtochty. He ached all over, sun-sleepy, sun-tired, yet vaguely refreshed and his sins forgiven. Then he found where his head still rested, heavy, and started up, Ellen moved at last and cried out at a sudden sting of cramp.

—*Why didn't you wake me? You must feel half-dead*.

She said, with a pretence at perky Scots, *More whole than half, but you slept so sound*, and stood up beside him, dark as him. With the drowse still in his eyes he smiled at her: *That was nice of you*.

She said absently *I thought you were going to kiss me, don't bother now, there still are some oranges! . . . But what wouldn't I give for a cup of tea!*

He thought it must surely be late by now, but she showed him her watch, only four o'clock, they'd have plenty of time to get back to Auchinblae and get a bus to Duncairn in time, the last passed through at six o'clock.

So they sat down, yawning, and ate the last orange, and Ellen began to speak about Socialism and the world revolution that was coming soon when the workers were led in a sane way to power, no blood and mess, reorganizing things for the good of all, building great healthy cities, schools (what fun there would be in gutting Duncairn!), endowing the sciences, endowing motherhood, no more weeping and no more tears: *I couldn't go on living if I hadn't that belief*.

And the dark Scotch boy shook his head and said you could go on living though you might believe in nothing at all—like Chris; and that struck Ellen as queer and then as true, and then queerer still. Funny freaks the Scotch, rather dears sometimes. . . . And she stopped her mind bothering about them at all, only about Ewan, and peeped at her watch when he wasn't looking, then at the sun and as she did so a long, cold shaft of wind blew up the heath at their feet and they raised their eyes and saw the fringes of the darkness on the land, below them the Howe stirring as though someone had stirred a dark drink in the mixture. Ewan jumped to his feet: *Your watch must have stopped*. And took her wrist: *Let's see*.

The watch had stopped. They packed up the rucksacks and slung them on their backs, Ellen's mind in a flurry. Shouldn't she have done it up here?—she could, easily, nothing to have stopped her. Only—a mess; and she wanted it proper. What now, what the devil the best thing to do?

Ewan called to her not to take that way, the other was the nearest to Auchinblae, she cried back that here was a clearer track and he came to her side and they ran hand in hand, plunging and slipping from tuft to tuft, the woods stared up and came gambolling to meet them, bound on bound, Luther gleaming beyond, up in the opposite heights rode a castle, all curlecue battlements, a pork-pie in stone. Then it vanished from view as they still fell west.

Ewan said it didn't matter, over late now to reach Auchinblae, and looked worried a minute, and a clump of larch came and a shoulder of hill and, winding wide and deserted, the road. Ellen stumbled against him of a sudden dog-tired, the outing had won, not her, no need to go on with the thing to the end—oh, thank goodness, for she'd never have managed!

He said *Ellen!* in a strange, hushed boy's voice and put his arms under her arms, she saw his face suddenly blind, she gave a little sob, kissing he drew her tight and a wild fear came and struggled and escaped, she didn't want to escape him, hadn't done this to help him, she just wanted him for herself, for delight. And she held him away and told him that and he blushed, funny Ewan who could kiss like so! But his voice was cool and clear as glass: *I'm going to kiss you all over. Soon.*

She said that would be fun, trying not herself to go foolish again; and told him to sit down and asked what he knew of the countryside here, he didn't know much, two or three miles away was a little inn, he thought, he'd once seen it, picture-book place with honeysuckle in the summer. . . . She said *Oh Lord,* NOT *honeysuckle!* and he said he was sorry, but it wouldn't be out; and they smiled at each other, stared, laughed, kissed once—too damn dangerous more than once.

And then she remembered and sought out the wedding ring she had bought that day: *Ewan, will you put this on for me?*

When she woke near morning in the little inn-room he was sleeping beside her, hallowed and clean and made whole again, light faint on the dark face turned to her shoulder; and in tenderness she lay and looked at him and thought *Yes, that was fun, Oh Ewan, funny boy!*

He woke at her movement—quickly, at once, and knew her, put his right arm under her head, and said sleepily did he tell her last night that Yes, she felt as well as looked like silk? Some funny grain in skin-texture, no doubt: he'd find out some time, unless he first ate her. . . . And he'd forgotten to kiss her as completely as he'd promised.

But when he'd done that and slept again, Ellen didn't, holding him in a quiet compassion that he wouldn't have understood and would never know; and that didn't matter, she was his forever, in desire or hating, his till they ended or grew old and remembered, far off, the terror and wonder of those first moments that made you suddenly so frightened of God because there must be a God after all.

And Chris stood with gloved hands on the hot May railings and looked down at Duncairn where her marriage was waiting. What a reel of things in a short few months, what an antrin world that waited tomorrow!

Well, that had to be faced, and whatever else it would be (she thought, and smiled to her sulky self trigged out in the glass of the Windmill Steps) it wouldn't be the tomorrow she expected now. No tomorrow ever was though you planned it with care, locked chance in the stable and buried the key.

Tomorrow.

Ake.

Ewan.

Ellen.

Ewan and his Ellen. What had happened with them? Nothing but the thing that had happened so often as any fool of a woman might know. And now that it had happened— what came next? And she thought *Ah well, it's no matter of mine*, though her thoughts strayed a little even as she thought that, half in tenderness, half in anxiety, wondering what they'd said, what they'd done, what their compact was, not caring greatly they'd done ill by old standards though she hoped to God they'd at least been careful. And she minded their faces at breakfast that day and that look they'd exchanged while she sat and watched, Ellen's open and lovely, unashamed, Ewan's open as well, but the kind of smile that no lad ever yet kept for his lass. Grey granite and thistledown—how would they mix?

Oh, that unguessable tomorrow would tell!

FOUR

Zircon

THE HILL SLOPES were rustling with silence in the glimmer of the late June gloaming as Chris Ogilvie made her way up the track, litheness put by for a steady gait. On the bending slopes that climbed ahead to the last of the daylight far in the lift the turning grass was dried and sere, a June of drought and swithering heat, the heather bells hung shrunken and small, bees were grumbling going to their homes, great bumbling brutes Chris brushed from her skirts. Half way up she stopped a minute and rested and looked down with untroubled eyes at the world below, sharp-set and clear each item of it in that brightness before the dark came down, mile on mile of coarse land and park rolling away to the distant horizons that tumbled south to her forty years in the distant Howe.

She looked down at herself with a smile for her gear and then took to the climb of the brae again, following the windings of the half-hidden path, choked with whins and the creep of the heather since the last time men had trauchled up here. Then, greatly cupped and entrenched and stone-shielded, she saw the summit tower above her, so close and high here the play of the gloaming it seemed to her while she stood and breathed if she stretched up her hand she could touch the lift—the bending bowl of colours that hung like a meikle soap-bubble above her head.

Treading through the staying drag of the heather she made her way under the shoggle of the walls to a high, cleared space with stones about, to the mass of stone where once the astronomers had come a hundred years before to take an eclipse of the moon or sun—some fairely or other that had bothered them and set them running and fashing about and peering up at the lift and gowking, and yammering their little supposings, grave: and all long gone and dead and forgotten. But they'd left a great mass of crumbling cement that made a fine seat for a wearied body—a silly old body out on a jaunt instead of staying at home with her work, eident and trig, and seeing to things for the morn—that the morn she might get up and see to more things.

That the reality for all folk's days, however they clad its grim shape in words, in symbols of cloud and rock, mountain that endured, or shifting sands or changing tint—like those colours that were fading swift far in the east, one by one darkening and robing themselves in their grave-clouts grey, happing their heads and going to the dark. . . . Change that went on as a hirpling clock, with only benediction to ring at the end—knowledge that the clock would stop some time, that even change might not endure.

She leaned her chin in her hand and rested, the crumbling stone below her, below that the world, without hope or temptation, without hate or love, at last, at long last. Though attaining it she had come a way strewn with thorns and set with pits, like the strayings of a barefoot bairn in the dark—

She'd not failed in her bargain she told herself that night in the house on Windmill Place, been glad for the man with kindness and good heart, given that which he needed and that which he sought, neither shrinking not fearing. And he'd given her a pat *Ay, lass, but you're fine,* and thrust her from him, assuaged, content, and slept sound and douce, alien, remote. Her husband, Ake Ogilvie.

She bit her lips till they bled in those hours that followed, seeking not to think, not to know or heed or believe when every cell of her body tingled and moved to a shivering disgust that would not cease—Oh, she was a fool, what had happened to her that wasn't what she'd known, expected to happen? Idiot and gype to shiver so, she'd to sleep, to get up in the morning and get on with her work, get her man's meat ready, his boots fresh-polished, sit by his side and eat in a kitchen, watch his slobberings of drink and his mouthings of food while he took no notice of her, read his paper, laced his boots and went showding out to look for a job, a contented childe. . . . She'd all that waiting for her the morn, all morns : sleep and be still, Oh, sleep and be still!

And at last she lay still with memories and ghosts, Ewan with dark hair and boy's face, Ewan beside her, Ewan from the dust, who'd thought her the wonder of God in the wild, dear daftness of early love, Ewan whom she'd loved so and hated so, Ewan—oh, little need to come now, she'd paid the debt back that he'd given for her when they murdered him that raining morning in France, paid it to the last ounce, body and flesh. And then in the darkness another came, a face above her, blue-eyed, strong-lined, only a moment as that moment's madness between them long syne. Not in longing or lust had they known each other, by chance, just a chance compassion and fear, foolish and aimless as living itself. Oh, Long Rob whose place was never with me, not now can you heed or help me at all. . . .

Quiet and quiet, because not that third, not look at him or remember him. And she buried her face in the pillow not to see, and then turned and waited rigid : Robert.

And she saw him for the first time since he'd died Robert completed, who'd had no face in her memory so long, Robert with eyes and face and chin and the steady light of madness in his eyes. Robert not the lover but the fanatic, Robert turning from her coughing red in sleep in that last winter in Segget, Robert with red lips as he sat in the pulpit—she stared at him dreadfully in the close-packed dark, far under her feet the clocks came chiming while she lay and looked and forgot to shiver.

Not Ake alone, but beyond them all, or they beyond her and tormenting her. And she knew in that minute that never again in memory or reality might any man make in gladness unquiet a heart passed beyond lust and love alike—past as a child forgetting its toys, weeping over their poor, shattered shapes no longer, and turning dry-eyed to the lessons of Life.

Ewan tramped Duncairn in search of a job—he knew it would be too expensive a job to try and fight on the apprentice's rights which Gowans and Gloag had torn up with his agreement. No chance of winning against them, of course, they could twist any court against a Red. He told that to Chris, cheery and cool; but his coolness was something different now. Cold and controlled he had always been, some lirk in his nature and upbringing that Chris loved, who so hated folk in a fuss. But now that quality she'd likened to grey granite itself, that something she'd seen change in Duncairn from slaty grey to a glow of fire, was transmuting again before her eyes—into something darker and coarser, in essence the same, in tint antrin queer. More like his father he seemed every day, if one could imagine that other Ewan with his angers and hasty resentments mislaid. . . . She told him that and he laughed and teased her: *Only I'm a lot better looking!* and she said absently he would never be that, there was over-much bone in his face.—*And what job are you thinking of trying to get?*

He said he'd no idea, any old job, there'd likely not be much opening for a Red: *I'm sorry to have upset your plans, you know, mother.*

Chris asked What plans? and he asked with a grin hadn't she wanted him to be respectable, genteel, with no silly notions and a nice office suit? Chris didn't laugh, just said she hadn't known she'd mothered a gowk: if he knew as little of the beliefs that had made him a Red as he knew of her—faith, it would be long before he and Mr Trease ruled in Duncairn.

He sat and listened to that with a smile: *Faith, it'll be long anyway, I'm afraid. And as for what you call my beliefs, they're just plain hell—but then—they* ARE *real. And you ought to like them, you're so much alike!*

She asked what he meant, and he said *Why, you're both real*, and stood up and cuddled her, laughing down at her, Ewan who'd once had no sense of humour, had he found that in torment in a prison cell? *Didn't you know you were real, Chris, realer than ever? And stepfather Ake's pretty real as well.*

Real? She watched through the days that followed, manner

and act, gesture and gley, with a kind, quiet curiosity. Like Ewan he was tramping Duncairn for a job, she'd listen to his feet on the stairs as he went, and the stride never altered, an unhastening swing. And at evening they'd sit long hours in the kitchen, Chris sewing, him reading, hardly speaking a word, Chris because she had nothing to say, Ake because he'd no mind for claik. Then he'd drink his cocoa and look at the clock, and say *Lass, it's time we went off to bed*, and off he'd go, in his socks, no slippers or shoes, she'd follow and find him winding his watch, feet apart, independent, green-eyed, curled mousered, taking a bit glance at the night-time sky. And even while they undressed he'd say no word, getting cannily into the bed and lying down. Then he'd swing over on his pillow and off to sleep without a good night or a single remark: would a man be as daft as say good night to his own wife?

And Chris as those nights went by, padding at the heels of unchanging days, slept well enough now without fears at all on that matter that had set her shivering at first, she shivered no longer, he came to her rarely, eidently, coolly; and with a kind honesty, unhurtable now, she awaited him, paying her share of the price of things, another function for the woman-body who did the cooking and attended the house while he still kept up his hunt for a job.

Kisses there were none, or caresses even, except a rare pat as she leaned over to set a plate in front of him. They said bare things one to the other: *Ay, it's clearing. . . . Rain in the lift. . . . Eggs up in price. . . . That'll be Ewan. . . .*

She was finding ease who had known little.

The Reverend MacShilluck had never heard the like, he'd advertised for a gardening body and the morning the advertisement appeared in the *Runner*, the first to come in search of the job—now, who do you think the young thug was?

The housekeeper simpered and said she didn't know: could it be the young man was an ill-doer, like?

The Reverend MacShilluck said Not only that, far worse

than that, ahhhhhhhhhhhh, far worse. And the housekeeper said *Well, God be here. Was the smokie to your taste?* for she wanted away back to the kitchen to add up the grocer's account for the week and see how much she could nick on the sly and save up against the day that would come when she'd be able to clear out completely and leave the clorty cuddy forever. . . . But he was fairly in full swing by then and went on to tell that the young man who'd come was no other than that thug Ewan Tavendale who'd led the strikers at Gowans and Gloag's and been sacked for it, he'd been in the jail and yet had the impertinence to come looking for a job about a Manse. So the Reverend had refused him, sharp and plain, he'd seen the young brute was a typical Red, born lazy, living off doles and never seeking an honest day's work—

The housekeeper said *God be here, like that? Then he couldn't have been seeking the job at all?* And the Reverend MacShilluck gave a bit cough and said he would never trust a Red, not him; had he ever told her the tale of the way at the General Assembly he'd once choked off a Socialist, Colquohoun—shame on him, and him a minister, too! . . .

Miss Murgatroyd said Eh me, it was Awful, but had Mrs Colquohoun—oh, sorry, she meant Mrs Ogilvie—heard of the Dreadful Occurrence at Gawpus's shop? And Chris said she hadn't and Miss Murgatroyd said she didn't know how to speak, she was sure Mrs Ogilvie would understand her point of view and that she didn't really believe that young Mr Ewan had behaved like that. And Chris asked what was this about Ewan? and Miss Murgatroyd told her the dreadful story, just as she'd got it from that dear Mrs Gawpus that afternoon at the Unionist Ladies. It seemed that Mr Ewan had got employment in the basement of Bailie Gawpus's shop, and oh me, it was awful to tell the rest. He'd been there only a day or so when the other workmen in the basement had started raising a din because there wasn't a proper, you know, WC there, the Bailie had thought it would be just pampering keelies, wasn't there the yard outside? The Bailie had gone down to see what was wrong, and then he'd set eyes on Mr Ewan, so unfortunate, for the Bailie remembered him—he

had seen him when he was arrested for taking a part in that
dreadful strike. Bailie Gawpus hadn't known that Mr Ewan
was one of his employees, a foreman had engaged him—such
a nice man, the Bailie, but awful strict, a little stout, she was
sure it was his heart—

Well, he became Such Indignant at seeing Mr Ewan, and
sure that he was causing the bother, that he ordered him out
of the basement at once, he was so against the Communists
and the dreadful things they had done to the Common People
in Russia. He told Mr Ewan he was dismissed on the spot,
Such a Pity, Bailie Gawpus perhaps not as nice as he might
have been—in fact, Mrs Gawpus admitted that her husband
perhaps exceeded his powers, he laid hands on Mr Ewan to
push him out. And then—it was dreadful, dreadful, a man
old enough to be his father—Mr Ewan seized Bailie Gawpus
by the collar of his coat and ran him out to the yard at the
back, the Bailie almost dying of rage and heart-failure, and
showed him—you know, the place that those awful basement people Used. And he asked how the Bailie would like to
use it? And before the Dear Bailie could say anything at all he
was down on his hands and knees and his face being Rubbed
in It—feuch, wasn't that awful? Worse still, the rest of the
dreadful keelies came out from the basement and cheered
and laughed and when Bailie Gawpus got up to his feet and
threatened to send for a policeman Mr Ewan said there was
no need to do that, he was off to get one himself and report
the sanitary conditions of the place. So dreadful for the
Bailie. He'd to pay up a week's wages to Mr Ewan and
promise to have a proper WC constructed; and the Bailie was
just Boiling with Rage. . . .

Almost every night after that weekend in Drumtochty Ellen
would slip through her doorway, sly pussy-cat, and trip along
to Ewan's room, scratch on the door and be letten in, and
taken and kissed and looked at and shaken, because they
were mad and the day had seemed—Oh, so horribly long!
And Ellen would forget the vexatious Scotch brats whom she
tried to drum up the steep cliffs of learning, sour looks and

old women and the stench from the drains of the Ecclesgriegs Middle, the sourly hysterical glares of Ena Lyon—everything every time in that blessed minute when inside Ewan's door she was inside his arms, tight, arms hard and yet soft with their dark down fringe, Ewan's face bent down to hers to that breathless moment when she thought she would die if he didn't, in one second—oh, kiss her quick!

And he did, and her arms went up round his neck, fun, thrilly: you'd often wondered what men's necks were for. And the two of you would stand still, so cuddled, not kissing, not moving, just in blessed content to touch, to hear the beating of each other's hearts, each other's breathing, know each other's being, content and lovely, without shelter or shyness one from the other, blessed minute that was hardly equalled in all else, not even the minutes that followed it later.

But first she made tea on Ewan's gas-ring with the kettle and teapot they'd bought together in a Saturday evening scrimmage at Woolies, China tea, Ellen kneeling to make it, having made Ewan sit and be quiet and not fuss, tired out with haunting the streets for a job. And he'd say *But I'm not*, and she'd say then he ought to be—*Sit still and read and don't argue*. Ewan would laugh and drag down a book, silence in the room but for the gas-hiss, Ellen drowsy as she watched the bubbling gas-flame and the kettle begin to simmer and stir. Housekeeping comfy and fun, alone in a room with Ewan: though the house wasn't theirs, nor the room, nor the furniture, nothing but a sixpenny kettle and teapot and cups and saucers at a penny a piece!

She'd glance up at him, deep in his book, and not heed the book, but only him, nice arms bare and the curve of his head, strange and dear, nice funny nose, lips too thick, like her own, brown throat—she could catalogue them forever, over and over, and know a fresh thrill every word every time—oh, damnable and silly and lovely to be in love!

And they'd drink the tea in a drowse of content and talk of his books and the men of old time, the Simple Men who had roamed the earth before Civilization came. If ever men attained that elemental simplicity again—

And Ellen would rouse: *But then, what's the use? If we don't believe in that we're just—oh daft, as you Scotch people say, wasting our lives instead of—* And Ewan would ask *Instead of what?—Saving up to get married?* and laugh and hold her face firm between his hands, young rough hands, the look in his eyes that made her responses falter even while at his laugh and the thing he laughed at something denying struggled up in her, almost shaped itself to words on her lips. Sometime, surely—Oh, sometime they'd get married when the Revolution came and all was put right.

And sometimes, she'd feel just sick and desolate the way he would talk of that coming change, he didn't expect it would come in their time, capitalism had a hundred dodges yet to dodge its own end, Fascism, New Deals, Douglasism, War: Fascism would probably outlast the lot. Ellen said that she didn't believe that a minute else what was the good of all their struggles, what was the good of dissolving the League and both of them joining the Communist Party? And Ewan would smile at her: *No good at all. Child's play, Ellen, or so it'll seem for years. And we've just to go on with it, right to the end, History our master not the servant we supposed.* . . .

He'd fall to his books again, dryest stuff, economics she never could stick, she would reach up and catch the book from him and his eyes meet hers, blank a while, cold, blank and grey, horrible eyes like a cuttle-fish's—like the glint on the houses in Royal Mile, the glint of grey granite she thought once, and shivered. And he asked her why and she said she was silly and he said he knew that, eyes warm again, and they fooled about, struggling a little in the fading June night: and then were quiet, her head on his knee, looking out of the window at summer-stilled Duncairn, little winds tapping the cord of the blind, far off in the fall of the darkness the winking eye of Crowie Point lighting up the green surge of the North Sea night. And Ellen would say *Oh, aren't we comfy? Fun, this,* he'd say nothing, just cuddle her, staring out at that light wan and lost that bestrode the sky.

In bed, beside him, breathing to sleep, the little sleep after those moments that she still thought fun, she would tickle his throat with her hair, feel sure and confident as never in the light, here in the dark he was hers unquestioned, hers and no other's, breathing so, sweat on his brow, hair curling about her fingers from the dark, sleek head. He would stroke her with a swift, soft hand, like a bird's light wing, into that little sleep till somewhere between two and three she would awake, he wakeful as well, and they'd kiss again, cool and neat, and slip out of bed, slim children both, and stand hand in hand and listen, all the house in Windmill Place silent. Then they'd pad to the door and lug it open and peer out, nothing, the lobby dark below, no glimmer about but faint on the landing the far ghost-radiance of Footforthie. Ewan would open her door for her, sleepily they'd hug, and yawn at each other in the dark, giggle a bit because of that, and Ellen close the door and slip into her bed, asleep before she had reached it, almost.

But one morning she saw his hands cut and bruised and asked why, and he said oh that was from his new job, up at Stoddart's, the granite-mason's, he'd been taken on there as a labourer.

The table looked at him, the first any had heard: Chris asked if he liked it, were the other folk nice?

Miss Murgatroyd simpered she was awful glad he had found Respectable Employment, like. Such Pity not to be in the office though; they were awful respectable folk, the Stoddarts.

Mr Piddle said *he-he!* and ate like a gull landed famished on the corpse of a whale.

Mr Quaritch cocked his wee beard to the side: *You'll be able to study the proletariat at first hand now. Tell me when you get sick of them, lad. I might be able to find something better.*

Ena Lyon sniffed and said she Just Hated gravestones.

Ellen sat and stared in blank, dead silence, feeling sick and forgotten while they all talked. Oh goodness, hadn't they heard, had they all gone deaf? Ewan—EWAN A LABOURER!

July came in slow heat over Duncairn, and with it the summer-time visitors. John Cushnie took his feeungsay down to the Beach every night that his mecks would meet, in to hear Gappy Gowkheid braying his jokes in the Beach Pavilion, awfully funny, Christ, how you laughed when he spoke the daft Scotch and your quean beside you giggled superior and said Say he was sure the canary's camiknicks, she was awful clever and spoke a lot like that that she'd heard at the Talkies—though if you had mentioned *her* camiknicks she'd have flamed insulted right on the spot.

Or you'd take her down of a Wednesday afternoon, when Raggie's had closed, birring on the tramcars loaded for the Beach, wheeling out from Footforthie, there glimmering and pitching and reeling in the sun the Amusements Park with its scenic railway, Beach crowded with folk the same as the cars, you and your quean would sit and listen to the silly English that couldn't speak proper, with their 'eads and 'ands and 'alfs and such. Then off you'd get and trail into the Amusements Park, you'd only a half-dollar but you wouldn't let on, your feeungsay was so superior and you only the clerk in Raggie Robertson's. She was fairly gentry and said *how* she'd enjoyed her holiday away with her Girl Friend, they'd gone for a week out in the country, and the farmers were awful vulgar and funny. And you said Yes, you knew, hicks were like that, and she said *You've spilt it—with their awful Scotch words: Tyesday for Tuesday, and Foersday for Friday, and no proper drainage at all, you know.* And you said again that you knew; she meant there weren't real w c's but rather would have died than say so right out.

So you asked if she'd like the scenic railway, and she said *It's okay by me,* on you got, she screamed and grabbed you and the hair got out from under her hat, you were awful proud of her but wished to hell she wouldn't scream as though her throat were chokeful up of old razor blades, and clutch at her skirt, and skirl *Oh, stop!* Christ, hadn't she legs like other folk and need she aye be ashamed of them? So you gave her a bit grab about the legs and she screamed some more and hung on to you: but when the ride finished she was real offended and said she wasn't that kind of girl, *Don't try and come it fresh on me.*

You said you were sorry, so you were, and were just trying to make it up with her when she saw her friend and cried *Cooee, Ena!* and the quean came over, all powder and poshness, and who should it be but Miss Ena Lyon that you'd known at the lodgings in Windmill Place. She said she was just having a stroll about, and no, she hadn't a boy with her. And your quean giggled, and Miss Lyon giggled and you felt a fool, queans were like that; and as you followed them into the tea-tent you wished a coarse minute they'd stop their damned showing-off and be decent to a chap that was treating them—wished a daft minute you'd a quean who didn't care about Talkies and genteelness or was scared at her legs being touched or her feelings offended—one that would cuddle you because she liked it, liked you, thought her legs and all of herself for you, and was douce and sweet and vulgar and kind—like a keelie out of the Cowgate. . . . Christ, it must be the sun had got at you!

Your quean and Miss Lyon were at it hell for leather talking about their holidays and where they had bade, and how much they paid for digs in Duncairn. And Miss Lyon said she thought she'd move hers, the landlady had once been a minister's widow but now she had married an Awful Common person, a joskin just, that lorded it about the place and wasn't a bit respectful at all. Worse than that, though, the landlady's son was a Red. . . . You said that you'd known that, that's why you'd left, Raggie Robertson was dead against the Reds. . . . And your quean said *Don't be silly. Go on, Ena.*

And Miss Lyon said that another of the lodgers was a schoolteacher, Red as well, and she was sure there were Awful Things between them. She'd heard—and she giggled and whispered to your quean and you felt yourself turn red round the ears, what were the daft bitches gigg-giggling about? And your quean made on she was awful shocked and said she wouldn't stay there a minute, the place was no better than a WICKED HOUSE, just.

Miss Lyon said that she'd got no proof, of course, and your quean mustn't say anything, and your quean said she wouldn't but that Ena could easily get proof and show up the two Reds and then leave the place. And then you all talked together about the Communists, coarse beasts, aye stirring up the working class—that was the worst of the working class that they could bè led astray by agitators, they'd no sense and needed to be strongly ruled.

You told the queans that but they didn't listen, they were giggling horrified to each other again, your quean said *What, did you really hear the bed creak?* and Miss Lyon said *Yes, twice,* and their faces were all red and warmed up and glinting, they minded you suddenly of the faces of two bitches sniffling round a lamp-post, scared and eager and hot on a scent. . . . But you mustn't think that, they were real genteel.

For your quean was the daughter of a bank-clerk in Aberdeen and Miss Ena Lyon's father had been a post-master, some class, you guessed, you didn't much like to tell them yours had been only the hostler at the Grand Hotel, what did it matter, you were middle-class yourself now and didn't want ever to remember that you might have been a keelie labourer—Christ, living in some awful room in Paldy, working at the Docks or the granite-yards, going round with some quean not genteel like yours but speaking just awful, Scotch, no restraint or knowing how to take care of herself, maybe coming into your bed at night, smooth and fine and kissing you, cuddling you, holding you without screaming, just in liking and kindness. . . . Your quean asked *Whatever's come over you, red like that?* and you said *Oh, nothing, it's stuffy in here.*

And home you all went on the evening tram, your quean and Miss Lyon sitting together and your quean telling Miss Lyon what fine digs she had, the landlady so respectful, a perfect old scream: and Ena should wait about tonight and catch the two Reds and show them up, and then leave the place and come bide with your quean.

And Miss Lyon said that she would, too, she was sick of the place, anyhow—the dirty beasts to act like that, night after night. . . . And they giggled and whispered some more and for some funny reason you felt as though you'd a stone in your gall, sick and weary, what was the use?—what was the use of being middle-class and wearing a collar and going to the Talkies when this was all that you got out of it? And your quean, whispering some direction to Miss Lyon, turned round and said *Don't listen a minute*, and you nearly socked her one in the jaw—och, 'twas the summer night's heat that was getting you.

Chris's roses were full and red in bloom, scentless and lovely, glowing alive in the Sunday sun as she herself came out to the little back garden. Ewan and Ellen were out there already, their backs to the house, one kneeling one standing, their dark hair blue in the sunlight, young, with a murmur of talk and laughter between them. And she saw indeed they were children no longer, Ellen a woman, slim, a slip of a thing, but that pussy-cat dewiness lost and quite gone, Ewan with the stance and look and act of some strange species of Gallowgate keelie who had never hidden or starved in a slum and planned to cut all the gentry's throat, politely, for the good of humankind. . . . And Miss Ena Lyon was no doubt right in all she had said: Chris must tell them somehow.

But standing looking at them she knew that she couldn't, not because she was shamed to speak of such things to either but because they were over-young and happy to have their minds vexed with the dirty sad angers of Miss Ena Lyon, poor lass. She'd never had a soul slip into *her* room of a night, maybe that was the reason for her awful stamash about Ellen and Ewan exchanging visits. . . . She'd bade up last night, she had told to Chris, and waited on the stairs to confirm her suspicions. And sure enough it had happened again, oh, Disgusting, at Eleven o'clock Miss Johns slipping into Mr Tavendale's room. And she couldn't stay on any longer in a place like this, it was no better than a Brothel, just.

Chris had looked at her in a quiet compassion and said there was no need to stay even a week, she'd better pack and get out at once. Miss Lyon had stared and flushed up raddled red : *What, me that's done nothing? You've more need to shift those—*

She'd called them a dirty name, Chris had said without anger *You'll pack and be gone in an hour;* and left her to that and gone down to the kitchen and shortly afterwards heard a tramping overhead as Miss Lyon got her bit things together—thrown out of her lodgings for trying to keep keelies respectable.

Working in the kitchen with Jock the cat stropping himself up against her legs, Chris had thought that funny for a moment, then it wasn't, she'd have to ask the two what they meant to do. And she thought how awful it was the rate that things tore on from a body's vision, only a year or so since she'd thought of Ewan as a little student lad, her own, jealous when he talked to the pussy-cat: and now she'd have to ask him when he meant to marry!

So she'd made the oatcakes and scones all the lodgers cried for, Ake had come swinging in from outbye, out to buy his bit Sunday paper, no collar, his boots well-blacked, his mouser well-curled, he'd sat down and eaten a cake while he read. Chris had brought him some milk though he'd said he'd get it for himself, he'd taken to saying that kind of thing, queer, though she'd paid it little attention, looking at him quiet and friendly, just, this business of getting a job was a trauchle. She'd asked was there any sign of work and he'd said not a bit in the whole of Duncairn, and folded back his paper and looked up at her with green-glinting eyes as he drank his milk! *A job? Devil the one. And I'm thinking I know the reason for that.*

Chris had asked *What reason?* and he'd said *Jimmy Speight,* no doubt he'd sent a message all round Duncairn to the joiners and timber-merchants and such, warning them against employing Ake. Chris had said that surely he'd be feared to do that seeing that Ake knew the scandal about him, Ake had shaken his head, Ay, but he'd promised never to use that knowledge again and Jimmy knew that he'd keep the promise, a body must keep a promise made even to a daft old skate like the Provost.

And then he'd said something that halted Chris: *I'm sorry, mistress, that I drove you to marrying me.*

Chris had said *Why, Ake!* in surprise, and he'd nodded: *Ay, a damn mistake. Queer the daft desires that drive folk. I might well have known you'd never mate with me, you'd been spoiled in the beds of ministers and the like. I'd forgotten that like an unblooded loon.*

Chris had stood and listened in a kind surprise, beyond fear of being startled or hurt any more by any man of the sons of men who brought their desires their gifts to her. She'd said she'd done all she could to make them happy, and Ake had nodded, Ay, all that she could, but that wasn't enough, och, she wasn't to blame. Then he'd said not to fash, things would ravel out in time, he was off for a dander round the Docks.

So he'd gone, leaving Chris to finish the cooking and set the dinner and watch the taxi drive up and take away Miss Lyon's luggage, a pile of it, and hear the cabman ask if she shouldn't have hired a lorry instead? And Miss Lyon had said she wanted none of his impudence, she'd had enough of that already, living in a brothel. Chris had started a little, overhearing that, but the cabman just said *Faith now, have you so? Trade failing that you're leaving?* and got in and drove off.

And now, the pastry browning fine and Jock the cat purring away, Chris had come out to the noon-time yard to ask Ellen and Ewan what they meant to do over this business of sleeping together without the kirk's licence and shocking Miss Lyon.

But the picture they made took that plan from her mind, she saw now what it was they were laughing about, they'd gotten in the baby from over next door, the bald-headed father had been left in charge and had wanted to mow his lawn awful bad and the bairn had wakened up in its pram and started a yowl, frustrating the man: till Ellen looked over and said *Shall I?* And he'd handed it over, all red and thankful, and now Ellen squatted by the rose-bush, the bairn in her lap and was wagging a bloom in front of its nose. And the bairn, near as big and bald as his father, was kicking his legs, gurgling, and burying his nose and mouth in the rose, sniffing, and then kicking some more in delight. And Chris saw Ewan looking down at the two with a look on his face that made her stop.

Not the kind of look at all a young man should have given his quean with a stranger's bairn—a drowsy content and expectation commingled. Instead, Ewan looked at the two cool and frank, amused and a little bored, as he might at a friend who played with a kitten. . . .

And Chris thought, appalled, *Poor Ellen, poor Ellen!*

Gowans and Gloag's had quietened down after the strike, the chaps went back and said to themselves no more of listening to those Communist Bulgars that got you in trouble because of their daftness, damn't, if the Chinks and the Japs wanted to poison one the other, why shouldn't they?—they were coarse little brutes, anyhow, like that Dr Fu Manchu on the films. And wee Geordie Bruce that worked in Machines said there was nothing like a schlorich of blood to give a chap a bit twist in the wame. But you, though you weren't a Red any longer, said to Geordie that he'd done damn little blood-letting against the bobbies; and Norman Cruickshank took Wee Geordie's nose and gave it a twist, it nearly came off, and said *Hey, sample a drop of your own. Christ, and to think it's red, not yellow!*

You took a bit taik into Machines now and then for a gabble with Norman on this thing and that, the new wing they'd built, called Chemicals, where the business of loading the cylinders with gas was to start in another week or so. Already a birn of chaps had come from the south with a special training for that kind of work, Glasgow sods and an Irishman or so. You and Norman would sneak out to the wc for a fag, and you'd ask if Norman had seen anything of Ewan? And Norman would say he'd seen him once or twice at meetings of the Reds down on the Beach, he'd fairly joined up with the Communists now and spoke at their meetings—*daft young Bulgar if ever there was one, and him gey clever and educated, Bob.*

You said rough enough that you knew all that, and Norman looked at you queer and said Oh of course, you yourself had been a bit of a Red a while back and belonged to that league that Tavendale had raised. Why had you scuttled? Got the wind up?

You took him a smack in the face for that, he was at you in a minute, you couldn't stand up to him, the foreman came running in and pulled you apart: *Hey, what the hell do you think this is? Boxing gymnasium? Back to your work, you whoreson gets.* And back you both went, b'God you'd given the mucker something to think of, saying that you had the wind up—you!

It was just that you'd seen the Reds were daft, a chap that joined them never got a job, got bashed by bobbies and was sent to the camps, never had a meck to spend of a night or a shirt that didn't stick to his back. Och to hell! You wanted a life of your own, you'd met a quean that was braw and kind, she and you were saving up to get married, maybe at New Year and maybe a bit sooner, you'd your eyes on two rooms in Kirrieben, the quean was a two months gone already but you'd be in time if your plans came off; and you weren't sorry a bit, you'd told her, kissing her, she'd blushed and pushed you away, awful shy Jess except in the dark. So who'd time at all for this Red stite and blether that never would help a chap anyway, what was the use of getting your head bashed in for something worse than religion?

But that evening you and some of the chaps had a bit of overtime in the works, clearing up the mess of some university loons allowed down to potter about in Castings. You finished gey late and as you came out there was some kind of meeting on at the gates, a young chap up on a kind of platform, speaking low and clear, who could he be? And you and the rest took a dander along, a fair crowd around, Broo men and fishers, stinking like faeces, and a dozen or so of the toff student sods that had messed about that evening in Castings. The toffs were laughing and crying out jokes, but the young chap wasn't heeding them a bit, he was dressed in old dungarees, all whitened, a chap from the granite-works, no doubt, with big thick boots and red rough hands. And only as you got fell close did you see that the speaker was young Ewan Tavendale himself.

He was saying if the workers would only unite—when one of the university toffs made a raspberry and called *Unite to give you a soft living, you mean?* Ewan said *Quite, and you a hard death, we'll abolish lice in the Communist state,* and then went on with his speech, quick and cool, the students started making a rumpus and some of the fishers gave a bit laugh and started to taik away home at that, quiet old chaps that didn't fancy a row. But Norman Cruickshank called out to Ewan to carry on with his say, would he? they'd see to the mammies' pets with the nice clean collars and the fat office dowps. And Norman called to the Gowans' chaps: *Who'll keep order?*

Most of the others cried up that they would, you didn't yourself but taiked away home, you'd your quean to meet and were going that night to look at a bit of second-hand furniture in a little shop in the Gallowgate. Only as you turned the bend of the street you looked back and saw a fair scrimmage on, the whey-faced bastards down from the colleges were taking on the Gowans chaps, you nearly turned and ran back to join—och, you couldn't, not now, mighty, what about Jess? And you started to run like a fool, as though feared—feared at something that wasn't yourself, that leapt in your heart when you looked at Ewan.

Jim Trease said that was one way of holding a meeting, not the best, you should never let a free fight start at your meetings unless it was well in the heart of a town, with plenty of police about and folk in hundreds and a chance of a snappy arrest or so, to serve the Party as good publicity.

Ewan said Yes, he knew, but he'd taken the opportunity to stir up antagonism between the Gowans chaps and students. Deepening the dislike between the classes. Obvious enough that the day of the revolutionary student was done, he turned to Fascism or Nationalism now, the fight for the future was the workers against all the world. Trease nodded, a bit of heresy there, but true enough in the main. Anyhow, there was no great harm done, Ewan had barked his knuckles a bit, he'd better come up to the Trease house in Paldy and get them iodined. And maybe he'd like a cup of tea.

Ewan said he would and folded up his platform, the fight was over and the students had gone, chased up the wynds by the Gowans men. But Norman Cruickshank came panting back: *All right, Ewan?* and Ewan said *Fine. Thanks to you, Norman. When'll I see you?*

—I don't know, but to hell—sometime. Never heard anybody speak about things as you used to do in the Furnaces. And he asked what Ewan was doing now and Ewan told him he was a labourer at Stoddart's, and Norman said Christ, what a job for a toff, and Ewan said he wasn't a toff, just a worker, and Norman said tell that to his grandmother: only, where would they meet again? So they fixed that up, Trease standing by, big and sonsy, with the twinkle in his little eyes and his shabby suit shining in the evening light.

Mrs Trease held out a soft hand and said *Howdedo? . . . Jim, I'm away out to the Pictures. See and not start the Revolution without me, there's two kippers in the press if you'd like some meat, the police have been here this afternoon and the landlord's going to give us the push. That's all. Ta-ta.* Trease gave her a squeeze and said that was fine, so long as nothing serious had happened; and told her to see and enjoy the picture, who was the actress? Greena Garbage? Well, that was fine; and gave Mrs Trease a clap on the bottom, out she went, Ewan standing and watching. And Trease came back and smiled at Ewan, big, creased: *Ay. Think her a funny bitch?*

Ewan said No, she seemed all right, was she a Communist as well? Trease gave his head a scratch, he'd never asked her, he'd aye been over-busy, her as well, moving from this place and that, chivvied by the bobbies, her ostracized by the neighbours and the like, never complaining though, canty and cheery—they'd had no weans and that was a blessing.

Ewan nodded and said he saw that, there wasn't much time for the usual family business when you were a revolutionist.

And Big Jim twinkled his eyes and said No, for that you'd to go in for Socialism and Reform, like Bailie Brown, and be awful indignant about the conditions of those gentlemanly coves, the suffering workers. And Ewan grinned at him, he at Ewan, neither had a single illusion about the workers: they weren't heroes or gods oppressed, or likely to be generous and reasonable when their great black wave came flooding at last, up and up, swamping the high places with mud and blood. Most likely such leaders of the workers as themselves would be flung aside or trampled under, it didn't matter, nothing to them, THEY THEMSELVES WERE THE WORKERS and they'd no more protest than a man's fingers complain of a foolish muscle.

And Trease made the tea and they cooked the kippers and had a long chat on this and that, not the revolution, strikes or agitprop, but about skies and stars and Ewan's archæology that he'd loved when he was a kid long ago, Trease knew little or ought about it though he'd heard of primitive communism. He said he misdoubted they'd ever see workers' revolution in their time, capitalism had taken crises before and would take them again, it was well enough organized in Great Britain to carry ten million unemployed let alone the two and a half of today, Fascism would stabilize and wars help, they were coming, the wars, but coming slow.

Ewan said he thought the same, for years it was likely the workers' movements would be driven underground, they'd to take advantage of legality as long as they could and then prepare for underground work—perhaps a generation of secret agitation and occasional terrorism. And Trease nodded, and they left all that to heed to itself and Trease sat twinkling, his collar off, and told Ewan of his life as a propagandist far and wide over Scotland and England, agitprop in Glasgow, Lanark, Dundee, the funny occurrences that now seemed funny, they'd seemed dead serious when he was young. He'd tramped to lone villages and stood to speak and been chased from such places by gangs of ploughmen—once taken and stripped and half-drowned in a trough; he'd been jailed again and again for this and that petty crime he'd never committed, and in time took the lot as just the day's work; he'd been out with Connolly at Easter in Dublin, an awfully mismanaged Rising that. But the things he minded best were the silly, small things—nights in mining touns when he'd finished an address to a local branch and the branch secretary would hie him away home to his house: and Trease find the house a single room, with a canty dame, the miner's wife, cooking them a supper and bidding them welcome: and they'd sit and eat and Trease all the time have a bit of a worry on his mind—where the hell was he going to sleep?: and the miner would say *Well, look this way, comrade*, and Trease would hear a bit creak at the back of the room—the miner's wife getting into bed: and he and the miner would sit and claik the moon into morning and both give a yawn and the miner would say *Time for the bed. I'll lie in the middle and you in the front:* and in they'd get and soon be asleep, nothing queer and antrin in it at all, not even when the miner got up and out at the chap of six and left you lying there with his mate, you'd as soon have thought of touching your sister.

And Ewan laughed and then grew serious and spoke of his work in the Stoddart yard, he was raising up something of a cell in the yard, could Jim dig out a bundle of pamphlets for him? They'd all been Labour when he went to Stoddart's, but already he'd another four in the cell. Trease said he'd give him pamphlets enough, Stoddart's was a place worth bothering about, how long did Ewan think he would last before he was fired by the management? Ewan said he thought a couple of months, you never could tell, damned nuisance, he was getting interested in granite. And that led him on to metallurgy, on and on, and Trease sat and listened and poured himself a fresh cup of tea now and then . . . till Ewan pulled himself up with a laugh: *Must clear out now. I've been blithering for hours.*

But Mrs Trease came back from the Talkies and wouldn't hear of it, Jim would need a bit crack and a bit more supper, she thought there was some cheese. Greena Garbage had been right fine, cuddled to death and wedded and bedded.

Would Ewan stir up the fire a little and Jim move his meikle shins out of the way? *Ta-ra-ra, 'way down in Omaha*—

Trease twinkled at Ewan: *That's what you get. Not revolutionary songs, but Ta-ra-ra, 'way down in Omaha.* Mrs Trease said Fegs, revolutionary songs gave her a pain in the stomach, they were nearly as dreich as hymns—the only difference being that they promised you hell on earth instead of in hell.

And Ewan sat and looked on and spoke now and then, and liked them well enough, knowing that if it suited the Party purpose Trease would betray him to the police tomorrow, use anything and everything that might happen to him as propaganda and publicity, without caring a fig for liking or aught else. So he'd deal with Mrs Trease, if it came to that. . . . And Ewan nodded to that, to Trease, to himself, commonsense, no other way to hack out the road ahead. Neither friends nor scruples nor honour nor hope for the folk who took the workers' road; just *life* that sent tiredness leaping from the brain; that sent death and wealth and ease and comfort shivering away with a dirty smell, a residuum of slag that time scraped out through the bars of the whooming furnace of History—

And then he went out and home through the streets, swinging along and whistling soft, though he hardly knew that till he heard his own wheeber going along the pavement in front, the August night mellow and warm and kind, Duncairn asleep but for a great pelt of lorries going up from the Fishmarket, the cry of a wakeful baby somewhere. And he smiled a little as he heard that cry, remembering Ellen and her saying that Communism would bring a time when there would be no more weeping, neither any tears. . . . She was no more than a baby herself.

A bobby stopped in a doorway and watched him go by: there was something in that whistle that was bloody eerie, a daft young skate, but he fair could whistle.

It was plain to Chris something drastic must be done to reorganize the house in Windmill Place. With Cushnie first gone and syne Ena Lyon and Ake still seeking about for a job she'd have to get new lodgers one way or the other. But the price Ma Cleghorn had set on the house had made it for folk of the middle-class, except such rare intruders as Ake—and he'd come in search of her, she supposed, much he'd got from the coming, poor wight.

She asked Neil Quaritch when he came to tea, he looked thinner and stringier and tougher than ever, a wee cocky man with a wee cocky beard, pity his nose was as violent as that. Lodgings?—he'd ask some of the men in the *Runner*. Especially as they might never see Mr Piddle again.

Chris said Why? and Neil licked his lips and thought *Boadicea probably looked like that. She'd strip well—and damn it, she does—for Ogilvie.* Then he pushed his cup over for replenishing, they were sitting at tea alone, and told the tale about Mr Piddle that had come up to the office as he left. Mrs Ogilvie knew this side-line of Piddle's?—sending fishing news to the *Tory Pictman*? Well, he'd been gey late in gathering it to-day, doing another side-line down in Paldy, prevailing on a servant lassie there to steal him the photo of an old woman body who had hanged herself, being weary with age. Back at last he'd come to the office, *he-he!* photo in hand and all set fine, and looked at the clock and saw he'd a bare three minutes to tear down the Mile and reach the train at the Station in time. So he flittered down the stairs like a hen in hysterics and got on his bike and tore up the Mile, and vanished from sight, the *Runner* subs leaning out from their window and betting on the odds that he'd meet that inevitable lorry right now—it was an understood thing that he'd die under a lorry some day, and be carted home in a jam-pot.

Well, it seems that he reached the Station all right, the lorries scattering to right and left and Piddle cycling hell for leather, shooting through the taxi-ranks at the Station and tumbling into the arms of a porter. And the porter asked who he thought he was, Amy Mollison doing a forced landing? Piddle said *He-he!* and dropped his bike and ran like the wind for the *Pictman* train, he knew the platform for it fine, he'd to run half-way up to the middle guard's van.

Well, he rounded into No. 6 platform and gave a bit of a scraich at the sight, the *Pictman* train already in motion and pelting out of Duncairn toun. It was loaded up with Edinburgh students, clowning and playing their usual tricks, a bit fed up with their visit to Duncairn, they'd been leaning out to shout things to the porters when Mr Piddle came hashing in sight, head thrust out like a cobra homing like hell to the jungle with a mongoose close on his tail. And they gave a howl and started to cheer, Mr Piddle running like the wind by now to reach the middle brake. The guard looked out and yelled to him to stop, he'd never make it and do himself a mischief. But the van was chockablock with students, they pushed the guard aside, a half-dozen of them, and thrust out their hands, Piddle thought that fine, if only he could get near enough to hand up the *Pictman* packet to them. And at last, bursting his braces and a half-dozen blood-vessels, or thereabouts, he got close in touch—down came the hands, the students all yelled, and next minute Piddle was plucked from the earth and shot, packet and all, into the guard's van. And then the train vanished with a howl of triumph, an express that didn't stop till it got to Perth.

Chris sat and laughed, sorry for Mr Piddle though she was, poor little weasel howked off like that. Then Ewan came in and heard the tale and laughed as well, ringing and hearty, no boy's laugh any longer, Neil thought—far from that lad who'd once thought those silly happenings to folk had little or nothing of humour in them. Damned if one liked the change for all that, a difficult young swine to patronize, growing broader and buirdlier, outjutting chin and radiating lines around the eyes—Quaritch knew the face on a score of heads, he'd seen them on platforms, processions, police courts, face of the typical Communist condottiere, cruel and pig-headed and unreasonable brutes with their planning of a bloody revolution tomorrow when Douglasism were it only applied and the maze of its arguments straightened out would cure all the ills that there were of our time: the only problem was distribution, manufacture and function couldn't be bettered.

★

It was as though a great hand had battered, broad-nieved, against the houses that packed Footforthie. Windows shook and cracked, the houses quivered, out in the streets folk startled looked up and saw the lift go suddenly grey. Then, belly-twisting, the roar of the explosion.

Folk tore from their houses and into the streets, pointed, and there down by Gowans and Gloag's in the afternoon air was a pillar of fire sprouting a blossoming to the sky, it changed as you looked and grew black and then green, blue smoke fringe—Christ, what had happened? Next minute the crowd was on the run to the Docks, some crying the fire had broke out in a ship, but you knew that that was a lie. And John—Peter—Thomas—Neil—Oh God, he was there, in Furnaces, Machines—it was and it couldn't be Gowans and Gloag's.

Then, rounding into the Dockside way you found the place grown black with folk, bobbies there already crying to keep back, forward the left of the Works like a great bulging blister, a corral of flame, men were running out from Gowans clapping their hands to blackened faces, some screaming and stitering over to the Docks to pitch themselves in agony into the water. And as they did that the blister burst in another explosion that pitched folk head-first down on the ground, right and left—Forward, against the green pallor of the Docks, a rain of stone and iron stanchions fell.

And out of the sunset, and suddenly, the lift covered over with driving clouds.

. . . . . .

The *Tory Pictman* got the news from Duncairn over the telephone, clear-the-line, from Mr Piddle *he-heing!* like fun: all about the charred bodies, the explosion, the women weeping, the riot that broke out against the Gowans house up in Craigneuks when their windows were bashed in by Reds. And the *Pictman* printed a leader about it, full of dog Latin and constipated English, but of course not Scotch, it was over-genteel: and it said the affair was very regrettable, like science and religion experiment had its martyrs for the noble cause of defending the State. The treacherous conduct of extremists in exploiting the natural grief of the Duncairn workers was utterly to be deplored. No doubt the strictest of inquiries would be held—

. . . . .

The Reverend Edward MacShilluck preached from his pulpit next Sunday and said the catastrophe was the Hand of Gawd, mysteriously at work, *ahhhhhhhhhhhh, my brethren, what if it was a direct chastisement of the proud and terrible spirit of the times, the young turning from the Kirk and its sacred message, from purity and chastity and clean-living?* And Craigneuks thought it a bonny sermon, and nearly clapped, it was so excited; and the Reverend MacShilluck went home to his lunch and fell asleep when he'd eaten it and woke with a nasty taste in his mouth and went a little bit stroll up to Pootsy's room, and opened the door and peeped in at her and shoggled his mouth like a teething tiger—

. . . . .

Jim Trease said to Ewan they hadn't done so bad, twenty new members had joined the local, damn neat idea that of Ewan's to have the Gowans windows bashed in. Ewan was to take Kirrieben for the weekend meetings, he himself Paldy and Selden Footforthie. And be sure and rub in the blood and snot well and for God's sake manage a decent collection, he'd be getting in a row with the EC in London, they were so far behind with the Press contribution.

Eh? Of course the Works had been well-protected, that kind of accident would happen anywhere. But Ewan had been right, that was hardly the point, he could rub in if he liked that there had been culpable negligence. . . . Eh, what was that? Suggest it had all been deliberately planned to see the effect of poison-gas on a crowd? Hell! Anyhow, Ewan could try it. But for Christ's sake mind about the collection—

. . . . .

Alick Watson said in his barrack-room: *See what's waiting us in the next war, chaps? Skinned to death or else toasted alive like a winkle in front of a fire, see?* And the rookies said *Christ, they all saw that,* what was there to be done about it? And Alick said to organize and stick up for their rights, would they back him today down in the mess if he made a complaint about the mucking meat? They could force they sods to feed them proper, no fear of that if they'd stick together, no need to knuckle-down to the bloody NCO's. And if a war came and the chaps in the companies were well-organized: what the hell could the officers do to them then?

· · · · ·

Norman Cruickshank lay in the hospital and didn't say a word, quiet and unmoving, half of his face had been eaten away by the flame.

· · · · ·

Jess would never see Bob again. She thought at his graveside, decent in her black, *Young Erchie's been awful kind to me. Maybe the furniture me and Bob's bought will do if he's really serious, like.* . . . But she mustn't think of that, even with her Trouble, poor Bob that had been so kind and sensible even though he'd once mixed with those dirt, the Reds—

· · · · ·

Ellen Johns said, sick, it was horrible, horrible, *but, Ewan, you know that* THAT *was a lie. It was sickening of you to suggest that they let loose the gas deliberately.* . . . *Ewan, it's just cheating, it's not Communism!*

Chris had said *But, Ake, why are you leaving me?*

He'd tapped out his pipe by the side of the fire, *Just for what I've said, mistress: I want a change. So I've ta'en on the job of ship's carpenter, on the Vulture, bound for Newfoundland. That's all about it.*

She'd said But it wasn't all; what was this stuff about not coming back? And at that the Ake Ogilvie of Segget had awakened, a minute, as he told her why: that he'd never had a minute since his marriage day when he was a free and happy man, aye knowing how she looked on him, thought of him—oh aye, she'd done her best, he knew, it was just that the two of them never should have wed, *You were made for somebody different from me, God knows who, neither me nor Colquohoun. But it's been like hell, we just can't mix. Lass, do you think I haven't seen you shiver over things another woman would laugh at or like?*

She'd said that that was just foolishness, she'd liked him well and had aye done so. And he'd said she looked bonny standing there, trying to be kind. It was more than kindness he'd once hoped to get; and now they'd speak of the soss no more.

And he'd told her his plans, he was off in three days, and he'd maybe write her, had he anything to write about, when he got to Newfoundland or Canada. He thought of crossing over Canada and taking a look at Saskatchewan, plenty of work there for a joiner, he'd heard. Of what money he made he'd let her have half.

Chris had said quiet she wouldn't have that, if they parted she'd no need to live off him, they parted for good and all—if at all.

And Ake had nodded, Ay, that would be best.

So, watching from the doorway as he went this last morning, she minded in pity and smiled at him, kind. He hoisted the case on his shoulder and nodded, *Well, I'll away. Ta-ta, mistress.*

Her heart was beating high in her breast and her throat felt tight so that hardly she could speak: and all that meant little enough, as she knew. If she tried even now she could keep him by her—who would soon have so few to fall back upon. But he wasn't for her, she for any man, they'd each to gang their own gait.

She'd finished with men or the need for them, no more that gate might open in her heart, in her body and her soul, in welcome and gladness to any man. Quick and quick in the flying months she passed with hasting feet over ways that once had seemed ever-lasting: the need not only for a lover's caresses, but the need for anyone's liking, for care, kind words and safe eyes. . . . That dreadful storm she'd once visioned stripping her bare was all about her, and she feared it no longer, eager to be naked, alone and unfriended, facing the last realities with a cool, clear wonder, an unhasting desire. Barriers still, but they fell one by one—

She stared from the doorway, standing still, motionless, almost the last sight Ake saw, it twisted his heart and then left it numb. Ay, a strange quean, yon. And not for him. He'd thought that glimmer in her eyes a fire that he himself could blow to a flame; and instead 'twas no more than the shine of a stone.

Ewan at last had been fired from Stoddart's he told to Ellen as they drove from Duncairn in the little car they'd hired for the weekend. Ellen had hired it and sat aside now while Ewan took the wheel and a reckless road through the lorry traffic of Kirrieben in the whistling spatter of December snow. She'd been deep in thought: on the road, on herself, on the week-end that waited them in that inn in Drumtochty. Now she started: *Oh Lord, what'll you do now?*

He said he hadn't the ghost of a notion, something or other, and whistled to himself, dark and intent, growing tall, still slim, with the mouth that was losing its lovely curves, growing hard and narrow she suddenly thought: dismissed that thought—he was just Ewan still.

And some time she'd tell him. But not tonight.

For a while Ewan drove without saying more. Topping the Rise the storm had cleared, the snow no more than an inch or so thick scarred with the passing of buses and lorries, a lorry came clanging to meet them, chains on, and once the little car caught on a slide and skidded and galumphed a wiggling moment till Ewan's hands switched it into line again. Up here the full blow of the wind was upon them; behind, down in its hollow, Duncairn was a pelting scurry of flakes, browny white as smoke rose to snow and commingled and presently drew down a veil, capped with darkness in the early sunset, over the whitening miles of grey granite. Forward the country wavered and shook, no solid lines as they held the road, a warm, birring dot, tap-tap the hardened flakes on the shield. Ellen snuggled up closer to Ewan and he reached out a hand and gave her a pat and nodded thanks as she put a cigarette between his lips. She lit it and then said *Goodness, we're comfy. Wish we'd a car like this of our own.*

He said he'd have to get Selden's job for that: and he
doubted if it would be as easy next time! She asked what on
earth he was talking about and he steered through a drifting
drove of cattle, head down to the storm, drover behind, and
didn't answer her for a moment. Then he asked her hadn't
she heard the news?—oh no, she hadn't been down to the
Communist local for nearly a couple of weeks, lazy thing. *The
point is that Selden's bunked with the funds.*

—*Selden? With the funds of the Party?*

—*Every cent, and there was a decent amount. I thought it risky
to have him treasurer, and so did Trease, but he'd got in well with
the* EC *in London. Cleared us out to the very last copper.*

She said the man was a beast, it was filthy; but Ewan had
started his whistling again, hardly heeding her, only the road
and the car, he said Selden had shown a lot of sense in waiting
till the local had a spot of coin. Been sick of unemployment
and his wife wasn't well—her that used to be Chris's
maid—remember?

—*You speak as though you might do the same.*

He laughed at that, cheerfully, *I'm a Communist.* And fell
to his whistling again, but soberly. And when he next spoke
there was steel in his voice, the steel of a cold, unimpassioned
hate: *I could tell long ago that Selden would rat; you can tell a
rat easily among revolutionists—yeasty sentiment and blah about
Justice. They think they're in politics or a parlour game.*

And what did he himself think it was? But she didn't ask,
didn't want to hear more, wanted to forget Duncairn and all
in it and that dreadful paper they had made her sign. And
Ewan drove as though he owned the road and all the Howe
and half of December and had specially arranged the storm
effects, the storm coming rolling down from the Mounth and
pelting across the grey fields in wan tides, now snow, now
sleet, once, curling and foaming, combers of hail. The
shrouded farms cowered in by their woods, here and there a
ploughman wrapped to the ears went whistling up to the end
of a rig, the lapwings flying, *Lost; lost!* their plaint above the
wheel and fall of the snow.

Ellen drowsed against Ewan's sleeve, and woke and looked

out, they were past Auchinblae going down into the Glen of
Drumtochty, here no snow fell, far in the lift Drumtochty
rose with its firs going climbing to the racing clouds. She said
Remember that day there, Ewan? and told him to be careful,
he'd nearly turned the car in a ditch, kissing her, he laughed,
he'd remembered as well, something like a shadow went over
his face, not from it, and a moment she saw again the shamed
hurt boy whom she'd loved, still loved, deeper and madder
and worse than ever.

The landlady said God be here, they'd expected no visitors
on New Year's Eve, but they both were welcome. If they'd
wait a while she'd stir up those sweir meikle bitches the maids
and see that a room was set in order. Och, she minded the two
of them fine back in May and she'd known another thing
though she'd never letten on—that the two of them had been
on their honeymoon. Wasn't that true?

Ellen said it was, but the landlady was looking at Ewan,
hardly heard, she said he'd take a bit dram with her?—and
his good lady too, maybe?

So they sat and had their dram, all three, and the landlady
and Ewan were at it in a minute, gossip that somehow left
Ellen out, though she didn't know how, she was just as
interested in floods and storms and hens and chickens and
farm boys as Ewan was (and once a lot more). But as always
with the working people everywhere, however she dreamed
of justice for them, flamed in anger against their wrongs,
something like a wall of glass came down cutting her off from
their real beliefs, the meanings in tones and intonation, the
secret that made them bearable as individuals. But Ewan had
now the soap-box trick of pretending to be all things to all
kinds of keelies—That was damn mean and wasn't true,
there was no pretence, he WAS all things—sometimes,
frighteningly, it seemed to her that he was the keelies, all of
them, himself.

But they were served a warm supper ben in the parlour and
sat there thawing in front of a fire, resin-spitting, curling
bright amber flames up the wide lum, it whoomed in the
blasts of the storm driving night, hunted, down through

Drumtochty. Sometimes the whoom in the lum would still, then roust and ring as though the storm going by beat a great bell in the low of the lift. And Ellen felt happy and content again, sleepy as a cat, a little bit like one: and something a moment touched through to Ewan, a hand from other days, other nights, queerly. He said *You're thinner, you were always slim, but plump in a way as well that time we climbed the Barmekin.* She shook her head, she was just the same, only horribly sleepy, was he coming now?

He went to the window and looked out at the storm, solid in front of the inn it went by, speckled in the lights, a great ghost army hastening east, marching in endless line on line, silent and sure; and he thought a minute *Our army's like that, the great lost legion, nothing to stop it in heaven or hell;* and that thought lit him up a little moment till he closed it away in impatient contempt. Bunk symbolism was a blunted tool.

So he said he'd look in at the bar a minute, and sent Ellen to bed: looked a tired kid. When he got up the stairs in a half-hour or so the house was shaking in every gust, the candle-flame leaped as he opened the door, Ellen lying in bed in silk nightie, pretty thing, drowsy, she said *Hurry, it's cold.*

But soon it wasn't, the candle out, the lights from the fire lay soft in the room, he said *Warm now?* and she said *That was fun: remember the first time I said that?* And she laid her head in the hollow of his arm sleeping the New Year in.

The storm was over when they woke next day, breakfast ready and a tramp in the snow to follow, they climbed to the top of Cairn o' Mount, bare ragged and desolate under the snow, no exaltation of the storm left; around them, mist-draped, the jumble of hills. It seemed to Ellen the most desolate place that God ever made, and she hated it.

But Ewan said one could think up here and sat on a stone and filled his pipe, and dusted the stone clear of snow: *Sit down. I've something to ask you.*

She sat down and cuddled up close to his shoulder and said if the question was if she still loved him, the answer was in the affirmative, worse luck. And did he know he was, oh damnably thrilling?

He said *Listen, Ellen. About the Party. Why haven't you been to the meetings of late?*

She watched a puff of wind come over the snow, ruffling it like an invisible snake, nearer and nearer, and caught her breath, if it didn't reach them—for a luck, a sign. . . . It blew a white dust over her hands.

She said quietly as him *Just because I can't, or I'd lose my job.*

He said *Oh*, and knocked out the pipe and filled it again with the cheap tobacco, his suit was frayed and the coat collar shiny, she saw, sitting away from him: funny she had never noticed these things before. . . . *What's happened, then?*

She laughed and caught his shoulder *Ewan! Don't use that tone to me!* EWAN!

His face was a stone, a stone-mason's face, carved in a sliver of cold grey granite. *You might as well tell me.*

Suddenly frightened she stared at him, and told him she couldn't do anything else. The Education Authority had got to hear and had put the choice plainly enough. She'd to sign a paper saying she'd take no more part in extremist activities and stop teaching the children—what she'd been teaching them. *Oh, Ewan, I couldn't help it!*

—*Does that mean you've left the Party as well as left off attending its meetings?*

And then anger came on her: *Yes, I've left the Party! And it wasn't only that. I've left because I'm sick of it, full of cheats and liars, thieves even, look at Selden, there's not one a clean or a decent person except you and perhaps Jim Trease. And I've left because I'm sick of being without decent clothes, without the money I earn myself, pretty things that are mine, that I've worked for. . . . Oh, Ewan, you know they're hopeless, these people—the keelies remember you used to call them?—hopeless and filthy; if ever there's anything done for them it'll be done from above, not by losing onself in them. . . . Oh,* CAN'T *you see?*

He nodded, not looking at her. And colour came back into Ellen's cheeks—oh, he was going to understand! She leaned forward and told him all that she planned: he would get away from ridiculous jobs, Mr Quaritch had promised to find him another. They could save up like anything and get married in a year or so, have a dinky little flat somewhere in Craigneuks. Even that car down there at the inn—it had been hired with her money, hadn't it? Well, they'd soon get one of their own, you couldn't have any fun without money. And it needn't mean they must give up social work completely, there was the Labour Party—

He stood up then, dark and slim, still a boy, and brushed her off carefully, and the snow from his knees: *Go to them then in your comfortable car—your Labour Party and your comfortable flat. But what are you doing out here with me? I can get a prostitute anywhere.*

She sat still, bloodless, could only whisper: *Ewan!*

He stood looking at her coolly, not angered, called her a filthy name, consideringly, the name a keelie gives to a leering whore; and turned and walked down the hill from her sight.

The extremists were getting out of hand again said the *Daily Runner* in a column and a half; and Duncairn was the centre of their sinister activities. There had been several strange and unexplained phenomena in the blowing up of the new wing of Gowans and Gloag's: and though no definite charge might be laid at any door hadn't there been similar occurrences abroad inspired by the Asiatic party of terrorism? And what had followed within a few months of the explosion?—a soldier of the North Highlanders arrested and court-martialled for circulating seditious literature in the barrack-rooms—an ex-employee of Gowans and Gloag's. He had been dealt with with the severity appropriate to his case, but behind the muddled notions of Private Watson what forces were aiming at the forcible overthrow of Society and suborning the loyalty of our troops? It was true the soldiers had no sooner become aware of the contents of the leaflets than, with admirable promptitude, they had seized the culprit and marched him off to the guard-room. The tales of

the barrack-room riots in his defence might be discounted as
malicious gossip. . . .

And here the sub-editor who wrote the leaders stopped and
scratched his head in some doubt and stared at the Spring
rain pelting Duncairn and streaming from the gutters of the
grey granite roofs. He wondered a moment what had really
happened when the furniture was smashed in two barrack-
rooms and five rounds issued to the NCO's? Better cut out that
bit and keep bloody vague. Something about the absolute
and unswerving loyalty of our Army and Navy throughout
the hundreds of years of their history? What about Parker
and the Mutiny at the Nore? Or, closer in memory, the Navy
at Invergordon? Or the Highlanders in France? . . . Better
miss it all out. Some blah about the bloody hunger-march
now—

. . . In civil affairs the same state of things, culminating in
the organizing of this hunger march down through Scotland
and England to London. Hunger—there was none anywhere
in Duncairn. For their own ends extremists were deluding
the unemployed into the privations of a march that would
profit them nothing, a march already disowned by official
Labour—

.   .   .   .   .   .

Bailie Brown said Ay, B'God that was right, the Labour
Party would have nothing to do with it: if the unemployed
would wait another three years and put the Labour Party
back in power, their troubles would all be solved for them.
But of course it was no class party, Labour: wasn't it Labour
had instituted the Means Test? It stood for a sound and
strong government, justice for all, peace and progress, sound
economy and defence of our rights. . . . And hurrying to the
police court at ten o'clock he sentenced two keelies to two
months a-piece, for obstructing the police near the Labour
Exchange, and to show the low brutes what Reform would be
like—

.   .   .   .   .   .

The Reverend MacShilluck said straight from the pulpit we
could see the mind of Moscow again, deluding our unem-

ployed brothers, ahhhhhhhhhhhh, why didn't the Government take a stern stand and put down these activities of the anti-Christ? The unemployed were fully provided for and the Kirk was here to guide and to counsel. Straitened means and times were the test-gauge of God. . . .

And he wondered what Pootsy would have for lunch; and finished the service and got into the car and drove home, the streets shining white in the rain. And he let himself into the Manse, rubbing his hands, and called for the woman to come take his coat. But he heard no reply, the place sounded empty; and he couldn't find her ben in the kitchen or yet upstairs or yet in the sitting-room. In the dining-room he came on his desk smashed open and gaping, the Kirk fund gone, and where had the silver gone from the sideboard? But there in the middle of the desk was a note: *I've cleared off at last and taken my wages—with a little bit extra as a kind of a tip for sticking your dirty habits so long. Just try and prosecute and I'll show you up so you can't show your face anywhere in Duncairn—*

. . . . . .

In Paldy Parish and the Gallowgate, in Kirrieben, Ecclesgriegs and Lower Footforthie, folk stood and debated with a bit of a laugh this hunger march that the Reds were planning. And those that had jobs said *Christ, look out, they're just leading you off to get broken heads, they don't care a damn for themselves or any other, the Communionists, the sods aren't canny.* And those that hadn't jobs said *Maybe ay, maybe no. Who got the* PAC *rates raised if it wasn't the Reds, tell us that?*

Not that you were a Red, Christ, no, you had more sense, and you wouldn't be found in this daft-like March, you hadn't the boots for it for one thing. And the wife said *Mind, Jim . . . or Sam . . . or Rob . . . you're not being taken in by this coarse March of the Reds, are you now?* And you said to her *Away to hell. Think I've gone gyte?;* and took a stroll out, all the Gallowgate dripping and drookèd, most folk indoors but chaps here and there nipping in and out of the wynds and courts, what mucking palaver was on with them now?

Then, afore you could do a sneak back and miss him, there was Big Jim Trease bearing down upon you, crying your name, he'd been looking for you as one of the most active and sure of the chaps. The March wouldn't be a march unless you were in it to stiffen the backbone of the younger lads. And you said To hell, you hadn't any boots; and he said that they'd be provided all right and wrote your name down in a little book, and you saw Will's there and Geordie's and Ian's and even old Malcolm's—Christ, you could go if they were going; and it was true what Big Jim said, you wanted a pickle of the older men to put some guts in the younger sods—

. . . .

And in and out through the courts and wynds and about the pubs all through that last week were Trease and that mad young devil Ewan Tavendale, prigging with folk and taking down names and raising the wind to buy chaps boots. The bobbies kept trailing after them, the sergeant called Feet and a couple of constables, who the hell were they to interfere? They'd never let up on young Tavendale since he'd shown up the explosion at Gowans and Gloag's as the work of the Government testing out gas to see its effect in a crowded shed. So you guarded him and Trease in a bit of a bouroch, a bodyguard, like, wherever they went, young Tavendale whistling and joking about it, a clever young Bee—and Christ, how he could fight! They said he was a devil with the queans as well, though you hadn't heard that he'd bairned one yet.

. . . . .

Trease said the last afternoon to Ewan that he'd better get home and put in a bit sleep, he'd want it afore setting out the morn to tackle the chave of the march down south, the windy five hundred miles to London. Lucky young devil that he was to be going, Trease wished it was him that was leading the March, but the EC had given its instructions for Ewan and intended keeping him down there in London as a new organizer—right in the thick. . . . *And for God's sake take care on the line of march to keep the sods from straying or stealing or*

raising up trouble through lying with queans, they'd find the
Labour locals en route were forced to give them shelter and
help, never heed that, never heed that, rub it well in through
all the speeches that the workers had no hope but the
Communist Party.

Ewan said with a laugh that Jim needn't worry, rape
Labour's pouches, but not its wenches, he'd got that all
fixed; *well, so long, comrade. You'll lead us out with the band
tomorrow?* And Trease said he would, and then *So long,
Ewan,* and they shook hands, liking each other well, nothing
to each other, soldiers who met a moment at night under the
walls of a town yet unstormed.

The workmen from Murray's Mart had come up and bade in
the house all the afternoon tirring the rooms of their
furniture. Chris had made the two men each a cup of tea,
they'd sat in the kitchen and drank it, fell grateful: *You'll be
moving to a smaller house, then, mistress?* Chris said Yes, and
leaving Duncairn, and the older man gave his bit head a
shake when he heard the place she was moving to. He
doubted she'd be gey lonely, like. He was all for the toun
himself, he was.

Now, in the early fall of the evening, Chris went from room
to room of the house, locking the doors and seeing the
windows were snibbed up against the beat of the wind. The
floors sent up a hollow echo to her tread, in Miss Murgatroyd's room a hanky lay in a corner, mislaid, she'd be missing
it the morn and maybe sending for it. She'd said Eh me, she
was Such Sorry that the place was breaking up, but maybe for
the best, maybe for the best, she'd be Awful Comfortable in
her new place she was sure. And would Mrs Ogilvie take this
as a Small Bit Present? And this for young Mr Ewan, if he'd
have it?—two Awful Nice books about the ancient Scots,
such powerful they were in magic, Mr Ewan had once read
the books and So Liked them.

Chris closed that door and went ben the corridor, to Archie
Clearmont's, and peeped in a minute; he'd flushed, standing
in that doorway, trunk behind him: *I say, I'm damnably sorry*

to leave. Given you a lot of trouble, often. I say—and flushed again, looking at her. And Chris had known and smiled, known what he wanted, and kissed him, and watched him go striding away, and thought, kind, *Nice boy;* and forgotten him.

Nothing in here, nor in Mr Quaritch's, except the pale patches along the walls where his books had rested, still the fug of his pipe. He'd said *You were never meant for this, anyhow. Mind if I ask: Is your husband coming back?* Chris had shaken her head and said No, they had separated, Ake was settling in Saskatchewan. And Neil had fidgeted and then proposed, she could get a divorce, he had some money saved, get a decent house and he wouldn't much bother her. When she shook her head he gave a sigh: *Well, luck go with you if you're not for me.*

Mr Piddle hadn't bidden good-bye at all, he'd brought a cab and loaded in his goods, and gone cycling off in the rear of it, head down, neck out, without a *He-he!* And, queer, that had hurt Chris a bit she found—that the funny thing couldn't have said good-bye. The cracked pane in his window was winking in the light from the lamps new-lit outside as she looked round his room; then closed it and locked it. That was the lot. Oh no, there was one.

So she climbed up the stairs and stood in that, the room above her own, next to Ewan's, half-dark and quite empty but for its shadows. It had had no lodger a three months now, Ellen Johns herself had never come back from that week-end she'd gone away with Ewan: Ewan himself had come back mud-splashed as though he'd been walking the roads like a tink. And then next day a messenger had come with a little note, asking Mrs Ogilvie if she'd pack Ellen's things, Ellen was too busy to come herself and here was a week's pay in place of notice. And she hoped Mrs Ogilvie would be awfully happy. . . .

Chris had ceased wondering on that long ago; but now, going down to the kitchen where Ewan sat and the fire was whooming and the supper near ready, she minded it as in an ancient dream. As she closed the door Ewan looked up, he'd been deep for hours in papers and lists, marking off items of marching equipment, addresses, routes, notes for speeches: Chris had looked over his shoulder earlier and seen the stuff and left him a-be. But now, with that distant stare upon her, she asked if he'd ever seen Ellen since then?

He said *Seen whom?* and looked blank, and then shook his head. *Not a glimpse. Why?*

Chris said Oh nothing, she'd just wondered about her; and Ewan nodded, forgetting them both, finishing his lists while she laid the supper, the house unquiet without furnishing, filled with rustlings and little draughts. Then she called Ewan to supper and they ate in silence, night without close down on Duncairn.

He said suddenly and queerly *The Last Supper, Chris. Will you manage all right where you're going?*

She said that he need have no fear of that, she was going to what she wanted, the same as he was going. And they smiled at each other, both resolute and cool, and Chris cleared the table and re-stoked the fire and they sat either side and watched the fire-lowe and heard the spleiter of the wet on the panes. And Ewan sat with his jaw in his hand, the briskness dropped from him, the hard young keelie with the iron jaw softening a moment to a moment's memory: *Do you mind Segget Manse and the lawn in Spring?*

Chris said that she minded, and smiled upon him, in pity, seeing a moment how it shook him, she herself beyond such quavers ever again. But his thoughts had gone back to other things in Segget: that day that Robert had died in the kirk—did Chris mind the creed he'd bade men seek out, a creed as clear and sharp as a knife? He'd never thought till this minute that that was what he himself had found—in a way, he supposed, Robert wouldn't have acknowledged, a sentimentalist and a softie, though a decent sort, Robert.

Chris stirred the fire, looking into it, hearing the Spring wind rising over Duncairn, unending Spring, unending Spring! . . . . Rain tomorrow, Ewan said from the window, rotten for the march, but they'd got those boots. Then he came and sat down and looked at her, and asked her, teasing, of what she was dreaming. She said *Of Robert and this faith of yours. The world's sought faiths for thousands of years and found only death or unease in them. Yours is just another dark cloud to me—or a great rock you're trying to push up a hill.*

He said it was the rock was pushing him; and sat dreaming again, who had called Robert dreamer: only for a moment, on the edge of tomorrow, all those tomorrows that awaited his feet by years and tracks Chris would never see, dropping the jargons and shields of his creed, thinking again as once when a boy, openly and honestly, kindly and wise:

There will always be you and I, I think, Mother. It's the old fight that maybe will never have a finish, whatever the names we give to it—the fight in the end between FREEDOM *and* GOD.

The night was coming in fast Chris saw from her seat on the summit of the Barmekin. Far over, right of Bennachie's ridges, a gathering of gold cloud gleamed a moment then dulled to dun red. The last of the light would be going soon.

Alow her feet, under the hills, she could see the hiddle of Cairndhu, all settled for the night as she'd left it, the two kye milked and the chickens meated, her corn coming fine in the little park that ran up the hill, its green a jade blur in the soft summer light. Tomorrow she'd be out to tackle the turnips, they were coming up fairly choked with weed.

At first they'd been doubtful about letting her the place, doubtful of a woman body at all. But they'd long forgotten her father, John Guthrie, and the ill ta'en in which he had flitted from Echt twenty-three years before. To them she was just a widow-body, Ogilvie, wanting to take on the coarse little place that hadn't had a tenant this many a year. She'd moved in early in the April, setting the house to rights, working till she near bared her hands to the bone, scrubbing it out both but and ben, the room where she herself had been born, the kitchen where she'd sat and heard her mother, long syne, that night the twins were born. . . . And sometimes in the middle of that work in the house or tinkling a hoe out in

the parks she'd close her eyes a daft minute and think nothing
indeed of it all had happened—Kinraddie, Segget, the years
in Duncairn—that beside her Will her brother was bending
to weed, her father coming striding peak-faced from the
house, she might turn and see her mother's face. . . . And
she'd open her eyes and see only the land, enduring,
encompassing, the summer hills gurling in the summer heat,
unceasing the wail of the peesies far off.

And the folk around helped, were kind in their way,
careless of her, she would meet them and see them by this
road and gate, they knew little of her, she less of them, she
had found the last road she wanted and taken it, concerning
none and concerned with none. . . .

Crowned with mists, Bennachie was walking into the
night: and Chris moved and sat with her knees hand-clasped,
looking far on that world across the plain and the day that did
not die there but went east, on and on, over all the world till
the morning came, the unending morning somewhere on the
world. No twilight land anywhere for shade, sun or night the
portion of all, her little shelter in Cairndhu a dream of no-life
that could not endure. And that was the best deliverance of
all, as she saw it now, sitting here quiet—that that Change
who ruled the earth and the sky and the waters underneath
the earth, Change whose face she'd once feared to see, whose
right hand was Death and whose left hand Life, might be
stayed by none of the dreams of men, love, hate, compassion,
anger or pity, gods or devils or wild crying to the sky. He
passed and repassed in the ways of the wind, Deliverer,
Destroyer and Friend in one.

Over in the Hill of Fare, new-timbered, a little belt of rain
was falling, a thin screen that blinded the going of the light;
behind, as she turned, she saw Skene Loch glimmer and glow
a burnished minute; then the rain caught it and swept it from
sight and a little wind soughed up the Barmekin. And now
behind wind and rain came the darkness.

Lights had sprung up far in the hills, in little touns for a
sunset minute while the folk tirred and went off to their beds,
miles away, thin peeks in the summer dark.

Time she went home herself.

But she still sat on as one by one the lights went out and the rain came, beating the stones about her, and falling all that night while she still sat there, presently feeling no longer the touch of the rain or hearing the sound of the lapwings going by.

THE END OF
A SCOTS QUAIR
. . . . .

Grey Granite : Curtain Raiser

The following fragment is all that survives of the rejected Prelude to the novel. It is in NLS MS 26040(3–7), and is printed by kind permission of Mrs Rhea Martin, Gibbon's daughter, and the National Library of Scotland. It consists of five quarto pages of Gibbon's own first-draft typing. Typographical errors have been corrected and spelling brought into line with that of the first edition.

The City of Dundon stands midway the coast where they cease their speaking of beets and speens and take to a gabble of buits and spunes. To the north (but only if you're country and ignorant) they still bake cakes and the folk are meated often enough on a dish of sowans; to the south the old wives still cougg above a girdle set with fine baps of bannocks, thick with fat and dripping with grease. Along that coast in the trawler fleets you come to the city of Aberdeen, genteel with its fine university and proud with a clatter of awful trams, and as full of fine tales as an egg of meat; but if you sail south you come to Dundee, nestling and pressing like an unwashed bairn under the flow of the Sidlaws, dark, you may not see Dundee for a while for the smoke, but you'll smell it long ere your eyes light on it; and what there is there, and what it is like none know unless they're native to the place, or sent to the jail on an awful crime.

When that Greek man Pytheas sailed these coasts long syne, he halted his boat one season by a little place, a wide bay that stretched with a cream and a froth of grey waters, ebbing and swaying into red mists, late autumn, the waters flung long hands upon the beaches, tearing at his craft. But there he cast anchor, and landed his men, strangers came down to trade with them, dark, hairy men of that Pictish coast, bringing corn and the skins of beasts, and Pytheas and his men planted there corn and built them huts against the sweep and the ding of that ill coast's rains, pelting and salt-ridden, and watched the winter fade. Spring came with a whirling of sudden rains, and they took to the creaming seas again, and sailed north, out of the life of that land but that the Picts drifted here and built them a city of the long earth-houses, the dark broad men with their Kelt overlords, proud, with long, bronze daggers and curled hair, the men of the chariots and the red blood-sacrifice, kittle folk of a bloody mind and ill heart.

So here, where the Forthie meandered and spun with a seep of red clay down to the landfall of that lost childe Pytheas the little town crawled up into the years and the lights of history, dim and red-tainted, sometimes the outbye men came down to prowl the houses beyond the broch, till the city had a wall built round about, fit to repel the coarse landward men. Behind, on the hills, they built tall forts; and they lived and they died, worshipping their gods; and if it might be that a Dundon chief desired the wife of a Dundon pleb he stole her with unctuous voice and mien, being holy, a Dundon man even then would rape your pouches and cut your throat and tell you a funny joke while he did it, skilly and agreeable, and generally holy.

Well, this was fine, till the Norsemen came, with faces made of sour buttermilk, childes from the stinking straths and byres, squat and strong, black rotten their teeth, they never washed unless they were forced, and they'd better swords than the Dundon folk, so they couldn't force them, apart from the fact that they thought themselves water better used for sailing a boat on than bathing themselves in. So they fought together at that first raid, some of the Northmen got into a hall and found Red Kenneth, the Sheriff of that time, sitting at play at a game of board with his lady, the Red Ane; and the fine Norse childes bulged out their eyes, sore surprised to see a woman unlike their own, not fine and squash, with a face like a mat; and they stripped her, and she took long to die under the eyes of Red Kenneth, kept raving. But afore they could finish with him as well the Dundon folk were chasing them back to their ships, and they ran with their sour whey faces blood dripping, and scrambled away through the pound and roll of the Forthie, and that was the end of them for the time. But Red Kenneth was a mad[man] from that day, and his tortures the Dundon folk might not endure after the passing of a while, a little squire cut his throat one night and ran and hid in the Dundon wynds that led down to the burned shipwright's halls.

So Dundon was saved from the sour Norse childes, and rebuilt its kirk, and a Saint came there, a childe that cornered the droves of hogs that were pastured, black and grey they would grumph about, on the hills above Dundon itself. And he pressed the townsfolk sore for the prize of their meat, there were starving men about the wynds, some coarse creatures said that his throat should be cut. But instead he died and was made a saint. Good St Machar they christened the corp that had swollen fat on the profit of pigs, and they built a cathedral on his head and filled it full of those Catholic priests, awful creatures with brave gowns on that said when you took a sip at communion you really were eating Jesus Christ, they were awful ignorant folk in those times.

Well, the next thing that happened to Dundon toun was when Wallace came marching up from the south killing the English right and left, he fairly had the right way with vermin, him, and he came and chapped on the Dundon gates, and Dundon looked out and shook at the knees. For they had made pact with the English to kepp the port and give meal and milk in return for remission of all their taxes. So they parleyed till the Scots army lost its patience and battered in the walls, and went in and afore they had finished with that night's work there was surety of a plenty of a population of patriot Scots for the future, no doubt, though the sour folk that were to call themselves fathers were mostly at the time hiding up their lums. Those were fairly the times, there's little doubt, when Scotland had its glory bright and untarnished, folk went half-starved, when they weren't that they were being broken on the wheel or hanged at the tail of a cart of manure for stealing a penny's worth of meal, or led out and butchered on the dreich Mearns hills, in rain and the di[r]ty on-ding of sleet, white pelting, for the sake of Scotland and god and the wealth to fill up the gentry's pouches.

But trade was coming into the burgh from far and near across the North Sea, from Bergen, brought by the Northmen loons that had taen to carrying packs, not swords, as handless near with the one as the other, they couldn't cope with the Dundon folk, holy and solemn with great crude hands, they would dig in a pack, fell eident like, and get the packman to coup out his wares, and look at them all and walk round about and stare at the sky and scratch their heads and call the wife to bring them a drink (the Northman licking his dried up lips, the tink, as though he needed a drink); and syne's they'd say How much for the pock? and the Northman would say a half-angel, maybe; and at that the Dundon childe would give a groan and argue it out the lave of the day till the birds were heard singing bonnily outbye on the heaps of sharn at each door; and the Northman childe would be dead for sleep and sell the thing for a shilling, Scots, and take to his heels and across the sea and swear that what ever else he might do, try out a sail to Greenland or Iceland, or kill a bear with his naked nieves, he'd be hanged with a tarry length of tow afore he went trading down to Dundon.

They'd tell those coarse stories about their own selves, the Dundon folk, caller, clear-eyed, grey folk with a twinkle deep in Pict eyes, and think no shame. They went on with building their ship yards at last, fine boats, long sailors to the waters of the Baltic, where the beat of the sea on long, long swaps [?swaths] dreich under German suns, fine boats, folk bought them from far and near. And . . .

Notes

There are no entries for places on the map on p.vi but most are treated in notes to the Canongate Classics editions of *Sunset Song* and *Cloud Howe*.

p.1   *Windmill Place*. 'Duncairn is no imaginary city; Duncairn is plainly and visibly the Aberdeen that Grassic Gibbon knew as a reporter in his early working days, the Windmill Steps the very ones he lived at the top of in digs no doubt very like Ma Cleghorn's, the mile-long Union Street nearby the Royal Mile of Duncairn, Footdee and Footforthie conveniently in the right place, the Commercial Bank and the statue at the end of Union Terrace and Woolworth's and all the familiar landmarks which make Duncairn instantly recognizable as Aberdeen. Granite is quarried in the outskirts: Hazelhead and Rubislaw are not mentioned as such, but they could not be more clearly hinted at' (Ian Campbell, 'Lewis Grassic Gibbon and the Mearns', in *A Sense of Place*, ed Graeme Cruickshank, 1988, p.18).

p.2   *Mounth*. The great SE spur of the Grampian mountain system.

p.6   *the Broo*. From 'Bureau'—unemployment exchange.

p.7   *MacDonald*. J. Ramsay MacDonald (1866–1937), the prime minister. See note in *Cloud Howe*, p.219, Canongate Classics edn.

p.9   *War-horse out of Isaiah*. Perhaps Robert had used a large Bible with coloured illustrations.

p.14   *Howe of the World*. The Howe of the Mearns. See the map on p.vi.

p.18   *Dunedin*. The Celtic form of Edinburgh.
           Tory Pictman. Cf the *Scotsman*, 'Scotland's National Newspaper'—now far from Tory in the narrow party sense.

p.30   *Shaw*. George Bernard Shaw (1856–1950), the dramatist, essayist and pamphleteer.

Wells. Herbert George Wells (1866–1946), novelist, uto-
pian polemicist and popularizer of science. Both Shaw and
Wells had enormous influence on Gibbon in his early years.

p.31 *MacGillivray*. J. Pittendrigh MacGillivray (1856–1938),
poet and sculptor (he made the statues of John Knox in St
Giles' and Byron in Aberdeen Grammar School). He
experimented in mild pastiches of Middle Scots.

Marion Angus (1866–1946) has been judged by Roderick
Watson to be 'within her chosen range, technically the most
accomplished [poet in Scots] of her generation'.

Lewis Spence (1874–1955), anthropologist, poet, and gen-
eral writer. Miss Murgatroyd may have been referring to
*The Mysteries of Britain; or, the Secret Rites and traditions of
Ancient Britain restored* (1928).

Hugo MacDownall. A joke at the expense of Christopher
Murray Grieve ('Hugh MacDiarmid', 1892–1978), to
whom the novel is dedicated and with whom Gibbon
collaborated in this very year in writing *The Scottish Scene*.
See also the note in *Cloud Howe*, p.219, Canongate Classics
edn. Synthetic Scots was to be a deliberate creation, using
words and syntax from the past and from all dialects of the
Scots language.

p.32 *Edgar Wallace*. Wallace (1875–1932), an English writer
best known for his crime novels.

p.38 *The Slug*. The Slug Road runs from Stonehaven to near
Banchory on Deeside, and climbs to a height of 757 ft.

Dunecht. An Aberdeenshire village some twelve miles w of
Aberdeen.

Montrose. James Graham, Marquis of Montrose (1612–50),
Scottish general, supported Charles I after 1644 and took
and pillaged both Aberdeen (1644) and Dundee (1645).

p.39 *Blawearie*. The Guthrie farm-croft in Kinraddie, whose
lease was continued by Chris after her father's death and on
which she lived after her first marriage to Ewan senior.

Stonehyve. The traditional pronunciation of Stonehaven.

p.40 *Echt*. A village in SE Aberdeenshire, twelve miles w of
Aberdeen and two miles s of Dunecht.

The Hill of Fare. A broad-based hill on the border of
Aberdeen and Kincardine shires, 1545 ft at the summit and
some five miles NNW of Banchory.

The Barmekin. A conical hill (800 ft) near Echt.

p.41 *Cairndhu*. The farm-croft near Echt tenanted by John
Guthrie before the family moved to Blawearie. See *Sunset
Song*, pp.27–39, Canongate Classics edn.

p.42   *Excelsior*. The title of a poem by Longfellow which most children once learned by heart. It has an onward-and-upward theme, with lines such as: A youth, who bore, 'mid snow and ice/A banner with a strange device,/Excelsior! *and* Beware the pine-tree's withered branch!/Beware the awful avalanche!/

p.44   *Bennachie*. A rather sprawling hill with six summits (highest, 1698 ft) near Alford and Inverurie in Aberdeenshire. The song mentions a stream in the area: O! gin I were where Gadie rins/Where Gadie rins, where Gadie rins./O! gin I were where Gadie rins,/At the back o' Bennachie!

p.46   *gotten out his rag*. Made him lose his temper.

p.51   *Douglas Scheme*. The theory of social credit, which proposed that the government should distribute national dividends in order to spread purchasing power and thus increase consumption. Its leading proponent was Major Clifford Hugh Douglas (1879–1952). An attempt was made to put the scheme into operation in Alberta, and Douglas was made 'Chief of Reconstruction' to the state government there in 1935.

p.53   PAC Public Assistance Committees, which eked out unemployment and other benefits.

p.54   *plates of meat*. Rhyming slang for 'feet'.
        Up wi' the gentry, that's for me. A parody of the Burns song 'Up in the morning's no for me/Up in the morning early'.

p.55   *Arise, ye outcasts*. The beginning of one translation of *The Internationale*.

p.67   *Trusta*. A hill (1052 ft) in Fetteresso Forest, some six miles W of Stonehaven.

p.68   *rattle in the lantern*. Blow in the face.

p.72   *Spartacus* (d.71 BC). The leader of the slave revolt in Italy which began in 73 BC. He routed several Roman armies but was finally defeated and killed by Crassus. He is the hero of Gibbon's novel of that name.

p.73   *Parker*. Richard Parker, English seaman, led thirteen ships of the line and a number of frigates in a mutiny at the Nore from 10 May to 13 June 1797. He was hanged on 30 June.

p.91   *his Nannie was awa'*. Another Burns song—'My Nanie's awa'.

p.108   *presents on New Year's Day*. New Year was still the family festival in Scotland in the 1930s.

p.151   *Hill of Barras*. About three miles inland from the coastal village of Catterline.

The Pitforthies. Three upland farms (Hillhead of Pitforthie, Nether Pitforthie, and Upper Pitforthie), some three miles NNE of Arbuthnott.

Meikle Fiddes. A farm by the main Aberdeen road about one mile E of Drumlithie.

p.152   *Drumlithie . . . steeple*. In *Sunset Song* Drumlithie church is said to have no steeple (p.76, Canongate Classics edn). But see the note on p.216 of *Cloud Howe*, Canongate Classics edn.

p.154   *Glen Dye*. A rocky glen in Strachan parish, Kincardineshire.

Drumtochty. A hill and (nineteenth-century) castle about two miles W of Auchinblae in Kincardineshire.

Finella. See *Cloud Howe*, note on p.213, Canongate Classics edn.

Garrold Wood. Just S of Strathfinella and the Glen of Drumtochty.

Luther water. 'A troutful rivulet of Kincardineshire' (*Ordnance Gazetteer of Scotland*).

Dunnottar Castle. See *Sunset Song*, pp.125–6, Canongate Classics edn.

p.155   *Drumelzie woods*. About one mile W of Auchinblae.

p.161   *walls . . . cleared space*. Chris is climbing the Barmekin, which is 'crowned by remains of a prehistoric fortress, about six acres in extent, with concentric ramparts' (*Ordnance Gazetteer of Scotland*).

p.163   *Ewan, Long Rob, Robert*. The men in her life, for whom see *Sunset Song* and *Cloud Howe*.

Not Ake alone . . . 'She was' is understood—i.e., she was beyond not Ake alone, but beyond them all.

p.182   *Connolly*. James Connolly (1870–1916), Irish Labour Leader, organized socialist 'armies' and took part in the Easter rebellion of 1916. He was executed on 12 May.

p.193   *Cairn o' Mount*. In the words of the *Ordnance Gazetteer*, 'a mountain on the mutual border of Strachan and Fordoun parishes, Kincardineshire . . . it culminates about seven miles ESE of Mount Battock' (see Gibbon's map). There is a road from Forfarshire to Deeside over its eastern shoulder.

p.196   *Invergordon*. The Atlantic Fleet mutinied over a reduction in pay scales and resentment over harsh discipline from 16 to 21 September 1931. As a result, the Navy's cuts were reduced from an extreme upper limit of twenty-five per cent to ten per cent.

p.201   *that day that Robert had died.* See *Cloud Howe*, p.210, Canongate Classics edn.

Glossary

SND stands for *The Scottish National Dictionary*. Scots words which are generally known throughout the English-speaking world are not defined.

ahint, behind
alow, below
a-lowe, alight
antrin, strange, eerie
bade, stayed
bap, soft bread roll
bar (n), joke
basses, mats, rugs
ben, inside, towards the inner part of house
bide, dwell, stay
bigging, building
billy, fellow
birl, twist, rattle
birn, heap, pile, crowd
birring, whirring
blate, bashful
body, person
bourouch -och, crowd, heap, huddle; (v) mass together
bout, spell of work
braws, fine clothes
breeks, trousers
breenge, rush forward
brink, provide
broch, large round tower with hollow walls of stone
Broo men, the unemployed
brose, oat or pease meal mixed with boiling water
buirdly, burly, vigorous
byke, nest (of insects)

cadger, pedlar
calsay stones, cobble stones
cantrips, antics
canty, lively
chapp, knock, chime (of clock)
chave, toil, struggle
childe, fellow
chinter, chop, hack
claik, chatter, gossip
clorted, soiled
clour, strike
clype, inform
corp, corpse
creash, fat person
cry, call, shout
dander, saunter
darg, work
dight, wipe
dirl, shake, rattle
douce, quiet, respectable
dowp, posterior
dreich, dry, insipid
drouthy, thirsty
eident, busy, conscientious
eidently, carefully
fairely (*ferlie*), marvel, wonder
fash, bother, rush;
    (v) trouble yourself, worry
fegs, indeed, sure
fell, great, very
fettle, life, vigour
feuching, ill-smelling

215

flyting, scolding, joking

f[r]ere, companion, comrade

fusionless, pithless, feeble

futret, weasel, stoat

gait, way, road

gallus, bold, wild

gawpus, clumsy, stupid lout

get (giet), brat, bastard

gey, rather, very

girnings, whinings

glaur, soft, sticky mud

gleg-vexed, plagued by horse-flies

gleyed, squinting, dishonest

goloch, earwig, nincompoop

gomeril, fool, half-wit

gowk (v), stare foolishly; (n) fool

greeting, crying

guff, bad smell

gype, stupid lout

gypedest, stupidest

gyte, mad

habber, stammer, gabble nonsensically

happed, dressed

happing, covering, wrapping

haughs, meadows (often upland); valleys

haver, babble nonsense

heired, inherited

heuch, crag, cliff

hippens, baby's nappy

hirple, hurple, limp

hotter, simmer

howk, dig, hooded crow

jing-bang, whole lot, crowd

jookery-packery, trickery, underhand scheming

joskin, bumpkin

keelie, tough male slum-dweller

kepp, guard, restrain

kist, chest

kittle (up), start up, stimulate, excite

lair, bog down, stick fast, soil

lave, rest, remainder

lib, castrate

lift, sky

limmer, hussy, jade

lithe, shelter

loon, [farmer's] boy

losh! (interj), Lord!

lour, menacing blackness (of clouds)

lowe, glow

lum, chimney

malagarouse, dishevel, damage

marled, mottled, streaked

meck, halfpenny

mind, remember

mouser, moustache

mutch, woman's close cap

neb, beak, nose

neep, turnip

nick, police-station, prison

nip (n), dram (of whisky)

nout, ox, blockhead

orra, worthless, disreputable

outbye, beyond, out in the fields

paich, gasp, pant

park, field

peesie, lapwing

pieces, sandwiches, materials for picnic

pleiter (n), mess; (v) dabble aimlessly

pock, sack

press, large cupboard

prig, urge, plead

quean, girl

redd, tidy

reek, mist, smoke

rig, strip of land, field

runkled, wrinkled

sappy, plump, fleshy

scart (n), puny, shrunken

person

schlimpèd, stunted

schlorich, foul heap (of silver); disgusting mess (of blood)

scraich, screech

scrimp (n), thin slip

sharn, liquid dung

shoggle, sway

shoggly, shaky, wobbling

showd, swing to and fro, rock

skate, contemptible idiot

skeeter (n), diarrhoea; (v) slither awkwardly

skellop, long strip

skeugh, squint

skite, mad

slammock, hectic bout

slock, slake

slummock, lumpish slattern

smore, wind thick with fine rain or sleet

snell, biting, bitter

sniftering, snivelling

sonsy (of a lie), big, substantial

soss, mess, muck around with

sough, rush

sourock, sorrel; a perverse, surly person

sowans, sour pudding of oatmeal and water

spleiter, splash

squatter, scatter, flutter

st[r]amash, blind fury, uproar

steek, stitch, sharp pain

stite, nonsense

stiter, stagger

stound, feel painful

stour, dust, dirt, fuss, commotion

stravaigings, wanderings

sumph, slow, stupid person

sweir, relaxed; slothful

sweirty, laziness

syne, then; ago

tacketty, hob-nailed

taik, stroll

tanner, sixpence

tattie, potato

they, (a) those

thrawn, obstinate

tint, lost

tirr, tear off (skin), strip

trauchle (n), careless, incompetent person; mess; long tiring trudge; (v) drudge, trudge

trauchled, burdened, harassed

trig, neat

uncalsayed, unhewn, undressed (of stones)

unchancy, inauspicious, ill-omened

unsweir, hectically busy

vallay, valet

wame, stomach

weans, 'kids'

wheen, a few

wynd, narrow (winding) lane

wyte, fault, blame

CANONGATE CLASSICS
TITLES IN PRINT

1. Imagined Corners by Willa Muir
   ISBN 0 86241 140 8 £3.95

2. Consider the Lilies by Iain Crichton Smith
   ISBN 0 86241 143 2 £2.95

3. Island Landfalls: Reflections from the South Seas
   Robert Louis Stevenson
   ISBN 0 86241 144 0 £3.95

4. The Quarry Wood by Nan Shepherd
   ISBN 0 86241 141 6 £3.95

5. The Story of My Boyhood and Youth
   John Muir
   ISBN 0 86241 153 X £2.95

6. The Land of the Leal by James Barke
   ISBN 0 86241 142 4 £4.95

7. Two Worlds by David Daiches
   ISBN 0 86241 148 3 £2.95

8. Mr Alfred M.A. by George Friel
   ISBN 0 86241 163 7 £3.95

9. The Haunted Woman by David Lindsay
   ISBN 0 86241 162 9 £3.95

10. Memoirs of A Highland Lady Vol 1
    Elizabeth Grant of Rothiemurchus
    ISBN 0 86241 145 9 £3.95

11. Memoirs of A Highland Lady Vol 11
    Elizabeth Grant of Rothiemurchus
    ISBN 0 86241 147 5 £3.95

12. Sunset Song by Lewis Grassic Gibbon
    ISBN 0 86241 179 3 £2.95

13. Homeward Journey by John MacNair Reid
    ISBN 0 86241 178 5 £3.95

14. The Blood of the Martyrs by Naomi Mitchison
    ISBN 0 86241 192 0 £4.95

15. My First Summer in the Sierra by John Muir
    ISBN 0 86241 193 9 £2.95

16. The Weatherhouse by Nan Shepherd
    ISBN 0 86241 194 7 £3.95

17. Witch Wood by John Buchan
    ISBN 0 86241 202 1 £3.95